Matt heard the thrumming rise in pitch, quicken its pulse. Another disturbance started up on the other side of the room, people jostling, shouting.

And then, abruptly, people—*Lunars*—were hitting each other, throwing loose objects, swinging fists and furniture with complete disregard of mass and force.

An alarm sounded, and everyone stopped who could stop: it was an undulating whine, the Fire alarm, not the insistent on-off scream of Decompression.

And after that the confusion started up again, worse than before. Smoke was rising from the far plot of grass. Nobody seemed to be paying attention. Matt looked around, trying to find some sense or explanation. He saw none, as the smoke rose and spread.

"We've got to move," he said to the others.

"Where?" Cissa said.

"Not as a bunch," Matt said, thoughts racing. "Look, they're starting fights with groups. Scatter and we'll all make it. Go like blueshift now, stop when you're clear."

"But *where?*" Ciss said again, high-pitched, almost a scream.

"Train at three! Keep cool as you can till then, but *train at three!*"

Ruby pulled at Cissa's arm, and they were gone.

Also by John M. Ford

Casting Fortune
The Dragon Waiting
The Final Reflection
Fugue State
How Much for Just the Planet?
The Princes of the Air
The Scholars of Night
Web of Angels

JOHN M. FORD

GROWING UP
*W*EIGHTLESS

 BANTAM BOOKS

New York   Toronto   London   Sydney   Auckland

GROWING UP WEIGHTLESS
A Bantam Spectra Book

Publishing History
Bantam trade edition / November 1993
Bantam paperback edition / August 1994

ISBN 0-553-56814-0
Published simultaneously in the United States and Canada

Bantam Books are published by Bantam Books, a division of Bantam
Doubleday Dell Publishing Group, Inc. Its trademark, consisting of
the words "Bantam Books" and the portrayal of a rooster, is
Registered in U.S. Patent and Trademark Office and in other
countries. Marca Registrada. Bantam Books, 1540 Broadway, New
York, New York 10036.

PRINTED IN THE UNITED STATES OF AMERICA
RAD   0 9 8 7 6 5 4 3 2 1

This one is for
Donald P. LeWin, M.D.,
who kept the lights on.

GROWING UP
WEIGHTLESS

Hating the Earth was easy.

It was always there to hate, a filmy blue eye hanging in the black sky, winking side to side. Even on that high day of the month when the eye was shut, a blue halo, a crust of dirty air, stared on. It asked to be hated, sending its people who thought Luna's land was ugly and her cities strange and her gravity comical, sending its message that Earth was the source of all the life in the Universe as if nobody had ever been born on Luna or Mars or the Frames, never mind the Far Worlds, sending its stupidity and its lies. It was full as a pimple of trash and stink and jealousy, spitting them all by shipfuls at Luna, hating Luna for not being another piece of Earth itself, refusing even to call the world by its proper name, as if "Moon" meant "owned," as if gravity made property: what was there to do except hate it back?

Matthias Ronay sat in his best coldspot, looking up at the blue eye and hating it until his jaws hurt.

Then finally he looked down, to the Lunarscape under the eye, and felt better for what he saw there.

Matt sat, suspended, between two walls of the Copernicus A Port service building: two broad, smooth concrete slabs, a couple of meters apart, sloped at thirty degrees off the vertical. Between the walls was a network of structural glass rods, each as thick as Matt's thumb; he sat comfortably nested in the net on his folded jacket and a cheap Betacloth chair cushion, about two-thirds of the way to the roof, the floor some ten meters below him. He faced a strip of glass that was the whole reason for being here.

The clear glass strip was fifteen decs wide, and as high as the whole wall. It was left over from the building days, meant to give light and view to the construction crews after the outer shell was sealed. At the bottom was an old cylindoor, bolted now and caulked tight. There were similar leftovers all over the city. The glass was just as strong as the crete around it, the sealed door as safe as a blank slab. No one would bother with busting vacuum just to replace them. And with that Matt was entirely pleased.

Because for all that it looked on the nasty Earth, the window also opened directly onto the A Port.

The three-day-wonder shuttles from Earth dumped their trash on the little pads at C Port. B caught the system ships from Mars and the Frames and the Jovian moons; those were good ships, sometimes beautiful ships, but they only went out and back. Home traffic, suborbital hoppers and Big Dippers back from the water run, came down at Old Landing on the other side of the city; they were important, Matt knew, but they went nowhere at all—another Lunar city, a comet, *nowhere*. Copernicus A was the *real* starport, where the MIRAGE-drive ships on the Far Worlds trade sent down their shuttles, or landed themselves. And then took off again, to go where the strongest telescope could not find the Earth in the sky.

The watch on Matt's wrist trembled. It was time.

The beacons around the pad lit white, red, blue. A service buggy ran for shelter under the crete pavilion where the crash vehicles waited, just in case of the impossible. Strobes on glass-rod towers flared upward, spilling a little light from their metallized-glass bowls, but casting no beams in the clean Lunar sky.

The TECHNET said the ship was the *Eau Claire*, a real free trader, no home port, last stop Burgundy, eighty parsecs out. Matt wanted to grab his slate and read her data live: but if he touched the net Matt could be located—*He* could find Matt as easily as whistling a note. *He* didn't know about this place, and He wouldn't. Matt was not going to heat his own cold-spot.

The ship came down.

Eau Claire was a pipe-racker, eight fifty-meter lengths of tube making two # signs one atop the other. Four flare cylinders went through the junctions; they were burning hydrogen in oxygen, their exhaust bells blasting against gravity with flares that were nearly invisible, except for the dust they tore up from the surface as the ship settled down. Inside the tubes, four meters across, were crew quarters, controls, storage for delicate cargo. Less-sensitive goods were hung outside, in small pods and cases along the tubes, and big containers in the central square.

The ship seemed to be coming down at an off angle. Between two breaths Matt played it out crashing, in a burst of dust and debris and burning gas; and, alert as no one else in the city could have been, he would grab a suit of plate from the public lockers, rush to the site, aid in the rescue . . . earn the gratitude of *Eau Claire*'s master and crew. Earn an offer of a job. Earn his ticket to *go*.

All he needed was an offer. Matt was past his

hundred and fifteen thousandth hour, old enough for
an offer. With a promise of work, by Lunar law he
could leave his parents, leave the sight of the blue
planet, get out, gain orbit, grab outworlds, *go*.

Then the ship touched the pad. Matt shook with
imaginary shock of landing, and the play burst like
soap film.

He wouldn't really want to light out that way,
Matt told himself, as the starship's engines shut
down, the clouds of dust collapsed. He wouldn't, he
said in his head, want to win his ticket in the wreck
of a ship, in a master's disaster. He told himself that
three times over.

Ramp slots were opening around the pad,
trucks crawling from their tunnels. Along the pipes
of the ship, windows blinked as the crew moved from
landing to loading stations. A twin-racker would
have a crew of about forty.

Room and work for forty ought to mean enough
for forty-one, Matt thought. But he had asked the
question, asked it more than once since reaching the
hour of Go. One master had just smiled and shaken
her head. One had shown him all over his ship, given
him a piece of white coal from Saint Alexis (he had
traded a third of it for two slate memory modules, but
the rest was carefully hidden). The third had called
Him. There had been no reason for that; it was a law-
ful question anywhere to ask for work, but—

Matt's father had been in a meeting (as if He
were ever anywhere else). Not that He had said anything; no long careful argument this time, no explanation of why He was right and Matt was wrong.
Why should He? It had gone His way, and Matt had
learned something. Matt had *learned* that he wasn't
going anywhere, not this way. So He just let the silence beat in Matt's ears like the pound of blood in a
small dark room.

In another forty thousand hours there would
not have to be any sort of promise from a third party.

Matt could survive that long. He could last that long breathing vacuum, if only he could get out of sight of the Earth.

And everything Matt had ever read or seen or heard told him that people did what they had to, to survive. Even He couldn't argue around that.

Matt put on his jacket. He tucked up the pillow for his next visit, stepped off the support rod and skipped down the inner wall, barely touching the crete with his soft-soled boots, brushing the glass rods as he dropped between them. He hit surface with a light bouncing shock and ran between the walls.

The space between the walls got dim as Matt left the window strip behind. He came to his exit: he unducked, grabbed a glass rod with both hands and killed his momentum in a full-circle swing over the bar. At knee height, a half-meter square of plain gray plycore covered a hole in the inside wall. Matt went through.

He came out in a very dim room, a vacant retail space on the top concourse of the building. There were some Beta dropcloths piled and draped, a box of bolts and fasteners, an unmounted light fixture. At the front of the store, light leaked in a fine white grid around the edges of ply panels.

Above the loose lightbox was an open spot in the ceiling. Matt jumped into it, caught the edge of the glass-channel suspension grid and swung inside with no more sound than a door closing. Careful to touch only the grid, not the glass-foam panels, with fingers and elbows and knees and toes, he crabbed his way past lights and cables and ducts to the space above a toilet room. He listened: no whumph of toilets or hum of sinks, not a grunt, not a cough. Matt tipped up a panel and dropped through.

He whacked the dust off his jacket and slacks, walked to a sink and blasted his hands clean in the ultrasound. He looked in the mirror: in a corner behind him was an empty camera bracket, a pigtail of wires. Eventually there would be a pickup installed, and Matt would have to find another way to the cold. Which he would.

Matt went out onto the concourse. The building was A-framed, walls sloping up to meet in a long skylight. There were walks along both sides, a gap down the middle that looked down past two more decks to the transit level. Air vines curtained down from railing to railing. To Matt's right, the floor ended in a circular space, a stairway spiraling down the center, a curved band of window giving a general view of the three Copernicus ports.

A few people were standing by the window, looking out; they began to walk away, their step confirming them all as Lunars. The last person spotted Matt and waved. Matt knew him: Gordon Tovey, one of the Transport supervisors. He wore a ten-pocket Beta vest over a high-collared shirt in Transport red, red jeans tucked into heavy boots. The vest pockets were stuffed full of gear, still more hardware clipped and looped to his belt and jeans.

Tovey said "Hello, Ronay the Younger."

It was what he always said. He meant nothing by it, and Matt had decided it was all right for Gordon to call him that: it wouldn't always be so, but when the time came the explanation would too. "Hello, Gordon."

Tovey pointed out the window. "Surely you didn't miss the big one."

"Pickup to con-down."

"So what did you think?"

"Think?"

"Of the ship."

"Oh, well. She came in a little off true—but pipe ships don't handle all that smooth, especially doubles. And her last stop was Burgundy—"

"That right?"

"TECHNET. Which probably means from Dvor before, and maybe Churchill or Ananse before that.

She may not have been anyplace airless in—oh, five thousand hours at least."

"You do spend a little time on the net, don't you?" Tovey said, grinning.

"Oh . . ."

"Don't suppose you'd like a job?" Tovey said suddenly. He was not grinning now.

Matt felt his guts drop away. He could feel His hand in this, and if so it led to a bottomless well of plots—if He knew about Matt's coldspot—had always known—and this would be just how He would close in, from a dark corner—"Have you got a job?" Matt said, trying to sound eager.

Tovey scratched at his ear. "Usually do; Tracks 'n' Packs isn't much of a star role these days. Not like starships, anyway. I keep saying, there's not such a difference between ziplines and tracks, eh?" His smile seemed a bit awkward. Matt held his own face rigid. Tovey said "Any rate, I heard you were past your one-fifteen."

"Yes." *And who told you that?* "I've got to think about it, Gordon."

"I don't see any reason to hurry." Tovey pressed at his ear again, pulled a picsel from a vest pocket. "Tovey, go ahead. . . . Oh, doesn't it always? Details. Put 'em up." Matt could see the face on the palm-sized screen change to a technical-systems display. There was no sound; Tovey was sound-wired, the audio running up an implanted fiber-optic pipe directly into his auditory nerves. He could hear private and clear over any amount of background noise. "Oh, put a spitwad in it and hold your breath. I'm coming." He snapped the picsel shut, said to Matt, "Want to see the mess I've just tried to get you into? Quick, before that starship's crew finds out what we've shoved under their goods?"

Matt did and knew he couldn't, but he checked his timer just to confirm. "I've really got to be someplace, Gordon. Maybe sometime else?"

Tovey shrugged. "Next ship, next disaster." There was no malice in it, and it cut Matt open.

Matt said "Really. I have to go."

"I guess you do," Tovey said seriously, then "If you're late, blame me."

"Thanks, Gordon."

"Arigato, but I meant Tranny, not me personally." They both laughed. Tovey said "Would you tell your father—"

Matt froze.

"No, wipe that. Think about the job, though, eh?"

"Sure. And thanks."

Tovey went to the stairwell rail and jumped over it. He could get away with that: he had a job to get to. Nobody would give him hardpoints for risking himself and spooking the Slammers.

Matt took a long step to the edge, looked down. Tovey had landed three decks down and was loping off to wherever his mess was. His work.

Matt had been tempted for a vac-tight fact. Gordon Tovey had the freedom of Luna: the run of the tracks and tunnels, Tycho to Tsio and all stops and stations. Transport ran the well buggies that loaded and unloaded starships; a Transport load super was the first person a ship captain saw live on landing, the last before lighting out.

But if it was the freedom of Luna, it was the freedom of only Luna, the freedom to work under the Earth. Tidelocked.

It was, and this killed it deader than a soap sphere in vacuum, the freedom to take orders from Himself. And there the matter ended.

Matt jumped the rail. A deck and a half down, he drifted by a Slammer team, two adults and two kids. Matt knew what they looked like before he saw them, because they all looked alike—what Tani called a gestalt, all the bits streaming as a whole. They had cameras and sunshields and THE EARTH'S ROUND

AFTER ALL! shirts of Beta over their linty weed clothes. They had a stuffed plush Ango and a Name the Craters game card. Before they left they would have a pocketful each of degaussed tickets from Transport and hourly suit hire and a Skyhook match and the theatre or the ballet or the orchestra (choose one), and at the Port Duty Free shop they would each get a glass sphere of Lunar soil and vacuum, the adults a bottle of Authentic Moonshine white whiskey.

One of the kids gaped and pointed at Matt dropping past, and he grinned and waved and did a backflip before landing just right on his feet. Matt had seen their cameras, as he knew he would; that was all right. Sometimes you had to be careful—a news disc might get on the channels—but these were just going back to the Earth, and what happened to them there Matt could not even slightly care. If you were trying to live and run cool on Luna, knowing the difference was everything.

He was skambling now; a light-footed run with knees bent and head down, ducked and tucked. The idea was to put all your power into forward momentum, none into vertical lift. You had to be Lunar to do it right. It drove the Slammers crazy when you skambled by them, so of course you weren't supposed to do it, and you did it every chance you got.

Matt riffed up a chart in the slate of his brain. He was in the A Port Surface level. He had to get to Ruby's place on Sokoni plus seven. There were three thousand meters of travel tube between Port and Sokoni Tower; they had wanted the landings far out for some reason.

For a long time Matt had walked the distance, thinking it must be cooler than a railcar. Then he discovered there were cameras in both—and few enough people walked that when the sensors warmed to somebody in the passage, someone always took a look. In the cars, if you kept quiet, you might run the whole city unseen.

Matt had quickly come to understand that things didn't always play as they ought. No Lunar in the blue eye's sight expected things fair. It was when things played completely backward that he wondered about the world.

Matt slowed down as he came to the travel concourse. It was always full of offworlders; no place was hotter. He was traveling at a nice smooth walk when he got to the rail gates.

There were instructions in six languages for Slammers; Lunars knew the system. About a year ago Transport had put up signs in Sympla, the icon language they used on starships. The ship people liked it, so it must work well, but Matt wondered: didn't they talk on ships? In stories they talked, of course. In stories they explained things to each other that real crew would be black vac dead for not knowing, or else they explained them to planet people who had no business aboard except not to know things— space Slammers. What were *they* like, without a spit of gravity to hold them down and together?

It was a relief when the story ships got into trouble: then they didn't talk so much. Or they said useless things like "Another hit like that and we'll lose cooling in the MIRAGE cases!" when any idiot could see the cracks and the clouds of boiling wet-N; but then you could just flip the sound off and enjoy the story pure.

Matt reached into the inside pocket of his jacket. Lining the pocket was a sort of envelope, made of double-layer foil with a thumbnail circuit panel wired in. Ruby, who had made them for all the team, called it a Faraday Pocket; a-eyes couldn't see through it. Matt flipped his Transport tag out just before he went through the gate, and it passed him. Rubylaser had warned him not to forget. He never forgot.

With the tag read he was warm, gated and dated

precisely located, a hot spark on the lines. All He had to do was look. Let Him.

Between the gate area and the train tube was a spinney door, a frame of layered plates that would whirl in to seal tight if vacuum broke on either side. Older Lunars sometimes took a long arching step through spinneys—the guillotine gavotte—just in case, though Matt had never in his life actually heard of a serious decompression.

The tube was a broad oval, cut through the regolith with electron guns; the curved walls were still of burnstone, smooth and slightly glassy. The passenger platform was a slab of white crete notching the tunnel's corner. A glass wall ran the thirty-meter length of the station, dividing platform from train tube, doors marked off by strips of red-enameled metal. At the upline end, big digits counted down to the next train: 48 seconds.

At 30 seconds out a chime rang to wake up dozing passengers—that was clearly explained on the signs, but some Slammers never saw *anything*—as happened now: a fat man, two stuffed shopping bags hung from each hand, heard the bell and was touched off like a racing mouse. He practically leapt through the gate, the bags rising under thick-legged thrust, oscillating on the heavy slack couplings of arms; by the time he reached the platform he was a hurtling chaotic system, an insoluble n-body problem.

The fat Slammer saw the end coming, the glass wall rushing up on him. He tried to kill his velocity, tried, Matt saw with some surprise, like a Lunar, crouching and scraping his shoes on the crete, and he almost did make it—but there was really a lot of mass times velocity squared there, and he didn't handle the whirling baggage right, and space just ran out on him.

Slam.

The man bounced off the glass, and again off the floor, a wavefront of shopping bags expanding from the impact. They were still in flight when the train filled the tube, train doors mating to platform doors and sliding open. The fat man tried to get up and grab his property at once, and managed neither.

Matt looked at the train and the time and the struggling Slammer, and then at the few other people on the platform. The Slammers were hustling into the cars, trying to see the accident without looking at it. Most of the Lunars hadn't seen it to begin with, it happened so many times a day. A small, yellow-haired woman in a blue coverup and sticky sandals was kneeling, putting books back into a Beta sack.

Matt gathered up the nearest bag. It was full of food: wrapped sandwiches, liter flasks of Pepsi Musato, two entire boxes of Cadbury's Rego Crunch bars. Matt and the woman in blue came up on either side of the fallen man. "Careful, sir," Matt said, and they got him on his feet. A chime rang, and the woman waved and kicked the crete hard; she sailed into a car just as the glass doors closed. The train slid out.

The fat man stared after the train for a moment, shook his head, and said "Thank you, thank you so much. Can you tell me when the next train to the Hub is due?"

Matt pointed at the countdown clock. "About 500 seconds."

"Ah." The man pulled back his left sleeve. There was a long black case strapped to his forearm: a tasset computer, time digits showing through a window in the closed lid. "I have to be on a long-distance train at 1400. Do you think I'll make it?"

"You ought to," Matt said, "sir." There was only one train from Copernicus Hub at 1400 today, as Matt had excellent reason to know.

"Ah. Good. My luggage is already supposed to be on there, you see, and I'd hate to have to run after my dirty socks. Especially as you've seen how I run."

He smiled. Matt smiled too, trying to imagine the cubage of the man's luggage.

The next train pulled in. "This one will get you there," Matt said, and almost hung back, almost went to another car, but voidit he wanted to know. He followed the Earthman aboard.

Matt said "It's three stops to the Hub Transport Center. We're on Surface level here, but Hub will be sub-2; the TranCity trains leave from Surface . . . that's two decks up. There's a lift. And you can get a cart for this . . . your packages." Pause. The man was listening carefully. Matt tightened his chest and said "How far are you going?"

"The end of the line. Tsiolkovsky."

Breath. "Are you an astronomer?"

"Astrophysicist. My name is Yuri Korolev."

"Oh! I've heard of you."

Korolev's eyebrows went up. "Oh, of course. The crater, on Farside." He smiled. "The big fat one."

"No, sir. I mean, you, sir."

"That's very kind, young man . . ."

"Matt."

"Thank you, Matt, but I'm certain—"

"You wrote about MIRAGE tracing by Avakian shock. It was on VACOR TECHNET."

Korolev laughed out loud. Matt held still for a moment, feeling sweat on his ribs, and then Korolev reached out, clamped Matt's hand in both of his and shook it. Korolev's hands were strong, and surprisingly fine-boned for such a big man. "Matt, sir, I am so delighted to make your acquaintance. You must excuse me: I have a son, you see, just about your age, and he is about as interested in celestial physics as . . . as the far side of the Moon."

Matt nodded for want of anything better to do. Korolev had said Moon, yes, but he'd called it the far side. Not the dark side.

The train stopped at Verne Center. No one entered their car. The doors closed.

"Do you live here, Matt? Copernicus, I mean? I haven't been to the Moon before, you see, and I really don't know how much you people travel."

"I live in Copernicus. I've been to some other cities. Tycho, and Da Vinci/Crisium."

"To Tsio?"

Heartbeat heartbeat. "No."

"Ah. Well, I shall be there for . . . let me see, you'd say seven hundred hours? A month, on Earth?"

"A skyday."

"I see," Korolev said. He seemed to be filing the word away. "Well, if you should happen to be in Tsiolkovsky during that skyday, you will say hello to me? Pozhalasta?"

"Da gospodeen."

"Muy bueno. I have hardly been on the Moon two days, and already I am amazed by . . . no, I am not saying that right. After fifty hours here, I find Luna amazing."

Matt said "We call it the Moon sometimes," which was only true. Korolev hadn't pronounced it right—"Loona," like "lunatic," not properly with a short *u*—but he seemed to mean well enough. Through the car window, burnstone and cables shockwiped to glass and platform, and the sign for Sokoni Tower. "This is my stop, sir. Nazdrovye."

"Zero noise, Matt."

"Next stop for you, sir. Luna e irrashaimase."

Korolev waved as Matt got off. Matt waved back, and then left the station, fast as he could.

He tumbled up a ramp and was in Sokoni Split, the triple-height traders' zone, shopcent souk and streetfair all in one and outside of time. There were tables and tents and kiosks, crosstalk pitches and pleas crackling in the air, which smelled of food and incense and drifting pine from the Core beyond. There were openframe openstores, built of glass rods and modular connectors, that ran up and out as they pleased, dangling draperies and ladders—there was no rule that you had to make it easy for Slammers to get in; a couple of stores were hung from under deck 1, accessible only by an easy jump that no Slammer would ever try.

Matt slalomed through the sales, keeping low where the air was thick and aromatic. He didn't quite dare leap the rugmerchants; he pivoted sharp and got nearly tangled with a handscanner juggling glass bracelets and mekbits-as-jewelry down her bare arms. She boomeranged something around Matt's head. Lunars did that. If you were *really* Lunar, you were part of the show. And then Matt was through into the Core.

Sokoni Tower was the tallest building in Copernicus, third highest on Luna, a truncated cone rising eight levels above Surface. Its core was an open cylinder nearly eighty meters across, space from sub-1 at the bottom of the Split to the glass roof forty meters above.

Green vines and glass cables hung down the distance, and it was webbed across with bridges of crete stones and glass rope and pure prismatic crystal, meeting in microplazas and eyries. There were three dozen trees here; five pines, the oldest trees on Luna, lanced upward three-fourths of the way to the top. Sunlight stripped only of hard UV poured down from the roof and shot in from the walls through angled pipes. Birds in vivid colors flew and chattered. So did Lunars. Two, dressed brighter than the birds, were halfway up the space, hovering on their glassomer wings, having a conversation with two more people seated at a skywalk cafe.

The top deck of Sokoni was all public space, restaurants and viewrooms. Underpeak was where Ruby and her father lived. The circular hallway was crete painted with swoops of blue to keep it from being too damn plain, but the doors were all different: one hung with an embroidery, another faced with real wood veneers, another a metal sculpture. The door to

731 was a solid slab of red Martian sandstone nearly a dec thick. As Sam Rincon told the story, the door had gotten here at the end of a domino chain of bartered favors, talent for trix for time for transport for tonnage tick tick tick all the way home.

"Est' el gabacho, Rubylaser," Matt told the door, and a moment later it swung open, and Ruby said "Hello, Lonestar. Welcome once again to the dusty corner of the universe."

Ruby Rincon was slightly shorter than Matt, her skin much darker, her hair and eyes absolute gloss black. She was about six thousand hours older, and looked maybe twice that. She was wearing a Beta pocket vest, like the one Gordon had worn but in Physical Plant gold, over a loose white jumpsuit of Framespun silk. Some tools and a tasset were stuffed into the vest.

"Sorry I'm late," Matt said. "There was—"

"You're the first one here," Rubylaser said, "so late or early doesn't count. Coming in?"

The door closed, and Matt followed Ruby into the common room, a space five meters by seven. Its walls, like all the rooms' in the flat, were covered with architectural drawings: these were in Italian Renaissance style—Sam had shown Matt the books by Palladio—columns and arches, fountains and geometric gardens. In the perspective distance was a crumbling Roman viaduct. Engraved columns flanked a glass bubble bay looking out over Surface and sky, and the corner of a cloister pretended to frame a 5-up masterdeck, one side screen running with the pingline news.

The floor was covered with dark green carpet so deep that Ruby's feet nearly disappeared into it. The only other furnishings were two dozen cushions, each in a different fabric: Beta, burlap, Ango wool, satin, novylon, Burgundian linen—and as many colors and sizes—and a couple of little cubical tables Sam Rincon said were a famous design. One of the tables held a pile of mex, a mostly disassembled little roby. Ruby sat down next to it and poked at the parts.

"I met a Slammer in the tube," Matt said.

"Zounds, what news!"

"This was Yuri Korolev, the physicist. The one who's trying to use Avakian shock as a navigation aid."

"That right?" Ruby said, idly working the action of one of the roby's jointed legs. "What's Avakian shock?"

"There's a pulse of free atoms when a ship holes out. A wavefront."

Ruby put the mek down. "What kind of atoms?"

"I don't know. Something they can detect at Tsioleye."

"Tsio has the best Caesura spectrometer in this system. See-spec can detect *anything*, my dear standby processor. So this Slam you met gave you a physics lecture?"

"Laserlighto'lovely, the point is he was going to *Tsiolkovsky*. He asked me to visit . . . if I was going to be out there."

"I'm not going to ask because I know you didn't tell him."

"Well, I didn't, so I'm glad you didn't ask."

She looked at the roby bits, then finally said "Vack, it'll be on PhysNet," and looked up at him. "We've got a quarter at least before the others get here."

"And how do you know that?" he said, pleased that he'd brought something to interest her.

"Not everyone runs quite so cold as you, Lonestar. String pinged me, no explanation sagenlos. Raf's just checked out of the Maze. Cissa will be on time when it rains on Tycho, and Tani left a vue fifty ago saying she'd be a quarter late."

"A quarter exactly?"

"Tani." She crawled over to the deck, made a

nest of cushions. "Avakian shock, K. Now what was your Slammer's name? Kowalski?"

"Korolev. Yuri Korolev. Next you're going to tell me you don't know who Avakian was."

"I should," she said, fading him out as she brought the deck to life, "just to watch the reaction. . . . My room's open, usual rules." Then all five screens were running and Ruby was out of the conversation.

Of course Ruby knew who Avakian was. *Everyone* knew that. Leon Avakian was the A in the MIRAGE stardrive, the man who had blown a hole in the far side of Luna and opened up the way to all the worlds beyond the Sun. Avakian had himself come to Luna to live, just after Independence, more than eighty years ago.

Matt wandered along the hall, past the closed and inviolable doors of Sam Rincon's workroom and bedroom, into the large circular kitchen. Around its perimeter were renderings of a revolving restaurant Sam had designed for Herzl Frame. Sam called it the Ezekiel Cafe, though the owners didn't. Space spread out one way, the planet below, and all around the circle you looked down on the heads of the diners spin-stuck to the rim.

He went into Ruby's room. The walls here were an Escher construct: geometrical arches covered with tiny interlocking lizards, opening out onto something much like a Lunarscape. But each view was from a different angle, none matching, a maze of conflicting horizons. In each portal there was a sort of bird, sometimes up front, sometimes nearly hidden. Its body was unnaturally smooth and regular, its face nearly human, with a strange and unsettling expression.

There was an unmade bed, a wall closet, three cabinet desks. Every flat surface, including the floor and most of the bed, was covered with mex and papers and trix and tools and sausage sticks in various

stages of eaten. Usual Rules meant Free use of anything, food included, that wasn't on the red corner
desk or in a drawer.

Matt looked around a little, less because he was
interested than to have Ruby think he was. He
wanted to go running, that was what he was here for.
He fiddled with a wooden puzzle, stroked a lump of
pet clay that purred and flattened in response. A
quarter . . . he could have stayed with Korolev all
the way to his train.

He drifted out again, into the bathroom. The
lights came on and the door closed with a rather loud
click. The walls here were starship schematics, showing the conduits and ducts and structural members
that would be in and on the walls of a ship's head. The
fittings were actually Pullman-Stargold ship stuff,
but that wasn't unusual anywhere but Earth.

Matt sat down on the toilet lid. He was facing a
phone plate, some books, and an engraved metal
plaque that read

An architect

who does not believe

in privacy

may also lack faith

in keeping out the rain

It rained on Luna, despite Ruby's joke about Tycho.
Every hundred and fifty hours water misted down on
Copernicus's open spaces, Sokoni Core and the Hub
Amphitheatre.

Matt looked at the bathroom door. It was secure,
soundproof, would not open until he touched a button on the wall. He put his slate on his knees, folded
out the controls and switched in. Immediately it

downloaded Ruby's ping, telling him everyone was going to be late. He mashed the eraser and switched out into the cold again.

Matt got up, pressed the door button and went back to the common room. Ruby was still at the deck. Matt took another step, and then, just when it was too late to back off again, the master screen lit up with a vue from Sam Rincon.

"Hello, Sparrow. Got some good news for once: they decided to trade money for time and get things done out here. So we're already tying off: I'll be done in about a hundred fifty. So I'll be home early by half a skyday-hurray-olé." He held up a roll of drafting fillum and a flat black chipcase. "Full set of plans for you—and a surprise. No hints either. Love and sharp pencils, Gorrión."

Ruby sat very still, took a long breath; then her hands flicked over the keyblox, drew ten-finger sketches on the scratchpads, and the lapping subscreens flashed: master locator, local index, target. Matt started to speak, ask where she was going, but he didn't; he couldn't follow and didn't try. Matt could find out what he wanted to know—it was true that he spent a lot of time in VACOR TECHNET—but he couldn't touch Rubylaser, let alone catch her: she was as focused and unjammable as her lightname. In a luminous moment she was at scanl'ecran speed, sliding down a frictionless tunnel of data. She had found whatever she was looking for and was holing out again by the time Matt even recognized the net she'd been in. It was FRACTOR, the main distribution line from the orbiting Frames.

Then it made sense. Ruby was right; sometimes he didn't have all his brains switched in. Sam Rincon was on a Frame. He was bringing Ruby some new trix. He'd just dared her to find out what it was. And she had.

Matt said "So what's in the box, Rubylaser?"

"It's a surprise, Lonestar," she said, from the

other end of spacetime. "It's *my* surprise. . . . Short, short, *short!*"

Matt waited. Ruby shut the deck down with one hard swipe and turned away, her fists tight. "Aguila's coming back three hundred eighty early. You know what that does to the schedule."

He did, without asking how she knew so precisely. The plan did depend on Sam Rincon (only Ruby could call him Aguila, just as only Sam could call Ruby Gorrión) being aboard a ballistic shuttle, his schedule fixed by Kepler's laws, while the team was aboard the TranCity to Tsiolkovsky Station. Sam's schedule had been the thing that kept them running cool all the eighty hours out and eighty hours back.

Matt thought hard. Three hundred eighty hours. They could move up that much. The covers would have to be adjusted; Ruby would run the numbers just as she had before, and they—

Matt said "What about Raf?"

"I believe that's for you and String to work out," she said indifferently. "You can let Raf in on the discussion, if you want to."

"K. K. We'll work around this."

"My father isn't an *inconvenience,* Ronay," Ruby said, with a particular cold calm that Matt knew was fury.

"I didn't mean it like that," Matt said. "I'm sorry, Rubylaser."

"I think you pretty probably are. Do you want to tell them before or after the run?"

"I think . . ." He thought. "After. One run at a time."

A bit of the deck screen lit with a view of the hall outside the door, a person in the hall. "Light and color, Ruby," Cissa's voice said, and an a-vox followed with "Cissa Okuda identified."

"Prysis nonvocal," Ruby told the door, "Corbel," and it opened to let Ciss in.

Cissa was a centimeter or so taller than Matt, a little more muscular: she was first-generation Lunar. The full name her parents had given her was Cissa Luna Okuda; friends never used the middle word. Her hair was almost as dark as Ruby's, longer and straighter. She was wearing a peach-colored cotton coverall and a short cape of brown novylon; her skin was sensitive, and she couldn't wear Beta or wool. Under the cape was her slate, an artist's unit that could unfold to four times the usual size.

She looked around the room. "I'm *still* early? Or were we off for today? I've been using the board, haven't been listening."

Ruby said "Still early. What's on the pirinoshny?"

Cissa looked around. "Well . . ."

Ruby said "Oh, go show. You've got to switch in for the run, anyway."

Matt said "I won't look if you'd rather."

Cissa giggled. "All right, all right." She draped her cape over a large cushion, sat with the slate in her lap and unfolded it. The screen turned pearly, then showed a sketch of Copernicus Old Landing. "I was fooling with softness," she said, and Matt saw at once what she meant. The distant background, the sky and mountains, were sharp as nature, while a ship in the middle distance was slightly soft-edged, as if seen through mist, and the cranes and crawlers up close were smoky, translucent, almost unreal. There was a peculiar power to the image, though Matt didn't really understand why. He said "I like that," because that was true.

"Thank you, Matt."

Ruby said "You want a print?"

"Oh—well, if it's okay—"

"Printer's just sitting there. It's on this card?" She touched one of the memories in the slate's edge.

"Not yet. Here." Cissa pressed SAVE IT, took out the card.

Ruby accepted it with a sour look. "I can give you a chip that'll remember to do that for you."

"No. Thanks, no, that's all right."

"Yeah. Just be a tick. Want to put some drinks together?" She went into her father's office, closing the door behind her. Matt and Cissa went on into the kitchen.

Cissa popped a bin near the wet sink and took out some tubes of flavor concentrate. "Apple for you?"

"Yeah. And cola for Raf, black cherry for String-fellow."

Cissa sorted out the tubes. Matt tossed her some drinking flasks. She dropped a tube into one, connected it to the water tap and dialed. The digits on the meter ticked up.

She looked away from it, at Matt. Matt's head came up quick: Ciss realized what she'd done and at once turned back to the veedwater.

Matt said quietly, "You ought to take the saver chip."

"I don't want to save everything."

"Well, maybe not, but it's one of Ruby's own chips. She made it for Sam. I don't think he uses it all the time either, but Ruby'd like it if you took one."

"Oh." She shook one of the flasks. "Do you think everybody's going to be here soon, or should I stick these in the chiller?"

Matt looked at the time. "Better chill. I should have brought some water, but . . ." Ciss didn't seem interested, so Matt let the thought go. He didn't want to say that he hadn't thought of bringing water. It was the kind of thing He loved hearing Matt say.

Matt knew absolutely that Ruby's father, presented with Ruby's chip, hadn't explained why he didn't need any such thing.

People were different. As He would say.

Ciss was looking at him again, a stare that felt like fingers touching his face. Only his mother ever looked at him quite like that. And sometimes Ruby, almost, but Ruby's black eyes were as cool as the sky. Cissa's—it wasn't fair, he thought, that she should be able to tease him with nothing but her burnt-almond eyes.

Jack Stringer's voice came from the door. "Avast ye, lubbers, and stand by to be boarded!"

Ruby came out of the office holding the print, a big sheet of white fillum still smelling waxy-spicy from the printer. She handed it carefully to Cissa, told the door to let Jack in.

Stringjack was wearing a black judogi with a red belt, black tabi slippers. He was the tallest of them, 19 decs even, and the slimmest except for Tani. He had short, wavy black hair, a long sharp face, long hands and feet. His real name was Joshua Weiszäcker, but you never called him that, *never*. It wasn't the same as Ruby's private name, which was just private, or Cissa's middle name, the weariness over a bad joke endlessly repeated. He had thrown punches over it; if he couldn't do that he would storm out of the room; if that wasn't possible he would drop into a vac-black sulk. Nobody knew why. It wasn't something you could learn from the nets (and Ruby had tried); it seemed to Matt somehow beyond explanations (though Ruby just snorted at that idea). Jack String was just one of his lightnames; sometimes he was Solomon Jay, JJ Striker, Jackie Wirebird—you could really call him anything, except what it said in his card.

As Jack saw Ruby, he held out his black slate in both hands, and Ruby leapt and aimed a karate kick at it. Jack wheeled and jumped, kicking above Ruby's head; he touched the ceiling and stuck there spider-like a moment. Then he pushed down, dropping faster than Ruby, caught her in a hug and spun the both of them around. They separated, backed apart, and bowed to each other, slowly and formally.

"Hail to the sciences," String said, then turned to Ciss and Matt and bowed twice more. "Hail to the

arts, hail to the power temporal. Do we still await the
power spiritual? And . . ." The pause was very deliberate. ". . . the alien presence?"

"Was that maneuver part of what you've got set
up for him?" Matt said.

"Ah, no coaching from the audience. There'll be
sufficient surprises to come. Sufficient to settle the
issue as far as passages to the East are concerned."

"I don't suppose it's occurred to you," Cissa said
with moderate nastiness, "that you're setting Raf up
for serious revenge? If he doesn't go with us—no,
let's be precise, if *you stop him* from going, what's to
keep him from talking? Superheating the whole plan
to vapor?"

"Nothing physical," Stringjack said, not worried but some way from calm. "But everything else.
He's the one who wants so bad to be Lunar. I don't
care in the overall abstract whether he's Lunar or
not; but this mission is for Lunars, not Slammers,
and if he's one of the first and not the second he can
waterwell prove it or switch out."

Matt felt himself on the brink of saying something about the time crisis. He glanced at Ruby, who
was looking straight ahead: no, she wouldn't speak,
she'd given it to Matt to say.

No. Raf and Tani weren't here yet, for one thing,
and for another he was sure it was right to wait for
the end of the run. One set of problems at a time.

The truth, he thought, was that he just wanted
to say something to stop Jack. And stopping Jack
wouldn't help.

"Now you see it," Raf's voice said out of the air,
"2mg over c squared and now you don't."

Raf Economou had actually been born on Earth,
and still had part of a family there; there had been
some kind of family mess about a year ago, and now
Raf lived in Copernicus with an aunt and uncle. He
had white-blond hair, a broad square face, vivid blue
eyes; he was the shortest of all the team, and the

stockiest—all Earthborn muscle, which the thirty-plus hours a skyday he spent at the gym and in the Maze had kept and even built up.

Tani Case had found him in the Maze, just over eight skydays back. It was probably because it was Tani that they had paid any attention to him at all, gone to see him working (she said) as if he were trying not just to exercise into Lunar form but to evolve into it.

They agreed he had succeeded. Mostly they did.

He was wearing baggy Beta trousers tucked into goatskin boots, a light blue shirt of Ango flannel. He opened a zipper on the bag, then hastily closed it again on a damp gym outfit. The other side gave up a Medelec-Luna high-speed slate and three liters of water in a soft pack.

"Lordy, Raf, three," Cissa said, "we're all gonna sog out. I've already got some mixes cold."

"It's okay," he said, as she took the water back to the kitchen, then more softly, "Really, it's okay." He turned. "I'm not late?"

"No," Jack said, sounding entirely friendly. "No one's ever said you weren't determined to jump with the beat. You *will* be as determined in fifty hours?"

"Sure. Okage sama de."

"Bolshoi." Jack sat back in the view bubble, hands on knees, ankles crossed. "So all that perfect existence lacks is Tani."

"Five," Ruby said, watching a time display on the corner of the screen, "four, three—"

"Sing, Goddess, the anger of Peleus's son," the door said, " 'cause Helen's gone AWOL, it's time for some fun."

"Traffic must have been light," Matt said, and they all laughed.

"Did I miss something?" Tani said.

Ruby said "You were three seconds early."

"My soul was light."

Tani Case—Tatiana Casimirovna—was almost as

tall as Jack, and acutely thin. Her hair was naturally a light brown, her skin pale, but long time under glass had bleached the hair and tanned her cinnamon. More than once in Tani's company Matt had heard Slammer boue de bouche about how all Lunar kids were wispy and frail and had to live under sunlamps.

She was wearing a vest and slacks of metallized film, silver sandals, a long shawl of glassomer stained with the image of a slender-bodied winged dragon. She took her slate, a battered gray industrial unit, out of a Beta carrier bag, and handed the bag to Cissa, who started unloading biscuits and fruit.

"Orange?" Raf said, and Ciss pitched him one high and overhand. Raf flexed his feet and rose, without any visible effort of a jump, and caught the orange with two fingers and a thumb. "Ever in your debt, Cissa."

Matt glanced at Stringjack, who had watched the pass and catch with an intensely null expression.

Ruby went to the masterdeck. "K, team, there are minions of evil to be discomfited." She hit the pads as the runners hit the kitchen and bathroom; shortly all were equipped and seated among the pillows on the deep green carpet.

Rubylaser dealt out memory cards with the runners' names written on them, and a daisy to each. They loaded the cards and jacked in the daisies, making sure there was a line of infrared fire between them and Ruby's projector. Cushions were adjusted, plates of food positioned.

"Everybody comfortable?" Ruby said. There were sounds of agreement. Stringer said "We who are about to die say bye-bye."

"K. The windup . . ." Optical drives hummed. ". . . The pitch . . ." There was the sound of a bird, the whisper of wind through trees. ". . . *The hit.*" Slate screens flickered with color. World and time dissolved.

Lafayette Lonestar leaned against a tree, fingering the end of his bow. He had a clear flat shot to the road through Sherwood; he stood off the road, and in his Lincoln green was not to be seen by the casual eye. No one else was visible from Lonestar's position, but he was not alone in the wood.

And still more people were coming: seven on the northbound road. The tall one in the blue robe and fancy hat would be the Bishop of Falsdyke; the small plump woman in brown was his clerk, Sister Anne. A broadset, powerful-looking man with a trim black beard rode just behind them, wearing a steel cap and a black mail shirt: that was Eamon, the Bishop's bodyguard and strongarm. The other four were robed as monks, but if Lady Judith's information was right, they were soldiers, the robes hiding their weapons and armor, the hoods up to cover their unmonkly haircuts.

Judith was priceless to the rebels of the wood, Lonestar thought, but every day her real loyalties came closer to discovery, and in today's weather her title and land wouldn't save her from the rope or the axe . . . or the rack, or the stake.

It hadn't come to that yet: the Sheriff was a man of curious scruples about the Old Way. You could claim, as Bowstring did, that it was only because a witch-hunt would be run by the Church, out of the Sheriff's control. That was true. Still, if pushed enough he might try to destroy the outlaws through charges of witchcraft.

They were true, after all.

The Bishop's party was at close range now. Lonestar looked for the sign he wanted: saw it. He pulled an arrow from the half-dozen in the earth at his foot, nocked, drew, shot.

The black arrow swacked into the Bishop's saddle, a finger's breadth from his gloved and jeweled hand. One of the robed riders threw his hood back and showed armor: next heartbeat there was an arrow through his throat, from another bow than Lonestar's.

The scribe began praying. The Bishop's horse reared. Another soldier died. Eamon looked into the depths of the wood; his eyes narrowed. The touch of wit was on him. He whistled loud enough to be heard in Canterbury and wheeled his horse, crashing straight through the wood, straight toward Lonestar.

Lonestar took another shot. It struck Eamon in the heart. Eamon grinned and kept riding: his armor was better than it looked. Lonestar knew Eamon hadn't been whistling for joy. He grabbed his arrows and moved, as a dozen light footsoldiers scrambled up from a ditch by the road and ran to join the fun.

The wood exploded with sound and fury. There was a noise like a sudden gasp, and the third and fourth of the footmen fell over the corpses of the first and second. The Bishop turned, and turned, trying to find a living man to get behind. Sister Anne hugged her horse's neck. Eamon turned again and came thundering still toward Lonestar. So it was as he'd heard, Lonestar took an instant to think: this soldier was a different sort than they were used to in this war.

"This way, Sister," the scribe heard someone say. She looked down and saw a young blond man of noble bearing and dress, a squire or perhaps a young knight, holding to her horse's reins. She let herself be led out of the storm.

The Bishop had ridden a few yards, to within sight of the woodsedge. There was an awful slaughter going on among the foot troops. That was what they were there for.

Suddenly there was a black streak of cloud across the green-filtered sunlight—no, it was a slim woman, all in black, dropping from the trees like a scarf drifting down on the air. Red hair spilled from her black hood, and the upper part of her face was covered by a mask of white metal. The Bishop made a sign against the Devil. The woman drew a sword, kissed the cross hilt with a mocking twist of her lips, then tossed the blade up and caught it so that its point was horribly near the Bishop's throat. "Now that we've both said our blessings," she said in a soft clear voice, "I'm sure you'll want to continue your departure; and you'll go much faster without that weight in your panniers."

The Bishop hastily drew a sack of gold from each saddlebag and tossed them to the woman in black. The money seemed just to vanish out of the air, and the woman with it. Relieved, the Bishop spurred on. He was nearly out of the woods before he remembered what he was supposed to do next. He bent his head back and shouted as if he were preaching to the Lord Above directly.

Lonestar could sense Eamon still bearing down on him. The man was good, no question. But this was Sherwood. Lonestar leapt for a branch overhead.

Something blew past his face. He missed the grab, lost control of the tumble; his head struck a knot on a treetrunk and he fell down hard. Dazed, he seemed to float above his own fallen body as Eamon closed the distance. The guard wasn't a man, he was a war engine, a flanged iron mace in his hand, his arm recoiling like the lever of a catapult. Lonestar's right arm was extended, thrown out straight as he had fallen, and his bodiless mind saw clearly what Eamon intended. The mace could cave in his head like a rotten fruit, but it wouldn't. It would come down on his elbow, mangling the joint, splintering the ends of bones.

A dead rebel could be a hero forever; but a one-armed archer was nothing at all.

Lonestar tried to climb down out of the sky, back into himself, but he stayed stubbornly cloudborne. Eamon came on.

From above Lonestar's soul above Lonestar's

body, Matt wondered if Eamon was a machine now, an outfielder, or was Ruby's touch of wit running Eamon directly? Ruby-in-the-sky was allowing Matt-above-Lafayette to see this all happening, so presumably Lafayette-under-himself was going to survive to get the explanation from someone—but survive maimed? Or—

And then the Bishop's voice came across the trees, like a Mohammedan's call to prayer: *"A curse upon all rebels, long live the King!"*

Instantly Eamon stopped. His arm of destruction unwound. He smiled. And he turned and rode away. (Oh yes, Matt thought from inside Lonestar, Eamon had been witty then. Ruby would not have left that to automatics.)

Lonestar stirred. His vision was crooked. He felt a light touch on his shoulder, saw a deerhide boot laced high up a woman's leg.

"Theo," he said, and she helped him stand.

Theo wore a loose, short-skirted gown of daisy yellow and pale green. Leather braids twined up her bare arms, coiled around her throat and her hair; woven into the cords were bits of carved bone and wood and metal. She was holding a wooden tube, a little longer than her long-fingered hand. Nipped between two fingers was a sliver of wood, stained black, with two bits of feathers fletching it.

Lonestar said "You wouldn't have killed him."

"All this chivalry," Theo said, "though you're not a knight, and Eamon isn't a knight, and I'm surely not a knight." She looked at the dart and blowpipe. "But no, this one wouldn't have killed him."

"I feel stupid. I don't know what made me miss—"

"*I* made you." She pointed at the branch Lonestar had leapt for. There was a wooden-hilted throwing knife buried in it, just where Lonestar's upper spine would have been had he caught the branch.

"Oh," Lonestar said shortly. "He was ahead of me every move. It's hardly natural."

"It's not."

"Are you saying that the Bishop is employing a sorcerer?"

"No. At least, not as such. There are . . . gifts, talents, that some people have without actually practicing the Art. The Newer Ways have never quite known what to do with them."

Lonestar nodded. He turned to look where the man had gone.

Theo said "You're thinking you might be able to reach him. Bring him to our side."

"Is there someone who *isn't* a step ahead of me? What about Colin?"

She shut her green eyes for a moment. "Colin has it."

"Let's go, then. Oh . . . thank you, Theo. For the branch, I mean."

She inclined her head, saying nothing.

Theo had two horses waiting. As they mounted, they saw a kind of picture, as if clouds were parting to reveal a distant view: the survivors of the riding party were collecting their wits in the shade of a tree, safely beyond bow-reach of Sherwood Forest. The Bishop was there, and the trembling Anne; Eamon rode up last.

The Bishop said "Did you kill any of the rebels, Eamon?"

"No, my lord," Eamon said flatly, calmly. "They cleverly escaped me."

"I sometimes must remind myself that I keep you for your lack of cleverness," the Bishop said. "Ah well, there has been enough cleverness on both sides today. An investment of a mere handful of gold"—the surviving footmen looked at each other—"has purchased us the safe transport of the documents, eh, Anne?"

"Yes, Lord," the little nun said, "thanks to that

young gentleman. I was so frightened, I daresay, until he came to my aid."

"Exactly," the Bishop said, almost choking on his pleasure. "The Sherwood rabble fancy themselves to have morals, and will not—*what young gentleman?*"

Anne put a hand to her saddlebag, and then both hands to her mouth. The Bishop stared at the scribe, his hand coming up, and then Eamon looked at the Bishop with the same flat smile he had given the unconscious Lonestar.

Mists closed again on the farsight as Colin de Courcy caught up to Lonestar and Theo. Colin's smile was broad indeed, and he held a rolled and sealed paper aloft as if it were the lost sword of Arthur.

It was nearing dark, the moon just up, when they reached their destination: a two-story building, half stone and half wood, a garden to one side and an apple orchard to the other. It was an inn, or had been an inn, before a new bridge changed the course of the main road from London. Now it was a legitimate travelers' rest that travelers rarely used: which made it just the sort of place Lonestar and his fellow rebels needed. Because though their rebellion was in the name of the absent King, and the people and laws of England, they were by that King's regent and under those laws outlawed.

Some of the people supported Prince John. Some took the part of whoever was strongest, which in Nottinghamshire meant the Sheriff. Some were afraid and wanted no part at all.

They had good reasons for fear. People were taken on the road, or in the middle of the night, or went out a door and were never seen again. Some had in fact been rebels, or aided rebels; some had merely given a stranger a meal, or bound a wound, choosing to give charity without asking questions; some had done no more than end up on the wrong side of a rumor, or a vengeful lie.

A few of them did reappear, on a gallows, broken and tongueless. The Sheriff hated public expressions of defiance, even from someone about to die . . . or perhaps especially from those.

Some people always cheered when the body dropped.

Lonestar's company stabled their horses and went into the inn. In the slate-floored common room, there was a cool, smoky darkness above the roof timbers. The moon was framed in a window, seeming to rest on the apple trees.

An old woman sat in the corner of the room, in a long black dress and a heavy woollen shawl, rocking slowly back and forth. There was a tiny gray kitten, hardly bigger than a mouse, cradled asleep in her hands; with a fingertip she stroked the fur behind its ears. The woman did not speak; she would not, unless spoken to. And that one did very carefully, because she was in fact a witch.

Lady Judith of Huntingdon came out of the kitchen, carrying a tray of mugs. Colin tried to take it from her, but she ignored him and set it on the table. "Did you get the list from the Bishop?"

"Yes," Lonestar said. "We can be sure now that money, at least, will go to ransom King Richard."

"Good," Judith said, "good." She sank into a chair.

"Yet by your tone, milady," Bowstring's clear voice said, "there's something not good." She was sitting against the wall, still in her black clothes and hood but without her steel mask; her face was fair and quite beautiful. No one had seen her enter the room.

Lady Judith said "Robert Vaux has been taken by the Wallasey outlaws."

Lonestar slammed a hand on the table. Robert Vaux was well known as a favorite of Prince John's, a supporter of the Sheriff. Lonestar's band were among the very few who knew that was a carefully main-

tained disguise. Vaux had helped them, hidden them
. . . more.

But the Wallasey band knew the public face, not
the private one. And they were more outlaws than
rebels.

Lady Judith said "Can't he tell them who he is?
Who he really is?"

Stringer said "Now, that's a thing difficult of
proof."

Lonestar said "Even if he could make them believe him, he wouldn't. Vaux will let them kill him."

"Which they will," Theo said.

Colin said "Can't we speak for him?"

String, not unkindly, said "We do him no good
by that. Abel Miller leads in Wallasey, and he's to be
trusted, but you can bet your eyeballs some of his
people play both sides. If we tell them the truth about
Vaux, the word will reach the Sheriff. And there's not
only Vaux's life gone, but his family's as well. That's
why he'll die."

"You say that as if it's already happened," said
Judith.

String spread her hands.

Colin said "We have to do *something*. If Miller's
trustworthy, why don't we tell him?"

Theo said "He'd still have to explain it to his people."

"But we have to do something," Colin said, more
weakly this time.

Lonestar looked at the corner of the room. The
old woman was rocking contentedly, scratching the
sleeping kitten's head. She said nothing: she would
not, unless asked directly. And then, Lonestar well
knew, the answer would come crookedly, and it
would come at a price. Finally he said "There's no
choice for Robert Vaux, so there's none for us."

Bowstring said lightly, "Now which of the
many possibilities here is the only choice?"

"Rescue."

Theo said "Disguised," not as a question.

Colin said "As the Sheriff's men, so we keep Vaux's reputation safe."

"That ought to work," said String, "at least until the Sheriff notices that none of his men remembers rescuing anybody."

Lonestar said "No disguises, no fighting. I'll go alone. They'll give him to me without questions."

String said thoughtfully, "Yes, they will. And then what do we do with him?"

Lonestar looked at the witch again. The kitten was awake now, its eyes very bright in the candle-light. "We trade him for another prisoner."

String said "For whom, as if I didn't know?"

"Even I can guess that," Colin said. "It's a fine idea, Lonestar, but not for you. The Sheriff won't trade for you—"

Lonestar said "Prince John will."

"You can't bet your life on that," Colin went on. He leaned across the table. "It should be me. The Sher-iff doesn't care about me."

String said "The young man's absolutely right. . . . And no, Colin, that's not an eagerness to see you hanged."

Lonestar felt as if the cat's eyes were burning into his. The witch was just smiling. Lonestar knew he could ask her how to save Vaux's life and reputa-tion both, and knew that the answer would cost: he was trying to avoid compound interest by working the cost out for himself. And then he knew it.

"It can't be you, or any of you," he said firmly, "because I'm taking Vaux from Wallasey in what's supposed to be good faith. If I swap him at once for one of us, it looks as if that was the only reason I wanted him. But if you trade him later, for me, they can believe you had no prior plan."

"But we do," String said, "so damn Wallasey and all who sail in her."

"I agree," said Lady Judith. "How did Miller's

men get hold of Vaux to begin with? They kidnapped him, no different from the Sheriff's men."

Theo said quietly, "And probably thinking that was a fine fair game."

Colin said, with a touch of desperation, "But what if the Sheriff doesn't believe you were really captured against your will? You've escaped them so often —it makes more *sense* if it's me!"

Lonestar stood up. "I'll settle it with you over quarterstaves, Colin. Knock me out and you may go."

"You know I can't beat you with a staff."

"Unless you cheat," String said equably.

"Then it's settled. I'll leave at first light; I should be back with Lord Robert by sunset. Lady Judith, will you go to Vaux Manor, explain to Lady Vaux what's happened? When it comes to the trade, it can't hurt to have her protesting to Prince John."

"Of course, Lonestar."

Bowstring said "One last thing, before we all retire to pleasant dreams."

"Yes?"

"After the Sheriff misplaces his orders from Prince John and has you murdered in your cell— what do we do with Lord Robert then?"

"I'll be past caring. Won't I."

"I must go," Lady Judith said.

"Not now," said de Courcy. "Not alone, in the dark, surely."

"My people will worry."

Theo looked out the window, at the moon. Theo had the vision of a cat in the darkness. She held out a hand toward the sky, traced blue and gold light with her fingertips. "Not now. They know you're safe."

"Well," Judith said hesitantly, "thank you. Do you know, I've no idea which of my household practices your Art?"

"There are reasons for that," Theo said with a slight smile.

Lonestar said "There's work to do tomorrow. We should retire."

They went upstairs to their rooms, even Bowstring silently climbing the stairs in everyone's sight, leaving only Theo in the great hall with the old woman.

After a few minutes, Lonestar heard a knock at his door. It was Judith, Baroness of Huntingdon, and her hair was undone.

Matt-not-Lonestar rose above his runner self, said "Is this—"

"Yes, of course it's my idea," Cissa-eka-Judith said, laughing.

Matt thought that it wasn't fair: girls grew up faster. Their mothers *told* them things. "I meant, is this the homerun."

"Not quite," said Ruby-in-the-Sky. "You and Judith have a quite sweet, if brief, little rendezvous. And Theo, in addition to her studies, makes certain that Bowstring doesn't get ahead of your plans. . . . Which brings us to, yes, you get Robert Vaux away from his none-too-bright captors, and we pick up the action. . . ."

The door of Abel Miller's house crashed in under sword hilts, and one of the Sheriff's serjeants stamped in. "All right, scum, you're surrounded. You can come along and hang, or you can save us the trouble. . . ." The soldier looked at Lonestar, and his eyes flickered with the touch of wit. "*I* know *you*," he said.

"That's too bad," Lonestar said, his sword already out. The serjeant parried the blow at the last moment—did it expertly, and Lonestar knew they were in for a fight. He shouted "Get Robert Vaux away," not for the benefit of Miller's men but the soldiers', lest they kill Vaux as just another rebel.

" 'Ware the lord!" the serjeant called out, and struck at Lonestar. They met blades again, and again. "And *you*, sir—"

"And I, sir?" A parry, a disengage, another pair of blows. "You lean a bit into your swing, sir. Watch your head."

"I'll watch yours." A sweep, a leap. "I'll watch it on a pike's end all the way back to London. And there—" He swung hard, drove Lonestar back a step. "—I'll trade it for—" Another step. "—a knight's—"

He never finished the line, for at that moment the end of Lonestar's sword cut his throat. "And a good night to you too," Lonestar said. "I did warn you, about your head."

Lonestar felt a sudden pain in his side. He thought it was just a stitch, winding from the fight, and then felt the blood against his ribs. He staggered against a table. One of Abel Miller's men, a little fellow, was standing nearby, wide-eyed, with a stained knife in his hand.

"King John's pax," the little man yelled to the soldiers crowding into the house. "I have a countersign—I have a countersign!" He was an easy sword's reach away, but Lonestar's arm wouldn't move, and his legs were turning to mush. The traitor took a cautious step toward Lonestar.

A soldier fell across his path, an arrow sticking up from his body.

"Excuse me," said Bowstring from the window, "I didn't hear the countersign," and she put an arrow in the little man's right eye. "Thought it might get complicated," String said to Lonestar, "what with traitors about, and all."

Lonestar nodded. His strength was coming back; the wound wasn't too bad. He turned, saw Robert Vaux backed against a wall, looking numb. He grasped Vaux's wrist, said "Come on."

There was comprehension, no more. Wit was elsewhere occupied. Vaux followed.

Lonestar said "I wish you had . . . escaped in the confusion."

"I'm sorry," Vaux said. "It was all so sudden . . . and the fight . . . sweet heaven, you're hurt."

"I'll be all right. It's as well, really—it'll explain how you escaped me."

"But not me," Bowstring said from Vaux's elbow. "And it's me you'll be traveling with." String took Vaux's wrist. Vaux stared at her, at her gloved hand on his; then he gave a little gasp and fell into String's arms. Bowstring showed the drugged thorn between her fingers. "You aren't going to make me scratch you too, are you, O fearless leader? I wouldn't want you to bleed to death in your sleep."

"This is a double—" Lonestar blacked out then. But again he stayed aware, hovering, seeing the scene. Future explanations were being economized upon.

Colin came around the house, wiping his sword-blade clean. He started at the sight of Lonestar.

"He's just fainted," Bowstring said, with surprising gentleness. "Get him home, Colin."

Colin said "Why are you doing it like this?"

"Because I owe a little to Robert Vaux as well," she said. "My life, anyway, and that's as little as things come. Now go on."

"I'll get him home," Theo said, appearing from nowhere. "Colin, you go with Bowstring." String opened her mouth; Theo stopped her with a hard look. Then String said quietly, "I told you I'd not use the thorn on one of ours."

"I never said you weren't honest. But since you've made Vaux helpless, you're going to need some help. Colin will go with you—and remember what you promised about the thorn."

"Aye verily, milady," Bowstring said, with respect.

Colin and String hauled Vaux away. Theo bent over Lonestar, touched the wound in his side. Lonestar's spirit rejoined his body.

"What was all that about?" Lonestar said.

"Your plan, a few of the names changed," Theo said. "String was going to do it by whatever means, as you ought to know very well."

"Yes," Lonestar said wearily. "And Colin—"

"I asked the wise one," Theo said. "She said that Bowstring and Colin had to be kept together, or it would be death for both of them."

"That's *exactly* what she said?" Lonestar said, trying to see the trick he knew would be in the prophecy.

"Yes."

"And what about them dying together?"

"I don't know, Lafayette," Theo said. "Please don't talk now." She touched his cut side, and cooled the wound again. "We need to get back to the inn, get you properly mended. It will be dark soon."

"I thought you could see in the dark."

"Not anymore."

The witch's answers always had a price.

Darkness descended.

Matt looked up, gulped a breath. Tani was looking at him, still with Theo's eyes. "I thought we might really lose you there."

Jack said "And is that it?" He was already gathering his gear for whatever adventure was coming next for him.

"Wait," Matt said. His eyes were still deep-focused on his slate, and he couldn't read his watch. "There's something else." He told them about Sam Rincon, the 380-hour problem.

Before anyone's tension could wind any tighter, Matt said "We only now found out. Ruby hasn't had time to run the changes yet—how long do you think that'll take, Rubylaser?"

She said "Any changes to the schedules I've got stored?"

Slates were riffed. "No." "Nada." "No."

"I'm locked up the twenty-eighth and twenty-ninth," Cissa said, and Ruby scratched it in.

Jack, who hadn't touched his slate, said "I've got
—no. Nothing at this end."

"Logged and loaded. K, there'll be paks out for
you within fifteen hours. Everybody switch in and
get them, bien?"

They acknowledged.

Jack said "Does that conclude today's business?"

"I think so," Ruby said. "You're in some kind of
hurry?"

"Oh, as ever. De Courcy."

Raf looked up.

"As we're comrades against fate now, you'll take
no exception in my reminding you of our previously
scheduled social affair?"

Raf did the trick with his foot muscles again,
rising from his cushion as if weightless. From a position a dozen decs above the green carpet, he said "I
assure you, mon ami, if your resolution in the matter
has suffered no diminution, you will find me apt."

"Splendid!" Jack said, with what sounded like
genuine delight. "Then upon the plaza behind the
Carmelite Convent, two . . . jours Gasconnais from
now."

"A Gascon, sir, may have a mighty wish to dis-
tinguish himself."

Jack was animated now. He started to speak
again, then instead bowed deeply, doffing an imaginary hat, and said "Until then." The door let him out.
The corner of the master screen followed him practically dancing down the hall until he vanished around
its curve.

"Vivid," Cissa said. "That was Musketeer talk,
right?"

"Yep," Raf said, with a sidewise look at Matt.

Cissa said "That could be fun, Musketeers. They
had better swords then. And they didn't fool around
with bows in the woods."

"Fool around?" Rubylaser said, more curious than anything else.

Tani said "True enough, but they did shoot big gunpowder holes in each other from time to time."

"Oh, now," Matt said, "when did you ever hear of a Musketeer . . . musketing anybody?" This was beginning to interest him. Matt had read all of Dumas's Musketeer books, and *Scaramouche,* and more. He had loved them, and then hated them, and then loved them in spite of their associations.

Matt was also carefully watching Rubylaser, because Ruby pitched this particular game, and would pitch whatever it might become.

Ruby said "Who knows. . . . Maybe some alchemist will invent gunpowder. Or you'll all go to sleep in Sherwood and wake up four hundred years later." Her voice was sarcastic but her look was not at all. "I suppose I'm going to have to learn French?" She looked at Matt, a grin creeping up her face.

"Regardez-vous *moi,* Mam's'elle maîtresse de jeu? Ou renseignez-vous moi sur les alchimistes?"

Tani said "Oh, Monsieur Lafayette, vous parlez comme les chevaliers de Charlemagne, les beaux ideals de le chevalerie. Mais le grand Empereur c'est mort; la Cardinalle Rubylaser c'est maintenant notre maîtresse. Pardon, notre maîtresse de jeu."

Raf was laughing uncontrollably, bouncing on the cushions. Cissa had riffed up a tran'slater. Ruby turned to the masterdeck, arched her hands a meter above the boards like a mad organist, and shouted "Suddenly, the Sheriff locates your hideout and surrounds it with the entire levy of England! And some Genoese crossbowmen! And some Welshmen who've gotten fed up! Saladin brings the jihad through town looking for Richard and decides to help out! Clang, crash, swoop, *thwip thwip thwip* p'tang, you're all dead and John gets to be king forever!" She turned around, folded her hands delicately in her lap, and said quietly, "Now, Musketeers, you say?"

Raf, suddenly looking uncertain, said "We aren't *really*—"

"Not yet," Ruby said. "There's still some Destiny you haven't confronted yet. Besides," she said to all of them, "are you *sure* you want Stringalevio loose in a world where everybody duels everybody else, all the time?" After a long pause, she said "Always leave 'em thinking. Time is called, team. Remember, pak through in fifteen."

"Bye, Ruby. Thanks."

"Gochiso-sama deshita, Rubylaser."

Matt left with Raf. "What's your next stop?"

"I don't know. My folks want me back in about three. I guess I'll go to the Maze again."

"You ought to take it easy."

"String's not gonna let me take it easy."

"Stop. Come this way." Raf followed Matt onto a glass bridge, eight levels and thirty meters above the green Core floor. They sat down on the edge of the bridge. Matt said "Two data points. One, String's not going to set up something you can't beat. One point one, he doesn't cheat—ever seen him cheat?"

"No. But he can run pretty rough sometimes."

"Not the same thing. One point two, we'll all be there watching, and we'd see if anything went crooked. Jack's really good at laying Maze, *really* good, but nobody can lay invisible Maze. Tracking?"

"You lay it, I'll track it."

"Point two." Matt's mind made his mouth slow down. He wanted to say this exactly right, because saying it wrong could bust vacuum in all directions. "Jack doesn't shift easy. If you make it through—and we all know you will, I've seen you work more times than String has—he may not act a lot different, not right away." Pause. Breathe. Make the words work, this is live online . . . but don't give Raf a chance to block you. "Jack likes you more than you think, Raf. He runs with you, right? That means something. He's just . . . just Jack the Slash, that's all."

"Yeah. . . ." Raf looked over the edge. Matt could see the twitch around Raf's eyes as he did. It was just a plain fact that Raf had grown up eleven years on Earth, and on Earth thirty meters was a long way down. On Earth nobody could fly. But Raf just kept looking.

Matt thought for just a flash that maybe it was the keeping on looking that made Raf really Lunar, or at least not a Slammer anymore.

Raf said "And if I make it . . . and then after the mission . . . what'll Jack be like then?"

Matt wanted to say *I don't know.* He almost convinced himself that *I don't know* was the truth. But it wasn't—at least, not the whole truth, not enough of the truth. "Jack will still be Jack. We'll all still be us." He saw the trap then, and before Raf could spring it, added "And you'll still be Lunar. Because you are, right now. Whatever happens in fifty hours."

Raf smiled then, and still looked down. "Hey, that's what Theo said. I mean Tani."

"Same difference." They both laughed. "You were talking to Tani?"

"She talked to me. Thirty back. Said what you said, about Jack and the Maze and stuff."

"Is there anyone here who *isn't* ahead of me?" Lafayette Lonestar said in Matt Ronay's voice, and then there wasn't any more need or way to be serious; they were laughing and rocking, making stress rainbows in the sunlit bridge.

Raf pointed down. "Look, we're scaring the Slammers!" A couple of people on the grass below were staring and pointing upward. "Hey, Slammer! Wanna catch me? I don't weigh half what you think!"

Someone flapped up beside them, her glassomer wings sparkling. "Want to watch yourself, friend?" she said, and pointed to the flight instructor's patch on her jacket. "In here you need a license to get airborne. Set of these doesn't hurt either."

"Prastityi pozhalasta," Raf said angrily. "I didn't know it was Earth *in here*."

"It's okay," Matt said quickly. He leaned toward Raf, spoke as if he were ignoring the flying woman. "We don't want to draw any heat. Not now. Not here." Raf was still red. Matt had an idea.

He sprang from the railing to the center of the bridge, pointed a hand at the woman. "More of your sorcery, de Winter?" Lonestar said aloud. "And in the very apse of the Notre-Dame! Even His Eminence the Cardinal could not pardon you that, though heaven knows you might seduce even him. De Courcy! Comrade, away! We'll fight this one when we have the proper weapons!" He dashed off the bridge, and Raf was right behind him. Somehow he managed not to look back.

They got down to the Splitlevel, breathless and delighted. "You're right, Lonestar," Raf said, "I wanna be a Musketeer. Even a Gascon Musketeer."

"You'll be a great Gascon Musketeer," Matt said, and then his brains caught up and he said "We've still got a couple of adventures in Sherwood."

"Sure. Sure-sure-Sherwood. You think I'd hole out on Rubylaser?"

"I don't think you'd ever hole out on anybody, Raf."

Suddenly Raf was clutching Matt's arm, hard enough to hurt. "Don't let me, Lonestar. Put an arrow in my back if you have to, but *don't let me*."

Matt felt his mouth dry up. He felt each of Raf's fingers as an individual bar of pain. He was frightened as Lafayette Lonestar could not be. "You won't . . . let anybody down . . ." Should he say Raf, or Colin?

Whoever it was let him go.

"I'm sorry, Matt. I wish . . . I wish sometimes I had parents . . . like yours. Like all the team's."

That made Matt's head hurt like vacuum breaking. Raf wanted—

Raf wanted parents who wanted him, didn't send him to another planet because their lives were suddenly too full for him. Raf was Lunar enough, that was true. He just wanted to be a little bit warmer than he was now.

Matt felt small as a dust speck in the Local Group of Galaxies. Somehow he, or Lonestar inside him, said "I ought to roll on now, Raf. Unless you want me to watch you, in the Maze . . . ?"

"No. No, thanks. You're right, I don't want to hurt anything, not now. See you there in fifty, right, Matt?"

"Forty-seven, Raf."

"Yeah," Raf said, and waved, and was gone through the Split. Skambling, of course.

Matt strolled on through the market, pausing every few steps, trying to decide where to go next. He bought a ten-cent stick of chocolate, nibbled half of it, then sat down in a corner with his slate on his knees. He tapped his fingers on the glass and resin, thinking, and then switched in and connected to VACOR TECHNET.

Matt riffed the Traffic tables, filtered for Lunar, again for Copernicus. There wasn't another starship arrival for over a hundred hours (he knew that, but there was always hope). A Big Dipper was arriving in orbit shortly, and hoppers would be bringing its load of water down to Old Landing in a few hours (not very exciting). In six hours the shuttle *Enterprise of England* would arrive from Earth (as if anyone cared).

He flipped back to the water ship, opened the tech file. It was a Dipper, that was all, a big blimp of aluminum and white glass and charged wire that went out, scraped stuff off a comet, came back and dumped its load. There were three dozen of them, cycling in and out. They were witless, mostly—a crew module could be attached, seeing a crew come back might be fun, but there wasn't one this time. They didn't land unless they needed repairs . . . Matt checked. The ship drew itself on the slate screen, with columns of tab data. There were some red lines that looked promising . . . no. Just maintenance, and they'd do that in orbit.

Matt ate some more chocolate and flipped to the TECHNET news pages. There had been a construction accident on a Frame, nobody killed; Kleistell announced some improvements in automatic pressure sealing; a baby had been born aboard ship near Mars (and what was that doing in TECHNET?). Nothing.

Then he felt a little cold, and checked the accident again. No, it had been on Larkrise, and Sam Rincon was working on Shomron.

He still felt cold. For a moment he'd run—no, he wouldn't want Ruby's father hurt, even a little—Sam wouldn't *have* to have been involved himself for a little problem to delay him a while; just a small delay, a hundred or two hours, nobody had been killed.

And twice in a few hours Matt had mindgamed a disaster, thinking to pick up something useful from the wreckage.

He folded his slate, tucked it away, and went down to Transport level to find a train from Sokoni, through the Hub, south to Verne Center: home.

Verne was the oldest large construction in Copernicus. A trench had been dug, over half a kilometer long and sixty meters deep; torches bored holes in the sides for cylindrical living modules. The trench got a barrel roof, of crete and metal and four kinds of glass, and the whole thing airtighted; a microwave arc melted a ribbon, and the Lunars moved in. You could see recordings of the whole process, and the ribbon, in one of the pavilions on La Place de Novembre. All the tourists went there, though not too many of them went to the Circle of the Names. You had to be Lunar to appreciate that.

Verne had gone up over seven hundred thousand hours ago. Now most of the homods were gone, moved to stations and towns around Luna, and a lot of the bore walls had been cut down to make bigger quarters.

Verne was deep: Transport level was sub-seven here, and the open part of the trench went five decks farther down. Passenger trains went through a glass tube at the east end, suspended above the floor on glass cables. Below, the trench floor was divided into three plazas, named and color-coded, separated by green linear parks. Plaza Jules Verne, the white zone, was just below the train tube; beyond was blue November, and still farther Willy Ley to the red west.

Matt slipped his travel tag back into its invisible pocket and slid past the Slammers who were pressed against the station wall, paralyzed by the view. He paused at the lifts, then, instead of going up and home, went down to the Plaza level, crossed Verne to Place de Novembre. He walked fast, but didn't skamble. Never here, where he could look up and see his own front door.

Small circular pavilions were set around the plaza, made of Lunar materials, black iron and Beta, crete and aluminum and stained glass. They housed exhibits on Independence, the Days of the Revolution. There were vues of rallies and council meetings, of the statement broadcast to the governments of Earth. One of the original six copies of the Charter hung in a glass envelope filled with helium. One whole pavilion held models of Tycho and Copernicus, the first cities, beneath their old dedication plaques. The slabs of gold-plated bronze were engraved with the names and flags of the founding Earth nations, the names of their heads of state. Both plaques had been cut down the middle with an electron torch.

Matt's favorite pavilion was the Economics exhibit. Glass spheres held Lunar wheat and ores, a spindle of Ango wool and another of glass fibers, all produced on the first day of Independence. On the wall were the first proof-struck Lunar coins, as well

as the Fiftieth Anniversary series, which had Ze'ev
Ben-Aaron's picture on the silver one-Kepler.

But the good part was Ben-Aaron's own original
slate—notebook computer, as they called them then—
next to an interactive display running a simple version of the economist's MOONGAME program. You
could touch the board and prove to yourself that
Luna could survive economically without the Earth
at all.

Learning MOONGAME was one of the first
things Lunar kids did on the nets; to beat it, you had
to know how to pull data from everywhere, and what
data to pull. But the display puzzled Slammer kids:
they thought it was some kind of adventure game
and seemed to expect a prize, or battle noises, or
something. Matt had seen them play for a few minutes, and get angry, and smash a fist into the
keyblock. Matt had complained about it to Ruby. Sam
Rincon, who was on the committee for public displays, asked Matt a few questions and made a special,
invisible change.

Matt pressed keys. Food, energy, money, oxygen, hydrogen, labor . . . Matt paused. *He* had said
something to Matt once, about there being only three
things—four?—that really counted. It had been another lecture, of course, what else could it be, but . . .

Matt couldn't remember.

Suddenly he was aware of being watched. Two
Slammer kids were standing by the door of the pavilion, looking intensely at Matt, at the display and controls. Without smiling at all, Matt blanked his entries
and walked casually out.

He strolled to the center of the plaza. On an in-
set disk of polished burnstone stood eight glass slabs,
each a dec thick, a meter across, five meters high.
They were engraved with the names of the 160 members of the Committee of Lunar Independence, the
framers and signers of the Charter. Refraction

through the pillars made the names glow with rainbow light.

Matt knew the Names. Most everyone did. They no longer meant quite what they had eighty years ago, when there were fewer than fifty thousand Lunars. Now there were almost a million, and any number of Ivanovs and Browns and Yamashitas who were not really descended from the Names. But all the Wynants were, and the Kerteszes, and the Havillands. And the Ronays.

Matt's great-great-grandfather Claude François Ronay was the third Name, third column. In the year of Independence itself his son Gérard was born, and a year later Gérard's sister Heléne, who had become captain of a starship and discovered three new planets. Gérard's oldest son was Claude François II, whose only child was He Himself. And then came Matthias Vincent Ronay. Who had no brothers or sisters to be Lunar after Matt went to the stars.

Matt wanted to know more about his great-grandaunt, what it had been like for her, why she had wanted to leave Luna (though he thought he knew), how she had done it. But the records, the nets themselves, were strangely, improbably thin about her. Matt knew that her ship was *The Duchess of Malfi,* knew its technical outlines and the names of its crew, knew where her planets were located and what they were like. Even He, who held the Name and the family like a religion, claimed not to know any more . . . but "claimed" was wrong, because He did not lie.

There was a little commotion in the Ben-Aaron pavilion, the sound of keys being struck violently. Matt grinned. From within the pavilion came a low, crackling, sinister hum, and the lights inside dimmed almost to red. The Earth kids nearly made orbit as they fled. The light had been Sam's idea; the sound was Rubylaser's.

Feeling much better about many things, Matt left the plaza and headed up to Sub-Three, North,

Blue Zone. He thumbed the lock, slipped quietly, quietly, through the door.

The Ronays' house was some twenty-five meters wide, four old bores knocked together. His father's workrooms took up half the space, but Matt still had a room bigger than some one-person apartments. Double-concave pillars, pieces of the old separating walls, were the only reminder of the old construction.

Matt listened for a sound from the study. Nothing. The music room was soundproofed with silicone and lead; nothing could get through there, *if* the door was shut. Matt took a step into the living room, his soft shoe making no noise on the woven rug. The furniture was of wood and Ango leather, the burnstone walls hung with photographs. There were two unlit screen displays; here, of course, there were no windows—

"Have you spoken with Gil Vela recently?" said Matt's father, seated in a brown leather chair against one of the curved columns, almost out of view. His tone was not accusing—was it ever?

Matt gulped his heart back down. "No. Why?"

"I haven't any idea why. But he's called for you, here, twice in the last six hours. You seem to be difficult to reach by the usual links."

"We were doing a game. Everybody's slates were jacked in."

"I'm not asking you to explain, Matt. I know very well Vela's aversion to leaving messages. I'm only reporting the calls."

"Thank you," Matt said.

"I was home," Ronay said, with no meaningful inflection. He stood up. Albin Ronay was a small man, only about a dec taller than Matt, with average muscles for a well-exercised Lunar. His hair was white-blond, his face broad and rather soft, his eyes a washed-out blue, with deep wrinkles at the corners. His hands were large and looked delicate; they were in fact very strong, as Matt had reason to know.

Matt had long ago riffed up an old picture of his father, from before Matt was born, conducting the Lunar Symphony Orchestra. Ronay then looked horribly like Matt now. Matt still looked at the picture now and then, stroking the wound.

"I have a meeting shortly," Ronay said. "Your mother will be home from work in five hours; we shall probably have dinner then. How are you doing?"

"I'll be okay."

"I *know* you'll be okay, Matt," Ronay said, with that terrible half-smile he had so often. "I just wondered if you'd like to eat with us."

"Maybe. I'm kind of tired . . . I'll tell you later."

Ronay nodded.

"I'll be in my room, Dad."

"I'll be in mine, son."

Ronay did not turn his head as Matt went away down the hall. He listened for the click of Matt's door, then went into the kitchen and counted out some water for tea.

That done, he carried the tall hot glass into the meeting room. The room was a flattened oval, five meters by three; one long curved wall was a single screen from chest height to ceiling, a row of smaller displays beneath it. The other wall had a chair, control boards in reach, and a photomural of Lunarscape, Copernicus city at one end.

Ronay sat down, looked at the time display near his right hand. He brought the room up; the lights dimmed slightly, the screen glowed a soft pale blue. A red block drew itself in the screen center, and wrote in:

SELENA

Translunar Conferencing System

The conference you have selected is

CLOSED

to general access.

Verifying access. . . .

Verified.

Good evening, Councillor Ronay.

The red block disappeared, and a green one appeared
in an upper corner. It printed title and date annotations for a meeting of Planning and Coordination Division, Water Board. The members' pictures began to
flicker in across the display.

Tracy Sorensen from Serenity City appeared
first, a thin woman with a perpetually tired look.
"Evening, Albin," she said. "And how has your day
been?" Her voice was a ride cymbal, slowly rising and
falling.

"Uneventful, Tracy."

The rest of the Board appeared, checkering the
screen image by image, filling in the score voice by
voice. C. C. Wynant from Mendeleev, an even-temper-
amented harp; Gus Felton, liaison from Transport,
the double-bass; Archimedes's Karin Karinovna, dark
and distant, a chiming celesta; Vargas, from Population Services, a brilliant silver flute; Da Vinci/
Crisium's Sobieski, a severe and elegant oboe; Jason
Olivetti, from Guericke on the at-large council, the
high sharp voice of the triangle.

The first violin was late as always. Finally he
filled his hole in the screen. Lawrence Duveen,
Tycho's member for Water, had a long, narrow face,
large dark eyes. A square black beard did a little to
smooth his looks, hide the severe hollowness of his
cheeks.

Ronay said "All members of the Board being
present, the meeting is declared in session." Vargas

started to put up a finger; Ronay said without pausing, "The primary purpose of this special session is to
receive and discuss data from the most recent cometary water flight. Gus, do you have those data?"

"Loading now." Felton's hands worked below
the screen image, and a panel irised open on first columns of numbers, then a graphic plot, rotating to
show three dimensions. "These are the first-reduction
figures on Comet Intercept ship number twenty-six."

Karinovna said "It's attractive, August. What's
it saying?"

Felton's jaw tightened; he made a noise, a plunk
of the low strings, then said "It . . . matches the pre-
vious reports." He leaned forward, stuck a hand into
the data display, following the colored curves with
his finger. "Component wear is still up in all areas,
and significantly up on the scoop equipment."

Sobieski said calmly, "Would you define 'significantly up' in practical terms?"

Felton reached forward again. The colored
graph was replaced by a large nested frame with the
Transport emblem: around the edges of the picture
were graphs and data blocks, connected by pointers
to a standard ship's data display from VACOR
TECHNET. "All major parts are still nominal—that
is, we consider that CI-26 can be relaunched following the usual maintenance cycle. We'll be replacing
more minor components than were expected."

"Are these VACOR numbers, or ours?" Olivetti
said, as a complaint.

"VACOR's numbers *are* ours," Felton said, as if
he were glad to have a positive answer. "We provide
them directly, and the TECHNET data format—"

Duveen finally spoke, smoothly, calmly, stopping all other activity on the board. "Gus. You said
you're going to recertify number twenty-six."

"Yes, for one more flight. It's the usual procedure; all the Dippers have to be recertified every time
they go out."

"Do you think twenty-six will pass the checks next time?"

"Almost certainly not . . . it'll need ground-based overhaul."

"That'll be a landing and overhaul after . . . how many flights since the last landing?"

"Two."

Karinovna mouthed a curse.

Duveen said "And according to the design specs, how many flights should a Dipper make between ground overhauls?"

"Five," Felton said.

Duveen said "Your witness," and sat back in his chair, hands folded against his chest.

Hastily, speed Doppler-shifting his pitch, Felton said "We're trying to get a closer fix on ion density and deflection coil wear, but instruments are expensive and crewed instruments cost more. The Sun's been active, too, as you all know very well, and we don't run *it*."

Cham Wynant said "One question: does this have any bearing on our local radiation hardware?"

"No. No, no," Vargas piped. "Phys-Plant and Population track those at *all* times."

Ronay said "Give us the water numbers, Gus."

Felton changed the data display again. "The blue curve is productivity, which since it varies with all the other factors is the greatest variable. The white arc is a weighted average. Breakthrough component is twenty percent—"

"Delete that," Ronay said.

Felton said "I'm assured that twenty is conservative."

"Not depending on breakthroughs is conservative. Remove it, please."

There was a general assent. Felton scratched the changes in. The blue-white curve bent down. Duveen sighed audibly.

Wynant said, with a terrible note-by-note precision, "If I am interpreting these figures correctly, Mr. Felton, the entire cometary water program is on an economic foundation that approaches the vaporous. Is that in fact your interpretation?"

Ronay was running his own filters on the data, as were Duveen and Sorensen, but they all knew what the numbers were saying.

It was Karinovna, who could read graphs perfectly well, who actually said it aloud: "Doubling in five years. In ten years, three to four times the present cost. After ten years, if no new source comes on line, the curve becomes exponential." The gorgeous sound of her voice almost made the message beautiful.

Sorensen said "Presumably getting the Dipper fleet working properly counts as a new source?"

"Yes," Felton said, "if new Dippers are built according to the original scheme."

Ronay said "And if we don't get them working right, how many ships do we need to build to stay even?"

Felton mumbled.

Ronay said "Excuse me, Gus?"

"It's—beyond our capacity. We couldn't build that many."

Ronay looked at Duveen; Duveen looked back, but did nothing.

Somewhere just below his screen image, Olivetti's hands moved violently. "So we're telling everyone the precise details of a Lunar crisis."

Duveen said "What?" almost laughing.

Olivetti said "I would like to suggest that we should be much more . . . careful with information on water production. Especially where the Vacuum Corporation of Earth is concerned."

Karinovna said in sharp high tones, "Take that up with Data Services."

"I will do that," Olivetti said, politely *fortissimo*, "but I see no reason to drop the subject here. Councillor Ronay: does this Board have control over the distribution of water information?"

"Provenance," Ronay said. "Not control."

"But it is an acceptable topic for our discussion."

Wynant said "What is there to discuss, Jason? You've stated your position clearly enough."

"Tracy, do you have anything to say on this?" Ronay said to Sorensen, who had shown no sign of interest.

"Uhm? D'you mean, should I explain to Jason why we can't kill a feed to TECHNET?"

Olivetti said "Yes, explain that," shrill, nearly untuned. "I'm only talking about keeping some maintenance information private—"

Lawrence Duveen said, with a wicked small smile, "You were never much skystruck, were you, Jason?"

Olivetti said "What?" He paused a moment, regathering momentum, and said "I suppose that means something," a deliberate quartertone short of irritation.

"It means you never sat by slatelight in your darkened bedroom, walking the corridors of the great faraway ships as revealed in TECHNET display, until you knew more about them than their masters and crews?"

What a way Duveen had with an aria, Ronay thought.

"Open data access is what TECHNET's *about*," Sorensen said, the cymbal brushing weary time. "Full engineering callouts on any ship you're sharing space with. No secrets, no unknown variables, no twiddling the veeders. That's what crews expect to find, and if they don't find it, they'll ask why. And VACOR will, with the utmost piety, explain that we're hiding the data, heaven alone knows why. Proposition, Jason: give me an excuse that doesn't sound crooked or crocked, and I'll call Data right now and pull the wire myself."

Olivetti said stiffly, "I will speak to Dataserve . . . to see if something can perhaps be done short of that."

No one answered that.

Wynant said "Now that we know where we're going with the Big Dippers, I believe we have to take up the subject of new production projects."

"Agreed," Ronay said. "Shall we discuss the CI-X program first, and then the Sunwells?"

"Fine," Duveen said, abruptly but quite warmly. "And after those?"

Ronay said, beating out the words, "I propose that we follow the CI-X discussion with an official poll of the Board on project funding. Is that acceptable?"

There were yeses and nods. Duveen said "That's fine, Albin. We've all got plenty of time."

The Comet Intercept-Experimental ships, the Super Dippers, were larger and more elaborate versions of the CI series, carrying a MIRAGE drive. They would travel to the Oort Cloud of comets, at ten times the distance of Pluto, and return faster than the Big Dippers could visit a single sungrazer comet—without traveling through the intervening space, avoiding the ions and particles and dust of the so-called vacuum. They also, it was suggested, would encourage Luna to start building MIRAGE drives itself.

Then came the antiphony. The ships themselves would cost several times as much as Big Dippers. They would need crews, the human operator the MIRAGE demanded, a few more people to keep that one sane. Crews needed life support and training and salaries, and sometimes they were injured or killed. And no one knew if they would really be cheaper to run than the present Dippers, let alone stay that way. Calling them Super Dippers was a kind of fraud, a false theme: they were not just a modification of the CIs, but a new design, and could be expected to run as rough as any new design.

Wynant voted first and firmly. "Recommend we

suspend funding to the program immediately, with a further recommendation that at the next Board meeting we vote on shutdown."

"That's it?" Felton said, reaching up from defensiveness into real anger. "Just blow all the work into vacuum?"

Sorensen said "There's still thirty kiloKay left from the last appropriation. Use that to make a new case for the project, if you can"—that last was a grace note, not unkind— "or find some new use for what you've done. I vote suspend."

"Suspend," Olivetti said.

"Suspend."

"Oh, yes, suspend," Duveen said.

"Suspend funding."

Felton said "Abstain."

Ronay said "I vote to suspend, and the recommendation is effective. Gus."

Felton grunted.

"Do the studies, as Tracy suggested. But I think it's unlikely that we'll provide any further money for this."

Felton said "As Transport isn't involved with any of the other—" He stopped entirely, leaving an utter silence. "As Transport isn't directly involved with the Sunwells, I'll ask you to excuse me."

"No," Ronay said shortly. "You're a member of the Board, and we still have business to conduct."

Duveen said softly, "Plenty of surprises still ahead."

"Very well," Felton said. "Let's talk about Sunwells."

Sunwells would be cones of magnetic fields and synthetic film, tens or perhaps hundreds of kilometers across, funneling hydrogen from the solar wind. Luna had plenty of oxygen, locked up in rocks. Bring in hydrogen, and they could make water until the Sun died.

A great many people were in love with the idea.

It was a great mental leap, an idea of pure space, not another mining operation or plumber's-nightmare surface plant. The artist's renditions of hazy purple sweeps across a Bonestell-black sky, blurring the stars, were undeniably beautiful. It was poetic: gossamer Moonflowers drinking nectar from the Sun. More practically, they could in fact be built and launched and served entirely from Lunar resources. The engineering was not completely blueprint and dream, since there were three companies building powersats and solar sailboats, each of which swore it could build the wells cheaper than either of the others.

Then the counterpoint pressed itself against the charming melody. No one had built a prototype. No one could simulation-solve the combined chaotic dynamics of solar wind, a giant flexible structure, and the gathered ionized vortex. To actually learn how much H_2 they would trap, how many people would die in the construction, and what the real costs would be, one would have to be built. To know how long they would last, and the price in money and lives of maintaining the funnel on station and drawing up the H_2, one would have to be kept working. To know how bad the navigational hazard would become, a lot of them would have to be built and kept working.

And yet it was so technically sweet.

The Board voted in nine-voice harmony to continue funding the project, and approve long-duration exposure tests of the available structural materials.

Ronay said "I believe that will conclude this meeting."

"The hell you say, Albin," Duveen said.

Ronay said "Shall we poll the Board?"

Felton said "I wouldn't miss this for anything. Vote to continue."

Tracy Sorensen said "*I* would. Dismiss."

Vargas said "Continue."

Karinovna and Sobieski voted to dismiss; Olivetti and Wynant called to continue.

Duveen spoke without any note of triumph. "We all have the reports on the Vacuum Corporation's IMT proposal. This project covers a great number of different points—"

"There's only one salient point," Karinovna said. Ronay agreed, but there was no use in saying so.

"I'll agree with that," Olivetti said. "This is Luna, and Luna is not interested in water from Earth."

Duveen smiled slightly and said "Karin, is that the point you had in mind?"

"No."

"Then it would seem there is more than one point for discussion here."

Ronay said nothing. They all knew perfectly well that there was only one important point in the VACOR plan, and it had nothing to do with where the water came from.

The MIRAGE stardrive did not have to be operated in deep space; it did not have to be mounted on a starship at all. The very first MIRAGE transfer— Avakian's prototype, that was not supposed to be a stardrive at all—had been from the surface of the Earth to the Lunar Farside. But for two reasons, the first Ingravity MIRAGE Transfer, ninety years ago, had been the last.

The first reason was that, operated in a gravity well, the drive unit and all that went with it arrived reduced to bits no bigger than a centimeter across.

But suppose you needed ores and undepleted soil, and had vast quantities of toxic wastes and radionuclide-salted earth to dispose of, as the Earth did have. None of those cargoes could be harmed by pulverization. Suppose you had oceans, and Luna was dry; drop a drive unit into the sea, and target it on a sealed Lunar cavern.

The Vacuum Corporation proposed to send Luna as much as two cubic kilometers of seawater. There were half a dozen ways to desalinate it: filters, hydrolysis, heat disassociation, simple evaporation in ultra-low pressure. In one great crescendo, two million million liters; it was almost beyond reason. It was enough to last for centuries if they pissed every drop at the sky. With recycling, even with relaxed controls—and Ronay knew that they would have to loosen them—it would last forever.

There was a second reason. MIRAGE would operate only if a conscious human being were present with the unit. No one was yet certain why, but it was a fact of the system: no remotes, no robots, no animals.

On Farside near Tsiolkovsky, where the Avakian prototype had holed out, there was a monument to a technician named Lochert, who had taken history's quickest trip to Luna. Under the stone was what of him could be scraped together.

"I understand the opposition to the idea," Duveen was saying, "and perhaps if I did not require three point two liters of water a day . . . or if only I and a few close friends did so . . . I might join that opposition myself. But I need the water. Nearly a million of us need it. Do you have another source? Ships, Sunwells? Fine; bring them on line and I will stand beside Jason in flipping a rude gesture to the Vacuum Corporation. But . . ." He sounded genuinely sad, as only strings are sad. ". . . they aren't on line. And all the citizens on Nearside can see that big drop of water in the sky every day, every dry day."

Vargas said slowly, drawing it out, "There is another possibility."

Ronay said "Do you mean controls?"

"There are two ends to any pipeline."

Ronay said again, harder, "Do you mean controls?"

Vargas nodded.

Before Ronay could speak, Duveen said "This Board is of course chartered to deal with production issues. Immigration controls are outside our provenance. And this meeting was specifically called to deal with water-production projects. With respect."

Vargas nodded again, said "Are we going to vote on the VACOR idea?"

There was a long pause. Then Karinovna said quite crisply, "I do not see anything to vote on. We lack the power to reject the proposal, and we aren't going to accept it tonight; it requires no technical studies; all we can really do, friends, is keep stalling it until our hand is forced by overwhelming events. Are we maintaining contact with VACOR?"

Ronay said "I'll talk with Lynch Ballantine."

"Then may I propose that we end the meeting now? Lawrence? Albin?"

Duveen said "I'm certainly tired enough."

Ronay polled the Board; they all dismissed. The images on the screen winked out one by one, until only Duveen and the data block were left; Ronay gave a command and the block vanished. Duveen's picture expanded. His eyes seemed more beautiful, enlarged; but the rest of his face looked sharper, harder.

Ronay said "Vargas is bluffing on controls."

"Bet a Kepler on that? Popsy's under ten times the pressure we are. They might *have* to set limits, just to prevent a bureaucratic breakdown."

"So we have a population problem *and* a labor shortage?" Ronay meant it as a joke, and Duveen took it so. Then in the middle of the laugh Duveen said "Albin. It's water."

"With a corpse floating in it."

Duveen sighed. "Every Lunar who dies gives his moisture back to the system. Your father did, you will someday—" He stopped, then said very, very tenderly, "You know you'd ride the bomb yourself."

"You know I've offered to," Ronay said, hearing his voice waver. "Ballantine just grins. Like a shark."

"I should consider that flattery."

"The whole thing's an obscenity."

"Well, yes, Albin, of course it's obscene. It's positively pornographic, and you can't make it into art. But the attractions of pornography aren't artistic, Albin. They're deep and compulsive and very often hateful to the people that hold them. Obscenity answers an inadmissible need." Duveen's eyes were cool and hungry, and Ronay felt a sudden twitch of pain.

"Get to the point," Ronay said.

"I wish you had the patience for my work that you have for your own. I always did," Duveen said, quite maliciously. "The *point* is that our neighbors have convinced themselves that they want and need IMT, and VACOR is going to get it for them. One way or another, with us or without us."

"I've no interest at all in what they do without us."

"We are not at war with the Earth, Albin; nor even with the Vacuum Corporation, even if both of them want to own us. And I would feel much safer against being owned if we were partners with either or both of them."

"You actually think they'll feel a debt to us, if we give them the sacrifice?"

"I actually think it's absurd for me to say anything, since we both know all the facts, since we both have to know them . . ." Another long sigh. ". . . and we both have to do something about them. What are we going to do, Albin?"

Ronay's wife was still at the hospital, an hour or more to go on her shift. His son was in his room, with every barrier raised. Larry Duveen was at Tycho, a quarter of Luna away. All these things, Ronay thought, were good and correct and as they should be.

He stared into the black pools of Duveen's eyes and said "We tell the Lunars how much their water is going to cost them, and we ask what they are willing to pay. Once we know that, we will know what we're going to do."

"I'm glad we're going to know that." The edge of sarcasm was invisibly thin. "You can do better, Albin."

"I think you enjoyed watching the meeting run out of control."

"Is that what it did? You're as close to a chairman as the Board has—surely it's you who should maintain control. Your *provenance*." After a two-measure rest he said "And you know I don't enjoy watching you lose control."

What a gorgeous lie that was, Ronay thought, and said "I'll talk to Ballantine."

"I suppose someone must. And given that you're the only one of us who can stand the sight of him, well."

"Good night, Larry."

"Good night, Albin. Give my best to Sonya and Matt."

"I will. And you should visit."

"And you." They neither would.

The screen went blank. Ronay leaned forward, looking at the floor.

Once he would finish a conference overcharged with energy, themes banging in his head, phrases and rhythms crackling off his fingers. Once the arguments over an issue were worth an oratorio; an issue as great as water, a symphony. He had been working on a symphony, with a movement all about water; once, once.

Now there was just a hissing in his head, gray noise.

His hand brushed the glass of room-warm tea beside the chair; it wobbled and he grasped it hard. A few drops escaped over the rim, drifting, tumbling. Ronay cupped his other hand and caught them, drank them salty from his palm.

Ronay thought about single drops of water,

clear ripples in the gray pool of noise. Suppose the movement began with one drop, one ripple, and moved upward and outward—

No. Not another mindless linear accretion of sound. There were already enough Ravellesque Boleroids to fill the Ocean of Storms.

He stood, turned to look at the mural behind him. The Ocean of Storms had never known water. Was there a possibility of dry water music? The flow of dust, waves of stone, the splash of an impact from the unblue sky.

There was a scratch of music in Ronay's mind, a squeak, a crack of woodwinds dissolving into bells.

And then a voice beside him.

Ronay turned. He saw Matt recoil a step from him. Ronay lowered his hand, which had been conducting the scrap of movement. He did not speak; if he asked Matt what he had wanted, Matt would inevitably have wanted Nothing.

Once Ronay had wanted Nothing. He had been in love, completely and transcendently and very erotically. He had also been as eager to die for Luna as D'Artagnan for France, under the musketry of the Terrestrial invader, in a boiling rush of translated water.

But there had never been any invasion troops, and there had been a need for new Lunars. So he had given up love to make new life for Luna . . . and yet now, after fourteen years with Sonya, he loved her, and Matt, as much as he once had wanted to die in the old family cause.

He did not want to die for a trillion liters of seawater. He did not want anyone to.

All that went by in a single mindbeat. Then Matt said "Dad?"

"Yes, son?"

"You said once . . . there were three things . . . I think it was three things, that Luna is made out of. What were they?"

Ronay heard music then, for many voices. It was old music, written long ago, when the Moon had seemed a simple place; that didn't matter. "Four things." He waved a finger toward the ceiling. "Air and light." He picked up the glass of tea. "Water." He pointed at Matt. "And people." He sat on the arm of the chair, bringing himself a little lower than Matt. "With air and light and water, and people to work with them, we can make anything else we need." Ronay wanted to ask why Matt had asked him this, and did not do so.

He handed Matt the glass. Matt took it, automatically; he was a Lunar being given water. "And . . . money?" Matt said. "We need money, right?"

"Air and light and water and people," He said quietly. "Suppose you had money, all the money there was, but no . . ." He put a finger into the glass of tea, flipped a lazily floating drop onto Matt's nose. ". . . water." Matt tried to keep the laugh in as he touched the drop down to his lips.

"Now," He said. "Could you drink the money? No. And you need thirty-two hundred cc's a day, every day. So you'd have to buy water from someone who did have it. At whatever price they wanted to ask, because you *have to* have those three liters."

"But wouldn't somebody get the water, if you had money to pay for it?"

"Maybe. Probably. Are you willing to bet your life on it?" He looked hard at Matt, like one of Ruby's villains, and Matt laughed again—but the look stayed hard, and the laugh failed.

"Thanks, Dad," Matt said, and started to get up, but His hand closed around Matt's and the glass, and the glass nearly slipped away; Matt couldn't move, because spilling a whole glass of water in front of Him wouldn't—He wasn't looking at the glass, why would He have to, He was looking straight into Matt, and said "There are things you mustn't sell for symbols," whatever that meant. Was He talking about Sympla, the starcrews' language, was that it?

Ronay took away the glass of tea, drank from it. "Are you okay for money?" he said.

Matt kept himself from smiling. So He thought that was what it was about? Matt thought for just a moment that he ought to ask for some cash. They needed hard money for the coming trip, because cash didn't trace back down the wires, and they had already piled up all they could without raising their parents' suspicions—but He had said it Himself: there were things you didn't take money for. "I'm fine, Dad, sure. Thanks for—telling me about the things."

He nodded, still propped against the meeting-room chair, still holding the half-full glass of tea, as Matt walked back to his room.

Matt shut the door, dropped the latch silently, silently. He shook.

He looked at his timer. Ruby's pak, with the new trip numbers, ought to be on the wires by now.

Matt's room had a three-up deck, the main screen built into the wall, framed in white steel. A star mural covered another wall. The others were all shelves, loaded to tumbledown with his books, ship models, artifacts from all the cities of Luna and seven other stars. Matt wanted, now and again, to do the room as a ship; people did that, you could get all the stuff easily. But it would be too obvious. Like a good coldspot, like a perfect plan, it meant nothing if you gave it away.

Matt docked his slate with the big deck, switched. Ruby's message was there; Matt cut it to slate memory, leaving no other copies. Then he pinged Gil Vela.

The screen showed rows of theatre seats, empty except for one. A man sat in it, feet propped up on the seat in front, a program booklet covering his face. His chest rose and fell slowly.

"Vela," a voice said. The man in the seat did not stir: it was only a stock image.

"Gil, it's Matt. My—I heard you called."

"Oh. Yes."

Matt waited. Finally he said "What is it, Gil?"

There was still no answer for a full minute. Then Vela said "Can't break things off just now. Come by tomorrow sometime . . . after ten, okay?"

"Sure, Gil."

"Right, Matt." Vela switched out.

Matt shrugged to himself. He tapped his fingers on the board, wondering what to do next. He loaded a tutorial on Sympla, stuck a pickup to his throat so he could just subvocalize the responses. It wasn't as good as actually being wired, of course. But Matt's mother had said No She Was Not Going To Operate On Him and that was that.

Symbols flashed on the screen. Docking Port. Emergency Control. Weapons Station.

They got faster. You are wanted on the Bridge. Bathroom. MIRAGE activation in eighteen minutes. Thrust Direction.

Faster still. Make a food selection—Unpressurized Cargo—You have received your maximum radiation allotment for this shift—Fragile Components.

Faster: Flightrecorder Unidentifiedvesseltostarboard Ejectionport Theatmosphereisbreathablewithmasks VACORTECHNET Wearecarryingnocontraband Hightemperaturegas Thishabitatwelcomesyou—

Matt stopped. He was breathing hard. His throat hurt and he felt sweat on his back. The clock said 2565, almost midnight. The twenty-fifth and last hour of the Lunar day ran for seventy-two-and-a-half minutes, making the full calendar day just one twenty-sixth of a skyday. All the new worlds used the system of long or short last hours, so that a minute was always a minute, a standard hour was the same everywhere in the human universe; but it was a Lunar invention.

Matt switched out, undressed and crawled into bed, feeling entirely sleepy. Tomorrow he would go and see Gil Vela, and find out—

Suddenly he thought he knew what Gil wanted to talk about, and knew he wouldn't sleep at all.

But he did.

A little past 0830 he got up, letting the sonic shower shake him the rest of the way awake. The door to his parents' room was closed. In the kitchen, he put in an earplug and dialed a music channel. Moving silently to the private beat, Matt knocked together some eggs, Ango milk, and a tomato in a shallow pan, folding the omelet pretty near perfectly and slipping it in one easy motion onto a plate. He sat down with it and a mug of tea, and got an adventure show on the wall screen to eat by.

Finished, he put the utensils, plate and mug in the washer, peeled the organic film liner from the pan and tossed the sheet into the bin for compostable waste. He checked the kitchen for any remaining trace of his presence, slung his slate and went out.

Matt took a train to the Hub, went up to Surface. The Slammers were thick as ever here, lining up at the Skyhook arena to buy tickets and place bets, shooting stills and vues of everything and each other, asking directions to Transport, Moonwalks, the toilet, "a good place to see the Earth from" as if the damned thing ever moved, *always* lurching, stumbling, slamming. And it was absolutely the last place to do anything that might upset them. Matt spent the time until clock ten not upsetting them.

Matt went through an archway beneath a long, narrow display board, dark now. Instead of going through the darkened glass doors beyond, he turned sharp left and stopped at what looked like a blank wall; he said "Hi, Naomi. Here to see Gil." The panel slid open, revealing a little, cluttered office. A woman sat behind a desk; on the wall behind her, a screen showed Matt and the entryway behind him.

"Hi, Matt. O'genki desu ka?" Naomi was short, heavyset, with very black hair, a sharp nose and a perpetual grin. She was wearing a gray Beta kaftan and a wrought-iron necklace.

"Fine, Naomi. Is Gil in his office?"

"On stage, I think. I know he's expecting you; peek first, but I think you can just go on out."

"Tak."

Matt threaded his way through the plycore labyrinth of backstage: dressing rooms, prop rooms, showers, the smells of paint and metal and makeup. Somebody carrying a bundle of swords and a severed head waggled an elbow at Matt, who waved back.

He stopped at the right wing door. The warning signs were off, but he took a look through the peephole anyway: nothing. He went through the wing, onto the half-thrust stage.

The stage was lit but bare, the house lights down. Matt looked out at the empty seats, saw no one. He looked left, right. Nobody. He tilted his shoulders, said "Now is . . ."

No, it wasn't right. Gil would be furious; Matt wasn't performing, he was just acting.

He humped his back, just a little, put a hand in a pocket and let the arm hang limp. With his other hand he gestured in the air, shaping a throne by pantomime. He touched an invisible crown, then stroked his withered arm again.

"Now is the winter of our discontent," Matt said, an angry man pretending to cheerfulness, "made glorious summer by this sun of York; and all the clouds that laid upon our house in the deepness of the ocean buriéd. . . ."

" 'Lour'd,' not 'laid,' " said thunder from above, "and it's 'the deep bosom of the ocean.' Otherwise, pretty good for a cold reading."

"Gil?" Matt said, feeling as if he could fall through a crack between boards.

"I'm in Control. Be right down." Matt looked up, saw a movement in the booth above the balcony seats. Gil Vela stepped into view, raised a hand and *flew* toward the stage.

Halfway down, Matt could see that Gil's raised hand was curled: he was sliding down a glass cable, invisible in the stage lighting. Gil let go above the stage, dropped with barely a thump. "Hello, Matt," he said genially, "sorry I caught you in rehearsal, but I couldn't resist." Matt knew he meant it. Gil always did.

Gil Vela was a full two meters tall, trim and all muscle. He was almost completely bald; an old long scar (covered in performance by a wig or makeup) ran down his right temple. His nose and chin were big, his eyes a deceptively mild brown. He looked very much like a pirate in an old picture. He was wearing a belted jumpsuit of undyed white Beta, leather gloves and low boots. He showed the palms of his gloves, which had pieces of glass channel attached. "Like the entrance? I don't know what to use it for yet, but I think you'll agree it's impressive."

"Yes," Matt said, "it's good. Probably even better when you're in the audience, looking the wrong way."

Vela nodded gravely. The seriousness stayed as he said "Do you know what I called about?"

"The season?"

"You know that Oki and Clara are turning nineteen, so they're out. Oki at least is joining the adult company. And Pru's family just got word that they're moving to a new world, I forget which—"

"Burgundy?" Matt said, tense as the glass wire overhead.

"Yes, that's it. Did Pru tell you?"

"There's a starship just in. Its last stop was Burgundy. The message must have come with it."

"Black space's intelligencer." Matt didn't get the reference, but Vela just went on. "At any rate, I've got three slots to fill. *Maybe* four, once we see what the final receipts look like." He gestured backstage. "So I guess we'd better talk, right?"

Matt followed Vela to the manager's office, a room four meters by five that had almost enough free floor space for two people. The rest was taken up by scenic models, stray props, framed and unframed pictures, book-bound scripts, ribbon-bound scripts, loose scripts and extremely loose scripts. Overhead was a glass-channel panel grid, with panels only here and there; more stuff was piled up there.

"Sit down, Matt. You don't mind if I take off the people suit?"

"No, of course not."

"It's not a part of the audition, Matt," Vela said with great gentleness, and plopped down in a big leather armchair on casters. He unbuckled his suit, opened a long diagonal zipper from right shoulder to left hip. Underneath it, he was wearing a black silk T-shirt and shorts.

Vela put his left hand through the open zipper, to his left shoulder. His knuckles worked beneath the fabric, and there was a dull click. His right arm dropped away from the shoulder, still suspended by the Beta sleeve enclosing it.

He stood up and peeled out of the jumpsuit down to the knees, placing the loose arm on the desk beside him. Then he sat back down and disconnected his right leg at the hip, his left at the knee. He tucked them under the desk, still upright, like a pair of boots, and turned to face Matt.

"Want something to drink?" Vela said.

"No, thank you."

"Extra grouse. Now, you've been in the training group long enough to know that I don't grade you—if I don't kick you out, it means you're good enough to stay, right? But when it comes down to cases like this, I've got to make choices. Understood?"

"Yes."

"So for the purpose at hand *only*, I figure you're . . . no, the hell with that. I figure you're in the top three, leave it at that." He rapped on his single knee with the knuckles of his single hand. "In fact, I'm going to ask you not to ask the others about this. Somebody might have reasons to turn the offer down, and those reasons wouldn't be any of anyone else's business. Can you live with that?"

"Sure," Matt said, feeling suddenly uneasy, thinking of the possibility of reasons of his own.

"And thus to terms and conditions. The Young Company does either two major productions or one major and two minor; same number of performances per play as the adults, but fewer shows a week and a shorter season. Once you're in, you're in for the whole season. This is a youth-terms contract," Vela said levelly, carefully, "but it's a real contract." Matt knew that Gil Vela could do anything at all with his actor's voice, and he was sure that what Vela was doing now was telling the truth and expecting it in return.

"I understand that," Matt said.

Vela gave a small nod. "Important point number two: you get a salary, but it isn't a large salary, because plain and simple the YC doesn't pull in that much money. Rather than spend our limited subsidy money on you, we assume you'll continue to live at home. I'll make that even clearer: it's *not* enough to live on, unless three or four of you get together to starve as a group.

"Which leads directly to big point the third: if you join the YC, the relationship between us changes, and you have to understand exactly how it changes." He put his elbow on the arm of the chair, leaned his head against his hand. "In the school group, we can be pals, you and I, because we're really just knocking around the idea of acting. If somebody's not really interested in working, they usually just leave, or I can say thank you, goodbye now, write if you get work." He smiled. Matt smiled too.

"But in a production company, that's out. It's oyabun-kobun, and no points for guessing who's who." He looked unhappy, not a common expression for Gil-not-acting. "I don't mean not friends: I'm not the kind of director who wants to be hated, but I *am* the boss.

"And being oyabun," he said, velvet over riveted steel, "does not mean that I assume, replace or otherwise alter the relationship between you and your parents."

Abruptly Vela shoved his chair back and sat up straight. "So you see, it's an utterly lousy deal that nobody in his right mind would swap for a glass of recently used water."

"What," Matt said, "and give up show business?"

Vela laughed from the bottom of his lungs. "I think that's the answer I was looking for," he said. "So. Shall I have Naomi do the papers?"

Matt felt a weakness in his belly, just a millimeter short of nausea. Two offers in two days: both good, but both so very Lunar. . . . At least as a Transport intern he could get out of Copernicus. This didn't even get him out of the house.

He knew that actors went to the sky. There were at least a dozen starship touring companies; the other worlds loved them, needed them, paid them wonderfully well (or so they said). He knew too that he would need a reputation for one of them to take him on; time in the Young Company, time with the main group, time, time, time.

"I need some time," Matt said, hoping to conceal his confusion from the man who had taught him acting.

"How much time?"

Go for orbit, Matt thought, and said "How much do I have?"

"I thought it might go like this," Vela said, with what might have been kindness had there been any room in the words for it. "And therefore I called you in first, the day I knew how many openings were available. Do you know why I did that?"

Matt had several notions, but was afraid to choose one. "No."

Vela's voice became cooler, more distant. "You're not the first in the class. I think you know that." He didn't wait for a response. "I also think that the reason you're not first is that you're not focused on any particular goal . . . which, please believe me, is not bad or wrong at thirteen years old.

"I would like you to take the job because I think it would give you a goal. And I'm not at all surprised that for one blind instant you jumped at it, and now you want as much time as possible to chew it over. So I'm giving you all the time I can give you: the two days until the next group session, on top of the half-skyday everyone else on the short list will have to get their lives in order."

For just an instant Matt found himself hating Gil Vela: the second-guessing, the "knowing" Matt better than Matt himself could—it stank of Him.

Matt forced the thought down, tried to think only of numbers on a clock face. Four hundred fifty hours. Matt realized that he hadn't studied Ruby's revised figures on the trip times. He didn't know how the curves would fit, and there wasn't any way to run the digits now.

It didn't matter anyway: the courses were set and the fuel spent. If the vectors collided, that was simply that.

"Thanks, Gil," Matt said.

"I appreciate the thanks . . . but it's going to be a while before you know if you mean it. Maybe quite a while."

The anger spiked again. "Thanks anyway," Matt said over it, and stood up. "Was there . . . anything else you wanted to talk about?"

"No. There wasn't anything else. Da svidanya, Matt." He levered himself up on his half leg, grabbed the overhead grid and chinned himself; hanging by his chin, he reached even farther up, groping for something stored in the loft.

"Dasvidanya, Gil."

Gil grunted through his load-bearing jaw.

As Matt made his way out of the office minefield, Vela hiked himself up again on his elbow, said "Ping if you think of something to do with my swell entrance, okay?"

"Okay."

As he passed Naomi, she said merrily, "Will we be seeing a lot more of you soon?"

Somehow he didn't cry; somehow he said "Never, never, never, never, never," just as he had heard Gil do it in *King Lear,* and under cover of her laughter he escaped alive.

He went to a farther corner of the Hub, away from the crowds, bought some orange juice and a pastry. He paid with his card, not cash: he didn't mind if anyone knew he was here, he had a right and reason to be here.

He folded out his slate and read Ruby's numbers. She had cut things tightly, but he supposed she hadn't had much room to cut. They had to complete the trip while Sam Rincon was absolutely absent, or lose the only definite coverage for their own absences. They had to start the covering process early enough for it to sink in slowly with their families. And they had to arrive by night: Tsiolkovsky Observatory did not shut down, the stars were still there, but there was no chance of the Sun interfering with things if it were down.

And the Earth, Matt thought again, was never there at all.

It was a little after 1100. Under the new figures they were to be on the 1400 TranCity in three days: seventy-eight hours from now. Eighty hours later they would be in Tsio.

And nobody in the world would know.

Thinking about the trip made Matt think about Raf. He had promised Raf that the Maze run would be fair. He meant to keep the promise. He started to ping Stringer, then stopped. Someone else, Matt thought. They all knew he wanted Raf to win. Ruby was the least involved (at least, she said so), but Ruby's interest in the Maze was mostly theoretical: she liked to watch, to get information for her own mindruns.

Matt sent a ping down the wires. The screen wavered and cleared; Tani Case appeared, her head sideways, pillowed on grass. "Good day, Lonestar."

"Hello, Tani. Look, you know Raf's running Jack's Maze in about thirty . . ."

"Of course I know." She frowned slightly at him, which looked very odd in 270° rotation. "You're looking most exceptionally serious, Lonestar. What'cha want?"

"I want you to see if Stringer's set it up fair."

The frown bent farther. "You know he will."

"Yeah," Matt said slowly, "you're right," knowing she was. "I'm sorry."

She stopped frowning. "Wait a moment." Her hand closed on the side of the screen, and there was a dizzying swoop as she sat up and swept the slate into her lap. Behind her, a peacock was strutting and screaming. "I'll ask him to let me take a look. *Not* because it's not going to be fair. Just because I want to, right?"

Matt nodded.

"Yeah," Tani said, from far away to somewhere even farther. "Con Dios, Lonestar." She switched out.

Matt had barely finished the juice when his slate beeped. It was Tani. "Stringfellow's way ahead of you.

He *wants* me to run his latest masterpiece. But I'm supposed to do it at sixteen-hundred today."

"Today?"

"He actually sounded eager. Well, almost eager."

"You're going to do it?"

"Lonestar—" She put her palms to her temples and shook her head from side to side, making a noise of brains rattling loose. "Message when I'm done," she said, and was gone again.

But there wasn't a message. Matt was up until midnight again, reading, playing, fidgeting. He left two pings for Tani, but nothing came back. There was nothing at all until 1500 the following day, in the lobby of the gym at Copernicus Old Landing. The site of the duel.

Raf was, not surprisingly, already there, in an open jacket and trunks of shiny light-blue novylon, worn white sneakers. He was on the gym floor, doing exercises that Matt supposed Raf would describe as "loosening up," but that almost made Matt sweat just to watch.

Cissa Okuda came in, in a long pink sleeveless dress and sandals, nibbling grapes from a woven bag wrapped around her wrist. She spotted Matt, slipped around to join him without letting Raf see her; quickly, she pulled a paper pad and a charcoal from the bag, did a sketch of Raf in motion. It seemed to Matt to catch the action completely in just a few lines. She tucked it away just as quickly, handed Matt a handful of grapes. "Bribe," she said. "You didn't see that."

Matt took the grapes, not entirely sure why.

Tani arrived, dressed in baggy Beta-plains and sneakers. She looked tired, and Tani Case hardly ever looked tired. She waved at Raf, sat down with Cissa and Matt.

Matt said, below Raf's hearing, "Did you—"

"I ran String's Maze," she said flatly. "I failed it,

but Jack told me exactly why I failed it, and it's fair. And that's all I'm going to tell you."

Cissa looked puzzled. Matt felt that way, for what he supposed were completely different reasons. "Okay," he said. "So where's Jack? It's almost—"

Tani said "I imagine Jack's in the chamber. I imagine he's been there since we finished last night."

Matt got up, went toward the Mazeroom door at the back of the gym. String came out, closing it behind him with a squeal of rubber on rubber. "Hello, Matt. Welcome to the Convent of the Carmelites, Lunar Chapter. Everyone *is* here, I trust?"

"Yes—"

"I knew it. Sorry to be a little late myself. Last fine adjustments."

Jack was wearing a dusty black coverall, traction-soled tabi. He had a deep-pocketed work belt around his waist and shoulders, a long loop of electric wire trailing from a shoulder strap, and his hair was in crazy shape. At his knees he had pads with large resin hooks, to hang from the rods while working. Matt thought that was odd. String had complained more than once that anyone who needed hanger-ons was no Maze tech at all.

Matt looked back at the others approaching. Cissa still had the puzzled expression. Tani's face had smoothed out, which Matt found quite a relief. And Raf was just a humming machine.

Ruby appeared then, in a red leather jacket and slacks. She seemed possessed, distant, expert; but Ruby ought to look like that.

"We would put you off no longer, mes amis," Jack said lightly, "from that satisfaction we have promised one another for so long. By your leave, do enter . . . freely, and of your own will."

Ruby snorted softly.

Jack pushed the door in; there was a rubbery squeak. All Maze chambers were the same, give or take a few meters: plain rooms, this one ten meters high by sixteen square. The ceiling and floor and walls, doors included, were covered with half a dec of Insulastic. The floors were piled calf-deep in a foam-pellet packing material called blowpop.

"Mind the step," Jack said, and hopped down half a meter from the doorframe. He had swept the blowpop away from the door in a semicircle.

Matt took the long step and looked up, expecting to see an impressive Maze. He did. They were already *in* it.

"Well?" String said.

Matt nodded, trying to take in the scope of what Jack had built.

The first stage in laying Maze was clipping the rods. Every chamber had a good supply of construction rods, hexagonal shafts of structural glass one and two and three meters long, and buckets of coated metal end connectors to assemble the rods into space frames. The components were common all over Luna, used for sales booths, temporary storage, construction falsework, everything.

The second stage was to put in walls and floors: solid plycore panels installed with edge clips, or Betacloth tarps with eyelets and glascord lacing around the edges.

The third stage was running. Someone started a clock, you went in, went through, came out. If you were really a Slammer after all, down in your springs and wires, you hit all the walls on the route, skidded on the floors, missed the climbs and jumps; you came out late, sometimes bruised, frequently the wrong way. Which was what the white drifts of blowpop were there for.

The fourth stage . . . well, there wasn't a fourth stage. Not openly, anyway. But for Mazemasters like Stringjack, there were tricks, tunings, special ways of using the equipment beyond its supposed limits.

Like the panel clips. The fittings that held the

plycore sheets in place were completely rigid in all directions. But there was a particular part, a U-shaped pipe clamp, ordered by number from Central Supply to some neutral address or just lifted off a construction site, that would hold the edge of the board tight while letting it swing like a door. Or a seesaw, or a trapdoor. And the stringing on the Beta tarps could be adjusted from crete-hard, to trampoline, to breakaway. For Stringjack the possibilities of glass and ply and Beta, cable and clip and the odd bit smuggled in a gym bag, were as limitless as polymer chemistry.

Jack's Maze filled almost the whole room but for the little swept area where presumably the team was to stand and watch. There were towers to the ceiling at each corner of the room, connected by bridges along the sides, and a pair of diagonal tunnels that crossed over-and-under at the very center, a long way above the floor. String must have gotten parts from at least one other chamber, maybe two—as well as a number of bits that were even farther from standard than his usual.

"It's a Stage Five, isn't it," Matt said, very softly, to Jack.

"Oh, I think maybe a Six," Jack said, proud, not quite smug. "It's a Maze, at any rate. Wasn't that the deal? The challenge? The proof?"

Jack turned to Raf, said in an efficient but perfectly friendly manner, "It works like this." He took a little gray resin box out of his tool belt. On its top were a slotted opening, a red-domed light and a large red button. "There are twenty of these, scattered—oh, all over the place." He twiddled something on the underside of the box. The light began to flash and a pinging, a little below a scream, came from the grille. "After it starts, you have fifteen seconds to get to it and do this." He pushed the button and the box was quiet. "Tell me what happens then."

Raf said "The next one starts."

"Full points. Fifteen seconds to reach that one, and then fifteen to the next, and so on, round and round Robin Hood's barn. Miss one and you're out."

"And there are twenty."

"Exactly twenty. Five minutes all told."

They had all run Maze at all-stops-out: five minutes of it was a long, long time.

Raf said "What if I get there early? Does the extra time add up?"

"Good question. No."

"Then let's do it." Raf stripped off his jacket, looked at his shoes for a long deep breath, then leaned against the wall and took them off too, leaving him in just the blue trunks.

Matt found himself staring at Raf for some bewildering reason. He supposed that any Lunar would have, at the broad hard build, the defined muscles that said Raf had been born in a full g.

Raf pumped oxygen for another minute, then said "Morituri te—"

"No, not that," String said, staring too, and with something strangely like respect in his voice. He stuck a hand into a tool pouch. "Ready. Set. *Go.*"

The beeping started, high in a tower at a far corner of the room. The light splashed against the wall. Raf jumped straight up, grabbed the edge of one of the diagonal bridges, threw himself inside and ran.

The sound of running stopped for a heartbeat, then started again. Matt knew what that meant: somewhere a section of floor was missing, and Raf had vaulted the gap.

They heard the slap. There was one second's silence, and then the tone started again from the other farside tower. Raf took the direct route through the connecting tunnel, hit the switch. Then the sound and light started up only a few meters directly below him. But the way must not have been clear: he swung out of the tower, pulled hand-over-hand *down* the column faster than gravity would have taken him, somersaulted inside and hit the button.

The tone came from the diagonally opposite tower, near the floor. Raf looked out, saw the deep sea of blowpop, slow to wade through, then braced his hands and shot straight across between Mazerods and floor. Hit.

The next box was on the other nearside tower. Raf climbed, crossed the bridge above them—

The floor at the center of the bridge split, swung down at both ends. Raf's feet stood on eight meters of air. There were eight seconds left. He grabbed the vertical rods to either side. The pieces he was holding came cleanly away, leaving him with a glass baton in each hand. Six seconds. He swept his arms forward in two great arcs, hooking the rods on the beam just in front of him, his chest hitting the dangling floorboard. Four seconds. With a gasp he pulled up. Three. Took a step. Two. Swung around the corner and hit the switch. Five down. Fifteen to go.

Matt understood now why Tani's test run had come so early. The superMaze was designed to self-destruct around the runner; as you learned a route it narrowed, vanished, turned into a trap. Panels slid past panels, floors fell away or rotated into walls, all to the beat of the light and sound. The Mazeparts hid and reflected the lights, echoed the pingers from all directions, so that Matt could hardly locate the boxes; how was Raf doing it, through the sweat in his eyes, over the cymbal and drum of his lungs and heart?

Still he did it. There were now four switches left, one full minute.

The top center bridge opened up and dropped Raf into the lower one; then the end of that tunnel farthest from the goal sprang free and collapsed, tumbling him away from the box. Raf allowed it, spreading his feet to catch a rod to either side; he coiled himself and sprang back up the tilted tube, hit the switch.

Matt looked around. Ruby's eyes were in rapid motion; she was trying to beat the system in her mind, guess what it would spring next. Cissa was counting seconds on her fingers. Tani looked a little bit sick. Jack's face was barren. Raf made it to the eighteenth switch with two seconds to spare.

Tani walked out of the room, shuffling through the pellets on the floor, climbing awkwardly to the door.

"This," Jack said, clearly not worried that Raf might hear, "is where Tani lost."

"Okay," Ruby said, perhaps not to any of them, "is it the second-guessing, or the *not* second-guessing?" Matt thought he understood what she meant, but there was no time to think much.

The next box was on the very top of the structure. Raf bounded up to the top of the highest tower, ran across a single rod toward the flaring light. He leaned toward it. There was a click and a whirr, and a filament cord yanked the box another three meters ahead. Raf launched himself toward it, landing on a horizontal Beta sheet.

It gave way, all the lacings at once. The tarp was hemmed with elastic, or springs, or memory wire, something contractile, so that as Raf fell the Beta was tying itself into a bag around him. The ping went on.

It was five whole seconds before Matt was aware that the sound was coming from a new location. Raf had gotten the nineteenth switch in the last instant before the trap sprang.

Raf, bagged and air-resisting, took four of those seconds to fall the nine meters to the floor, landing in a slow splash of white pellets. The Beta bundle bounced and twisted on the floor, but only buried itself deeper in the blowpop; Matt wondered what would have happened if the bag had closed on Raf's neck.

Then Jack said, quite loudly, "Raf! You have five seconds to turn off the last unit."

Four. The bag stopped struggling.

Three. Stillness.

Two. Raf's muffled voice said "*You* turn it off, Stringer!"

String held up the pinging gray box, the same one he had used to demonstrate, pressed the button. The light faded, the pinging stopped. "Right answer, Raf." He splashed across the floor, unfastened the bag.

Stringer said "Welcome to Luna," and then took a quick two steps back. Raf finished freeing himself, stood up, then sank down, hands on knees, breathing hard.

They looked at each other for some time, Raf, shining with sweat, sitting on the Beta afloat on blowpop like a magic carpet, String tall and cool in his blacks and work gear, the twentieth pinger still held loosely in his hand.

There were *exactly* twenty, Matt remembered String saying. Not twenty in the Maze, not twenty and this, or any other variation of twenty.

Ruby had seen it before he had, of course, before even seeing the last trap in action. She'd known what String would demand as a last real proof that Raf was really one of them, part of the team.

The door screeched open, and Tani sat on the sill. "Well?"

"Well," Jack said.

Matt said "Showers, Raf? And then what?"

"Shower, yeah. And then—"

"Ice cream on the heights of Sokoni," Stringjack said, "I'm buying. And, vack, we know what then, don't we?"

Raf said "Tsiolkovsky."

"Absolutely damn right!" Matt said.

Raf stumbled toward the shower room. As the rest of them left the chamber, Ruby pointed a thumb at the fabulous Maze, folded in and collapsed on itself, and said "Do we just leave this here?"

"Somebody probably said that about ancient Rome too," String said. "Let's just leave it for the Vandals."

The house was dark when Matt got home. "Room low," he said, and a dim blue strip of ceiling light traced the path to his door. He listened: there was no sound from the conference or music rooms. Nobody home. He tossed himself against a wall, walked it with his hands. His vision was full of phosphene stars. He felt nearly free, almost to the sky, next to nothing. He tumbled down what was for the moment a starship corridor, to what would pass for a crew cabin, through pale metal light to red worlds and gold and white, and small black stones with life inside, and blue worlds that were not the Earth.

Matt's door closed and the blue light faded. Albin Ronay, sitting in the dark corner of the living room, did not stir for several minutes. He knew perfectly well what he had just seen: he was Lunar-born, he had danced on the ceiling. If he had moved just now, made a sound or movement, he would have brought Matt back to gravity. Spoiled the dance, ruined everything.

He got up slowly. The room lights had been told to ignore him. He glanced at the watchboard—three small points of light on the apartment plan—and went into the bedroom.

Sonya was sprawled on her side, tangled in the sheet, a foot over the edge of the bed. That wasn't to be spoiled either, Ronay thought. He stepped into the bathroom to undress, sat down lightly on the opposite edge of the bed, stretched out as easily as he could.

Sonya opened her eyes, not moving beyond that, waiting for the shudder and sigh that would mean Albin was asleep. He stirred, shifted; then it came. She moved so that their shoulders touched. That was right: pulse, breathing, warmth. He had always been generous with his touches, his sounds. Now she was connected; now she could sleep. Even during the long early phase of inducing him to seduce her, there had been no shortage of reassurances that he was real, definite, palpable.

She eased just a little tighter against him, then let it rest. She had to be up and out long before he would.

Seven hours later, Albin woke, alone, but with a memory of pressure. He picked one of Sonya's red hairs off the pillow, rubbed it between his fingers.

He gulped down some juice and a soft-cooked egg, pulled on a jacket, felt in a pocket for his Transport tag and went out. There was a bad morning's work ahead.

The Vacuum Corporation of Earth had its main Lunar office at Copernicus Old Landing, east of the Hub, on the third and topmost level. The building, a square flat slab with angled walls, had been overdesigned and overbuilt. The curved hallway Ronay was in now had heavy reinforced columns intruding on the smooth walls, like the ribs of an ancient animal. There had been a plan to add levels to it as the city grew, piling up a ziggurat; there had been fears a ship might crash through it. But materials and architecture and city planning had gone in other directions; the traffic stayed on beam and gradually shifted to the newer ports.

So concrete and metal, broad air ducts and the passage of time had made it quiet here. Some Lunars were uncomfortable in Old Landing: they needed more reminders that air and machinery were running. Ronay passed through a spinney door: there were more of them here than elsewhere in the city, another old fear. Ronay's generation didn't really think about decompression very often—though let the alarm sound, the on-off scream designed to hammer into your bones even if the air had gone thin—and they would remember.

There were in fact plenty of Lunars who had never heard the alarm except in a drill, never seen a spinney iris shut in earnest; and many who thought the name referred to the rotary action of the door plates. Actually, they had once been called sphincter doors. Politeness had worn the word down.

Ronay thought about a symphony again, the one he had no time to think on just now: he thought of another paradoxical movement, to go with the song of dry oceans. Luna was silent: but no one living could ever know that silence directly, because buildings were alive with hums and hisses and rattles, and helmets roared with seashell noise. Dry water and loud silence. Two more movements.

Two more movements and no time at all.

There were brushed-metal letters embedded in the wall:

the vacuum /corporation

Next to them was a panel of black glass, flush with the white curve. In the glass were tiny, luminous starpoints. As Ronay reached for the control, the door slid open without any sound.

"Good day, Albin," Ballantine said.

Lynch Suárez Ballantine was often taken for a native Lunar by people who were not. He was tall, and moved with perfect grace in Lunar gravity. But his form—triangular upper body, strong, slightly bowed legs, certain manners of reaching and turning —was Terrestrial. He wore a loose, open-necked white shirt, brown moleskin trousers and leather slippers. A broad leather belt had a tasset computer and some other gadgets attached. His face was smooth, a light copper; his gloss-black hair started on the very top of his head and fell straight down to his collar, like a hood. His eyes were a startling, luminous, misfit light blue.

"Let's come in from the cold, Albin." Ballantine's voice was an even upper baritone: most people found it beautiful. To Ronay it was *too* modulated, a man using an instrument, playing it from somewhere other than the heart. And then too, Ronay knew what the instrument was used for. He nodded and went in.

The outer office was all blue-gray fabrics, glass and gray metal, smooth shapes and darkened displays, controls turned to zero without a fingermark on them. From the evidence here, The Vacuum Corporation's business might have been anything, or nothing. Which some people would have called a fair assessment.

"Jori says hello," Ballantine said as they walked through. Jori was a systems operator who was sometimes in the office, in a blue-gray outfit with a metal VACOR badge, installed as another bit of furniture. "She loves you, Albin." He smiled at the slight turn of Ronay's head. "A visit from you is worth the day off." He touched one of the boxes on his belt and a piece of the wall swung inward. "After all," he said offhand, "she's not going to serve any purpose with you here, is she?"

They entered a glass-sided corridor that ran through a much broader glass dome: an observatory that extended up above the roof of the Landing building. It looked unused: chairs were stacked on tables, there were no telescopes in sight. Ballantine looked straight ahead, never glancing at the windows.

"Did Sonya's conference go well?" Ballantine said.

"I believe so."

"There's a certain . . . well, let it wait a moment."

Beyond the dome were more doors along a curved metal corridor, and the sound of machinery.

Ballantine grasped a handle and swung the last door open.

The room beyond was softly, yellowly lit by brass lamps. It had oak paneling to waist height, green felt above. The chairs were wood and brocade. There were glass cases on the walls: most held swords, antiques and modern fencing weapons. In the center of one wall were three Olympic medals, two gold and a bronze. There was no view of the outside, no displays or controls in sight. From one corner, a hall went a few steps and turned right. Ronay supposed Ballantine's private quarters were that way, but in the five years of their acquaintance he had never asked or been told.

"Do sit down, Albin," Ballantine said, and shut the door. The silence that followed was completely un-Lunar. "Tea should just be ready, beside your chair. Unless there's something else?"

"Not just now, Lynch." Ronay sat down, opened a cabinet beside the chair and took out a hot cup of tea.

Ballantine sat, produced a squat glass of brown liquid. "Luna should really learn to make whiskey . . . it's a craft with long, fine traditions. Teaches planning for the future. And it couldn't possibly taste any worse than that Moonshine swill you sell the *turistas*. Cheers."

"Cheers, Lynch."

"As I was saying, Dr. Parker is about ready to do an exploratory on someone with his teeth. Can you give me a hint why he wasn't invited to the conference?"

"I don't have any responsibility over Medical Services."

"I just thought you might have spoken recently with the Chief of Exosurgery for Copernicus." There was no irritation at all in his voice.

"I have. Not about that."

"And your son? How's Matthias?"

"He's fine, thank you, Lynch."

"Any time he wants a discount on TECHNET use, ask, will you? He'd have to agree not to resell the data, of course—we have to maintain a balance of payments *somehow*."

"I'm sure he'd appreciate that."

"I see there's nothing at all I can sell you, Albin. I'm getting old, I shouldn't wonder. If you'd rather have that iced, it *can* be arranged."

Ronay sipped his tea. "It's fine."

"Fine," Ballantine said, very gently. "It's fine that everyone's fine and everything's fine. Only I am grown coarse with idleness and disuse. Let's see, then, if I have any systems still operational. What do you want to sell me?"

"The Board has voted to ask for another Waterhole study. So I'm here to ask for it."

"Congratulations, Albin. I'm sure you worked very hard for it. How much time are you authorized to buy?"

"Six months."

"It's getting more expensive to think up numbers. The digit foundry will want about half a million, but we can probably shop that down to two hundred thousand. And your share . . . twenty percent?"

"It's usually been ten."

"The Corporation is always looking for something new and different. Say fifteen. That's thirty thousand from Luna."

"Keplers?"

"Whatever. How much is a ton of oxygen snowballs bringing these days, Albin?"

"Would you take it in FLOX?"

"Not without a great deal of argument with the Corporation. Can you offer it that way?"

"Not without fighting the Oxygen Board."

"Stalemate, then." He took a slow swallow of his drink. Ballantine drank Terrestrial bourbon whiskey, nothing added. He made an issue of it whenever possible. "Are you sure you won't have something stronger? You know breaking the social contract has never meant much to *me*."

"They'd find out."

"Yes, of course they would. Connections. Do you have the thirty thousand, Albin?"

"There's that much in discretionary."

"Then I suppose that's all but the shouting. Come and watch."

They crossed the hall to a small room completely lined with equipment: boards, meters, loose wires, handwritten notes stuck everywhere, an eleven-up monitor bank. "Sit down," Ballantine said, and touched some controls. "Usual arrangement: if you want one of the smaller screens on the large display, just call its number. You're fully isolated."

"Am I?" Ronay tried against odds to make it a joke.

"I don't lie, Albin." Ballantine sounded slightly hurt; Ronay thought he might actually be, but he left it there. "I'll see you shortly."

Ballantine went out. After a minute, the large central display and five of the smaller screens around it lit with the VACOR trademark.

It *had* been meant as a joke, about isolation: surely there was no purpose in hanging Ronay out as a dumb-show observer to a VACOR conference. Surely it was outside Ballantine's brief to have a silent auditor. Ronay had known, as much as anybody knew, Lynch Ballantine for the five years since VACOR had sent the man here. He did know that Ballantine had a strong, even severe, code of ethics. Not lying was one point of it. But the others could only be made out dimly in Ballantine's depths, by a kind of echo-ranging.

There were five faces on the five small screens. Besides Ballantine, Ronay recognized Karl Burton, one of VACOR's flying squadron of area managers. They were all wearing high-collared jackets with dark-hued ascots, the current Terrestrial business style; Ballantine had put on a maroon shirt or robe that wrapped to his neck.

The faces occupied the top-left corners of the displays, covering about two-thirds of the area. Down the right side and across the bottom were small indicators: color bars, dials, digitals. Along the very bottom was a blue stripe with a marching line of periods, then . . . TEST . . . TEST . . . TEST . . .

"I believe we are ready for your report, Mr. Ballantine," Burton said. He was a large man, not fat but massive. He looked like a lump of rock half carved, half weathered into shape, and his voice was like crunching gravel.

Ballantine said "Luna, Decisionlink twenty-two, re Waterhole." He was precise, not at all deferential.

Then the telltales along the screens began to twitch and flash, and all five people began to speak at once, and that was the last Ronay understood of the conference.

That was not strictly true. He could still read a little from the sounds of voices, the angles of faces. But most of the conversation was being conducted on the little indicators, and what those meant was being defined as the conference went on. A deep blue flash at the same time as some numbers might mean "These are worthless, but they're what we'll put in the annual report"; between two different people, at a different conference, the same flash might say "Bet your life on these, because I am." The blue text line scrolled transport capacities and commodity prices and production quotas and once the *en clair* message *NOW* WHO'S KIDDING WHO? between Ballantine and someone else, though with no indication of who had sent, who received.

It went on for about twenty minutes. Ronay sat and watched it all, as he might have sat through a strange opera in an unknown language.

Karl Burton blinked out; the rest went on for

another minute or two—and Ronay supposed that if he understood anything of bosses and employees, he understood what was being said *then*—and then all the screens went dark.

Ballantine came in, in his casual clothes again, the robe tossed over one arm.

"Well?" Ronay said, feeling not at all angry and wondering how he was intended to feel.

"The short reply is that you may have a five-month environmental study, which will cost you twenty-five thousand Keplers now"—he paused, pure dramatic effect—"*or* twenty thousand NA dollars at the end of the study."

"How much is that in real money?" Ronay said, still calm.

"That's the trouble with short replies: they always oversimplify." He gestured across the hall. "Let's sit down first."

"No."

"Well, let's sit down *somewhere*, Albin."

They went back to the observation dome, sat in the light of the low Earth.

"All right," Ronay said, feeling his mood darken, "I've watched the play. Now you can tell me what it means."

"The system's called Princeps. It's available for license."

"From VACOR?"

"If I say yes, do you automatically say no? You're still using SELENA—which is no more than a minor upgrade of MIT's old ATHENA IV system. Heavens, Albin, your *children* use more advanced stuff to play *games* on! But then, I hear you're trying to develop a locally grown version of TECHNET."

"I'm not with ComServ. That, or buying a new conference system, would be their responsibility."

"Advertising isn't mine," Ballantine said lightly. "And I wouldn't get a commission if you bought it. Just as I won't get one on the water, when it finally comes roaring in."

"Returning to the conference . . ."

Ballantine sat back, folded his hands. "How long will it take to finish preparing the cavern at Archimedes?"

"Ten thousand hours. Plus or minus two thousand."

"I told them I thought a year; that's acceptably close. Very well. The Corporation wants construction resumed. Within the next kilhour."

"Or?"

"Or they blow off the study. They announce that you're stalling, which you are, and that Waterhole is tabled until Luna shows some serious interest."

"There are people who consider that exactly what I've wanted all along."

"I know that," Ballantine said quietly, "but I'm not that stupid and neither are you."

"You can't *force* us to build the reservoir. And there's damn little point in sending the water up here without it."

"*Albin.*"

"*What?* You can ruin my position, you've always been able to do that—"

"Farthest thing from—"

"—but I'm not the sole and exclusive obstacle, am I? I answer to PlanCord; the reservoir, if and when, will be built by Physical Plant's people out of their budget. If I changed my mind, I couldn't *order* it to happen. I don't believe you don't know that."

"I do. Karl Burton doesn't. He lives in a world of vice-regency. Where would he learn otherwise?" Ballantine leaned back, tilted his eyes skyward. "Speaking of whom, I require another large whiskey to wash his taste away. If you really refuse the hospitality of the lounge, please wait here for me."

Ronay shook his head and followed Ballantine back to the comfortable Terrestrial chairs.

"Here's to dual citizenship," Ballantine said, and took a long sip from his glass. "You're aware there are five territories in North America alone where this small pleasure voids my medical coverage? No moon is an island. Fortunately the Corporation doesn't care."

"Considering that you export the stuff . . ."

"*Control* the export. Yes. At least the Corporation is not hypocritical."

Ronay said "Ameribucks are cheaper than Keplers right now, Lynch, isn't that right?"

"About eighty cents to the Kepler, I believe. I can go across the hall for a current quote."

"No thank you. So we can pay twenty-five kiloKay now, or sixteen in six months. I didn't think delayed payments were supposed to be so advantageous."

"Perhaps if you thought of it as a commodity future. The futures market is so damnably tricky. You're a commodities man, of course."

"What do you think is going to happen in six months?"

"What *I* think doesn't matter. What the Corporation thinks—pardon the term—would be confidential."

Ronay sat, waiting. His fingers slipped on the wet glass of tea, and he fumbled to avoid dropping it.

Ballantine glanced up at the mounted swords. He held his eyes unnaturally wide, as if he were afraid to blink. "Matthias wants to get on a ship, doesn't he? Of course he does . . . what else should any intelligent child that age want, but to strike out from home—over hill, over sea, over sky? Spending all that time scanning TECHNET must be thin reward. What wouldn't he do to get his hands on a MIRAGE drive—even for an instant, one glorious instant."

Ronay's head hurt. He said, slowly, carefully,

"Do you spend a *great* deal of time monitoring individual net usage?"

"Knowledge is power. At least, properly filtered and correlated knowledge is power. Maintenance records, for instance. Have you looked at the figures on your Dippers lately? No, you haven't; you won't touch TECHNET at all. But August Felton of Transport does, obsessively. Volume discount for him. And coincidentally, he's seconded to the Water Board. . . . Don't flush, Albin: I *do* have dual citizenship, and even half-citizens are entitled by the Charter to know who's on what committee. Oh, and Lawrence Duveen's been looking as well. It all points the same way."

"What do you propose to do?"

"I didn't think I'd proposed anything. The data are there: I have no idea if the Corporation is aware of them. That's the truth, Albin: *I don't know.* If they ask me, I will tell them: but the Corporation is large and diverse and busy, and who knows what they might not notice on their own?"

"What does it cost to keep them from noticing?"

Ballantine turned his head, slowly, slowly. His eyes were blue electric arcs in a face like burnished bronze. "I am here, Councillor Ronay, to serve the interests of The Vacuum Corporation, and for no other purpose in heaven or earth. My own interests do not enter into it, and indeed are not *accessible* to you. *Or* to the Corporation."

Ronay almost said that he was sorry. But he wasn't sorry. Ballantine played with and twisted the people he dealt with—on Earth as on Luna, Ronay was certain—and he deserved a little of it back once in a while. What Ronay finally said was "What about everyone else's private interests?"

Ballantine laughed, a harsh sound but with real humor in it. His face relaxed. "Privacy dies unless it's tended and kept, Albin." He waved at the glass dome above them. "But if you would rather sit in the green-

house . . . Oh, my, is that the time?" There were no
clocks in the room; Ballantine hadn't looked at his
tasset. "I should see you out, lest people think we con-
spire against 'em."

They walked back up the corridor, to the office.
Finally Ronay said "Is there anything else, Lynch?"

"One small favor. If you see Gilberto Vela, ask
him to get in touch. Warn him that the news is bad."

"Who?"

"Vela. At the theatre."

"Oh." Ronay could not remember ever hearing
Gil Vela called by his whole name. He said "I will,"
there being nothing else to say.

"Thank you, Albin. And come again soon."

Ronay went back down the levels of the quiet
building, knowing that the third movement of the
unlikely symphony was a choral for voices and lumi-
nance organ. Ronay had learned long ago that he
was no lyricist, but it wouldn't matter: the chorus
would sing notes and syllables, counterpoint to the
flaring therelumin. Dry water, loud silence, senseless
speech. One more movement.

Down on the Transport level, Ronay was startled by what seemed to be two monstrous black
things wrestling in a pit, covered in blood and tar.
After an instant he saw that they were Transport
workers, grease and muck all over their red coveralls. There was a rope blocking the station entrance,
and an electric tractor was hooked up to a passenger
wagon.

"Where to, sir?" said a young man in red.

"Verne . . . no, just the Hub."

"This is to the Hub, sir; trains are running from
there. Would you like a map? Or directions?"

"The Hub will do, thanks."

"Leaving in just a few minutes, sir." The man
read Ronay's tag with a hand-held unit, waved him
aboard. The cart rolled off down the pedestrian tun-

nel, lights flashing and alarm pinging to warn anyone who might actually be walking in the pipe.

There were five other people on the cart. Three were a family of Terrestrial tourists; the mother was holding a toddler on her lap, pointing at the passing pipes and conduits. "Whoooosh, we go," she said to the child, "fast, *fast!*" The father looked straight back, doing a terrible job of hiding his grin. The other two, Lunar women, were chuckling softly.

The repairs shouldn't have taken place in the open, Ronay thought. There should have been some kind of view block; some plycore would have done it, kept the dirty machinery out of the open.

At the Hub, he watched the family go through the station gates, each of the adults holding one of the child's hands. When Ronay's grandfather was a boy, they had called people from Earth Toddlers. A generation later, Slammers had caught on. It was a circumspect bigotry. In the years just after the revolution, the insults had been more than casual. There had been accidents then too: always the sort of thing a careless Terrestrial, from a world with air and moisture and natural shielding against solar flares might suffer. There were people who believed that they all really had been accidents. Just as there were people who believed the legend of Execution Lock.

Ronay walked past Gil Vela's theatre, on to the east edge of the Hub, the Medical Center.

"Hello, Mr. Ronay," the woman at the front desk said.

"Hello, Violet. Could you check if my wife's busy just now, please? It's nothing urgent."

"Just a moment . . . She's in XR Three right now, but they should be finished in fifteen minutes or so. Would you like to wait in the gallery?"

"Sure."

The receptionist handed him a security tag, and he went down the green pastel corridor to the Sur-

gery wing. The operating-theatre gallery had two
rows of seats facing an overhead viewing window
and a set of screens repeating the OR working displays.

At one end of the room below was a patient, in a
sort of reclining chair, surrounded by hardware. A
wire tech and circulating nurse were in attendance,
and an anestech running an electronic pain suppressor. At the other end, Sonya Ronay Gurdzhian sat in
a chair rather similar to the patient's. A lightweight
metal frame circled her head, covering her eyes. A
white cable ran from each wrist.

This was exosurgery. A fiber-optic catheter had
been inserted through the patient's abdomen, and
was now somewhere inside his body, working. A
stereo camera saw through two fibers of the wire,
feeding back to Sonya's virtual-vision headset; another carried an illuminating laser that could be pow-
ered up to cut and weld. Three more ran to
microturbines for steering control. The cables could
mount any of a dozen other instruments: Ronay
could tell from the displays that this one carried a
dilating balloon and a tiny spray nozzle called a spin-
neret. Another screen showed the wire's-eye view, inside a large vessel, specks of cells passing down the
tunnel as the pulse drove them, *rush* tumble, *rush*
tumble. Ronay guessed Sonya had been relining a
weak abdominal artery.

The display was not how Sonya saw it, of
course. She had binocular vision through the goggles, not a flat screen: she *was* inside the artery, cutting, mortaring, smoothing by touch. Literally: her
hands were wired, an optical net implanted in them
(by the same technique) that fed control signals out
and sensation back.

She had shown him, once. Bill Blake Chamberlain, who had been Chief of Exo back then, fitted
Ronay with a set of drone gloves, clumsy spiders that
gave him the sensory feed. They ran vues first, so

Ronay would know what to expect. "Understand that it's not the same. You won't have control, of course, and it's coarser. A lot coarser. There's no substitute for the direct wiring."

Then Dr. Chamberlain drove the wire into Sonya's uterus, where Matthias Ronay floated and slept, six thousand hours into his conception. Bill took Ronay close—giving the boy a hug, he called it—the transducer pulling in double tympani, two heartbeats, vision wavering through fluid. The head and body were two worlds tidelocked, the eyes dark satellites . . .

Bill was Sir William now—no, William Lord Something since last year—and was retired to England. He had been given most of the operations starship crews had, to keep him alive on Earth: Sonya had wired him with a full biotelemetry net, one of the endosurgeons put in an Apparat Syertse, the cardiac booster the crews called a Russian heart.

Ronay sighed.

Sonya raised one of her cabled hands, gave a finger signal that was repeated as words on a data display: READY TO WITHDRAW. The wire tech took over then, reeling in the catheter, the view running dizzily backward. The screen went dark as the wire came out, and the circulating applied a pressure dressing. The anesthetist dialed down the pain suppressor.

Sonya leaned back in her chair, pulled the plugs from her wrists, took off the goggles. Ronay stood up and tapped on the observing window. Sonya waved and smiled. She held up a spread hand, then pressed thumb to fingers and twisted her wrist. Five minutes, coffee shop. Ronay nodded and went out.

The staff restaurant had originally been built with nothing but hard surfaces, someone's idea of hospital cleanliness, that reflected light and sound, an optical and visual noisetrap. So the room was retrofitted with draperies and carpets; but to Ronay's ear they didn't kill the noise, only wounded it, so that there was a continual strangled note of unresolved tension.

No one else seemed to notice. And the food was decent: hospital food had been a personal revolutionary crusade of one of the Duchesnes.

There was an area of small tables far apart, and another of long ones close together. At one of the big tables, eight or nine people were reconstructing yesterday's Skyhook game in detail. Ronay got a mug of powerful black tea and sat down at a small table.

Sonya came in then. Her hands were jammed in the pockets of her white jacket, her shoulders hunched absently. Her red hair was crimped at the temples from the working headset, and her dark eyes were a little bit red. She got a glass of milk and a cream bun from the counter, sat down across from Ronay. She wrapped a hand around his on the tea mug, cool over heat.

"That was good timing," she said. "We were in there over two hours. . . . So how was *your* day?"

"The usual performance. Lynch played his game and dared me to guess the rules. But we came to an agreement."

"And?"

"Lynch mentioned a conference. Someone you didn't invite. What was that about?"

"A husband trying to change the subject. What did Ballantine get from the agreement?"

"They want us to start lining the cave at Archimedes."

"I thought that was under way."

"It is. And I'm positive Lynch knows it."

"So?"

"*Lynch* knows. VACOR may not. And then—" He described the contract, the improbable currency discount.

Sonya scraped a bit of pastry filling from her

plate with a fingertip, sucked it. "You could buy some dollars now and bank them."

"We probably will," Ronay said, thinking that was exactly what Duveen would suggest—no, insist on. "The problem is still, what do they think is going to happen in half a year? Dollar up, Kepler down, or—"

Suddenly both her hands were on his. He felt the sharp touch of the induction buttons on her wrists, pressure of fingertips on knuckles. His head was quite clear, when he had not been quite aware of the clouds.

"Spasiba," she said. "I see better now."

"Your turn, then," he said. "Conference?"

"Ah. What conference, and who didn't I invite?"

"A surgeon. Porter . . ."

"Parker?"

"Yes."

She shook her head. "There were three doctors in from the outer planets. Eddie St. John at Medelec thought we should all get together and compare notes. There were two long lunches and a breakfast, we found out some interesting things, and Eddie sold some equipment. How did this become a conference?"

"I'm sure I don't know. Was it on a net?"

"It was *announced*. Parker could have come if he'd wanted."

"Who is he?"

"He invented the Parker Cannula, which was a great development twenty years ago. Everyone learned his name in school, but I can't think of anything he's done since. Is he *important* at VACOR?"

"It's possible. But it still doesn't make sense."

She smiled. "Khorosho, sreedya, I don't understand either. Do you feel like talking to Solly?"

"Hm? Oh. What does he want?"

"I don't know, but he's standing a respectful distance behind you."

"Oh," Ronay said quietly, and turned.

Sol Wasserstein, one of the Medcenter's three operating managers, was a plump man with a round balding head, round brown eyes, a button nose: he might have been laid out with a drafting compass. He was wearing a long, badly crumpled Beta lab coat (and crumpling Betacloth took effort) over a neat blue jacket and slacks.

"Hello, Sol," Ronay said. "Ma shlomkha?"

Wasserstein held up both hands in a shrug. "Wonderful. People are sick all over the place. Hello, Albin. Are you available?"

"Of course."

"Louise and I would like you and Sonya to come to dinner soon. And Matt too, of course—is he speaking to Tess now?"

Tess was Wasserstein's daughter, about Matt's age. Ronay could think of any number of possibilities between the two of them. "We'd be glad to. Pick the day—wait, I'll have a Board meeting tomorrow. Any time after."

"I've got two full wirings the day after," Sonya said.

Sol said "Three days, then?"

Ronay looked at Sonya. She nodded. He said "Three. Thanks, Sol. Best to Louise. And I'll see if I can round up Matt. If—something's happened with Tess—"

"Eh. I think she wanted to jump off Sokoni, and Matt insisted on wearing wings first."

Sonya burst out laughing. "I *told* you, Solly—one day—"

"Hey, *hey*. When I did it it was an *experiment*. And it was a great contribution to science, too."

"Oh?"

"Sure. It got me out of it. See you both soon, Sonya, Albin."

"Thanks again, Sol."

When he had gone, Ronay said "I feel like a

proper—well. I thought he was going to ask about water."

Sonya smiled, and Ronay was all right again. "Blood, maybe."

There was a joke half-formed in Ronay's mind, about blood and water; but he let it dissolve. "Well. More work?"

"A bit. Plans and talk, no more wirework today. I'll be home in four or five hours."

"All right. What shall we have for dinner, then?"

"Anything without noodles in it."

"Orange chicken?"

"Fine."

They stood up. Ronay gave her a long tight hug. A cheer went up from the Skyhook fans.

Ronay walked up to the Surface-level Hub plaza, to the darkened marquee of the theatre. Whatever business Vela and Ballantine had, it was unlikely to concern Lunar water, and therefore was not Ronay's problem. It was difficult to imagine what Ballantine's motive had been in bringing Ronay into it; convenience was just possible—in a databloat society, there was a whole metatechnology of getting messages through the noise, and choosing the messenger was one of them. Sheer malice in complication was never to be dismissed.

He went around to the office door, pressed the plate. Naomi, smiling as ever, let him in.

"Gomenasai, Councillor!" she said. "What can we do for you?"

" 'Mashta, Naomi. I'd like to see Gil, if he's available. Just for a few minutes."

"Surely. He'll be on the main stage. Do you know the way?"

"Well, no. Not from here."

"Oh, don't be embarrassed. Every theatre ever built has tales of people lost backstage. Ask Gil to tell you some." She gave him a quick list of correct turns.

After a few hesitations—was it right at the blue bulletin board or left at the light-green locker?—he passed between two racks of Betacloth and plycore scenic flats and was on the main stage itself.

It had an elevated platform to center rear; the whole floor was painted to resemble wood. Six brown ropes angled down and outward from a U-shaped piece some four meters above, anchored at the bottom to eyebolts in the floor. Gil Vela was dangling overhead, a rope under his artificial armpit, left leg off, right leg on.

"Albin! Hello! Won't be a moment." He stuck something into the support grid above the stage and glided down the rope. He stood quite stable on his single foot, one hand nonchalantly brushing the rope.

Something about the cords caught Ronay's attention, and he touched one.

"Yes, it's hemp," Vela said. "That's what the money goes for. I'd have built the floor out of real wood if I thought I could get away with it." There was not the slightest trace of rancor in his voice.

"What's the set for?" Ronay said.

"*The Fair Maid of the West.* This is the deck of a ship. When it isn't a tavern, or a tropical island."

"A pirate ship?" Ronay said, grinning.

"Yes! You know the play? Or—you saw it five years ago."

"No . . . just a stupid joke, actually," Ronay said, touching his leg.

"Oh. Yo ho to you too, then, and a harrrr-Jim-lad for good measure."

"Funny how pirates still say the same things," Ronay said.

"Oh, it all comes around. Have you noticed that people have started saying 'Lunna' again, just like forty years ago?"

"I've noticed. I wonder how long before we're Selenites again."

Vela said, with a flourish, "I'm holding out for Loony and Proud of It. Remind me to tell you sometime about the fabulous history of the word 'occupation.' What does bring you here, Albin?"

"Lynch Ballantine would like you to speak with him. He says the news is bad. He did not tell me what the news is, or why it's bad, nor did I have any expressed plan to visit you."

"Oh." Vela reclined against the rope, stood at a fifteen-degree angle. "Just his style to do it this way, isn't it?"

"Not unusual."

Vela looked at a time display set into his epoxy forearm. "Albin, at literally any moment the trainees, Matt among them, are going to be in here, to find out who's made the cut for the Young Company. Did you know that?"

"No."

"I'm going to have to ask you to leave, Albin." Vela sounded embarrassed. Ronay could not remember ever having heard that in his voice; his *characters'* voices, yes—Vela was a brilliant farce-player—but this was different in its high registers. Not an unstrung voice, but one trying to keep tune under strain. What, if anything, had he read into Ronay's not knowing that this was Matt's decision day?

Ronay said calmly, "You want him for the Company very much."

"Very much indeed, Albin—you understand that I'd throw out *any* parent who was here just now; you, Sonya, the Wynants, anybody. Understand?"

"Of course, Gil. And of course I'll go. Good day. Should I leave the way I went? To miss them?"

"Yes. They'll be coming in by the main doors. Wait: would you like to know what Ballantine and I were discussing? It was only money."

"Some other time," Ronay said, knowing acutely that it would amount to none of his affair and

probably nothing of consequence at all; just another
breath of vacuum that he had cared too much about.
He turned away. He had done it wrong, all wrong.
Sonya would not be home for hours; there was no
more comfort now. He heard the house doors open as
he disappeared into the wings.

Matt glided down the gangway. He saw a movement onstage, another above; he didn't see Gil. He
vaulted onto the stage, grabbed one of the ropes and
spun to kill velocity.

The cord scraped his hands like raw crete. He
wobbled to a stop, looked at his reddened palms.

Gil dropped straight down, landing one-footed.
"You'll get used to it," he said.

"This is—"

"It beats pulling glass fibers out of your skin
after every performance. Besides, I figured you'd be
tough, all that Maze running you do."

"Yeah," Matt said, meaning nothing. "What's
this for?"

"You. If you say yes." He grabbed a rope. "These
are ratlines. And chandelier cords, and jungle vines."
He pulled himself up one-handed, did a chimpanzee
routine. "You'll fight with cutlasses and rapiers—
that's for the gentlemen—and great big side-hammer
pistols that sound like nothing you've ever heard."

Matt cocked a finger. "Stand and deliver, sir!"
He dropped his thumb. "Fsst, *karooom!*"

"I should have known. Do your guns recoil?"

"What?"

"Kick. Newton's law. You're shooting a lead ball
as big as your thumb. That makes you a reaction motor."

"We're not really—"

"No, you're not really, but *they* don't know that.
How does a stage gun work?"

"Uhm."

"Actors," Vela said, with exasperation that was
awfully authentic. "We have had, oh, one or two

stagecraft sessions in the past year? *Anyway*, there's a strobe, and a puff of smoke oil past a hot wire."

"What about the—"

"Yes, some of the guns use flash oil, and make a big yellow *dangerous* muzzle flash. You can kill people with some kinds of makeup; were you paying attention then?"

"Yes."

"Okay." He shot up to the fly tower, came drifting down again. "Know what to do with this?" He had two broad, curved swords in a hand, his other prosthetic leg in the crook of his arm. He tossed one sword to Matt, who caught it, balanced it, as Gil attached his leg.

Stage swords always left Matt in shock for a moment. The quality, the *mass* of the thing—a slice of plycore, sure, but not just a stick waved in the park when no Lunar was looking, *definitely* not a touchpad on a slate in a game, even one of Ruby's—

"En garde," Vela said—well, of course—and extended his cutlass. Matt leveled his own, circled its point. With his left hand he caught one of the stage ropes, pressed upward. He and Gil crossed blades. A cut, a turn, a feint—

Gil was only playing with him, Matt knew. You had to attack the enemy, defend yourself, keep the big heavy blade under some kind of control, *and* use some kind of anchor, as they were using the ropes now, to keep Old Mister Newton from spinning you right off the stage. Gil made it look not just easy, but effortless: you could forget, as the audience was supposed to forget, that he was constantly vectoring himself down to the deck.

"You're . . . cheating," Matt said. "You're holding down the power on your legs."

"Am I?" Gil said, sounding surprised, and stopped moving to look down at his limbs. Matt aimed a thrust, but as he did Gil spun elegantly out of its way. "All's fair," they both said, and traded a few more blows.

It really wasn't like the game. But the game was set on Earth (or, Matt insisted to himself, a place *like* Earth). Nobody fenced on Luna.

The doors opened. "Hello, Blake!" Vela said, "Percy, Minnie," as more of the students came in. Matt saw that they were shuffling, all a little nervous; he understood suddenly that Vela had not told most of them—possibly any of the others—whether or not they had made the Company cut. He felt odd about that, and not entirely pleasant.

They all sat down, on edge. Vela stood on stage, half-leaning against one of the angled ropes. While the class was filing in, he had shown his usual merry-pirate face; now his look was curiously flat, empty.

"Don't settle in," Gil said then, and his voice was flat as well. "You all know what's due to happen today. There's no nice or kind way to put the knife in, so I'll make the cut quick. Jesse Straight Bow, Matthias Ronay, Persist in Justice Wynant, Caroline Tchernin, and Philip de la Fere, please keep your seats. The rest of you have my thanks and appreciation; our work is now over. Please leave by the plaza exit."

Matt thought that it was just like a construction blast, out on the crater's ringwall: a silent flash, and then after a long beat a tremor, more through your mind than your boots, more because you knew there was supposed to be a shock than anything actually felt.

Some people did stand to go. A few just sat.

Blake Macdonald stood up. He was slight, wiry, red-haired; his voice was squeaky, but he used his body as well as anyone in the class—*Blake* hadn't made it?

"What about next year's classes?" Blake said in his unoiled voice.

Gil didn't move. "The theatre is a fine hobby," he said, and the way he said it locked them all to him like ships on homing signal. "If you want to join an amateur group, there are several posted on the circuits, or Naomi can point you the right way." He paused. They all paused. "Those groups can do things I cannot do. And they don't have to do what I must. Goodbye."

More former students moved to go. Blake held still for a held breath, two. "Tycho—" There was another theatre at Tycho, not far away, as the train rolled.

Vela said and did absolutely nothing.

Blake held up his hands, and smiled, sort of. "Exit laughing," he said, picked up his gear and went out, without laughter from anyone.

And then there were just the six of them: Gil, Matt, and the other survivors.

Gil crossed his ankles, lifted his feet and slid down the rope to sit on the stage. "Now, ladies and gentlemen, for the tough parts.

"You can't do anything for the people who just left. You can't trade your positions for theirs; that's not the way I work. You can't make them feel any better about what's happened, and you'll only make things worse if you try. I've done this on a regular basis for a long old time, and I hope you'll act as if you believe me whether you do or not.

"Second tough bit. You know that making the cut today is an invitation to join the Young Company. You have four days from now to think about whether you want to accept the invitation. And *for* that hundred hours, I'm not accepting any answers, yes, no, or on a muffin with jam."

Jesse said "Gil, I want—"

"*No.* I know how much you all wanted this. I know how anxious you are to tell me yes."

Matt caught a short straight look from Gil and

understood that Gil was deliberately lying, and knew that *they* knew it.

"A bit of free advice, take it at face value. You may think you're going to wander between the winds for that hundred hours. The advice is, don't: and that goes double in a water pack for hiding from anyone who might talk you out of it. Do everything you'd normally have done in that time. If you *do* join the Company, you won't be that to the exclusion of everything else. Really." He smiled. "*I* don't get to, so why should I let you? Now, is that agreed?"

They looked at each other, nodded, mumbled agreement.

"All right. In that case, we have another . . ." He consulted the time display in his left arm. ". . . hundred thirty minutes of this class to use up. Everybody up here for warmup."

They did some mechanical stuff, lifts and stretches and braces, made a group pyramid and restacked it over and over.

"Okay, everybody loose?" Gil said. "Story time. Let's do . . ." He shut his eyes, folded his live leg up under him. "Games. Caroline: Teach us a game."

"Nonverbal?" she said.

Gil stood up straight, put two fingers to his lips and zipped them shut.

Caroline stood still for a moment, then began to wiggle with energy. She put her hands on Jesse's shoulders and pulled Jess over, then gently bent Jess's arms at ninety-degree angles, manipulated her by touches into a comfortable crouch with hands before her face. Matt was placed at the edge of the stage, facing Jesse. Phil and P.J. finished a square. She led Gil to its center, faced him at Jess, then raised his right arm and made cranking motions with it. She pulled Gil's hand a way back, snapped it forward. She kicked off from the floor and tumbled through space toward Jesse, dropped her feet to brake at the last moment before collision. She pivoted on a toe, put her hands together and dealt the air a great sweeping blow.

Then she took a long, vaulting step, landing near Phil in one, then another to Matt, one to Percy, and finally a long low swoop to Jesse, landing in a slide across the smooth stage floor.

"Baseball," Phil said suddenly. "That Earth game, baseball." An odd look crossed his face, and he said "We don't play that here."

Caroline said "Well, of course not! You're supposed to hit the ball as far as you can—*here*, you'd knock it halfway to Tycho."

"Or into low orbit," Percy said, almost giggling. Matt could feel his own energy rising. They were all spinning up.

Matt said "What do they call those long hits—flying balls?"

"Fly balls," Caroline said, and took up the hitting stance again. "Gil, are we verbal now?"

"Verb all you like."

"I'm going for a high, fly ball . . . a high fly ball!"

Percy picked up the rhythm. "High . . . fly . . . ball!" Phil did too. "High fly ball!"

"High! Fly! Ball!" they were all chanting now. "High! Fly! *Ball!*"

Caroline leapt, an impossible uncontrolled jump with the whole force of her body, as if Up went on forever. Philip's jaw dropped open.

Caroline caught the lighting grid above the theatre seats—no thump was heard—began to pull herself from rod to rod, toward the control booth at the hindmost top of the hall, calling out in a fading voice as she did so that she *was* a high fly ball, diminishing in a limitless sky.

She vanished into the booth, and a moment later her voice boomed over the speakers: *"And it's going, going, yes, it's over the wallanissgonnnnne!"*

"Guess we're warm, huh," Gil said, and slid down to the stage. "Jess, will you suit up?"

She skipped backstage. By the time Caroline had come down from the booth, Matt was helping Jess into the Stage Manager's vest.

The Vest was made of Ango leather and open-weave Beta, all a matte black that would vanish utterly in a darkened stage space. It had four keyblox, at left and right breast and thigh; cables jacked into finger-followers like blackened steel spiders perched on the backs of her hands. She bent an elbow, pointed a finger at the left wing light, raised her palm: the light came up, slowly. She snapped her fingers and it went black.

Gil was distributing prompters to the rest of them. They were small crescents of clear epoxy, trix visible within, that hooked behind the ear. An image pipe ran forward to just in front of the eye.

Gil handed Jesse a text chip and she slid it into a unit over her left shoulder blade. The prompters blinked on, spraying images onto the retina. Gil and Percy went around adjusting them, until everyone could see cool blue lines of playscript cleanly overlaid on the stage.

"Scene one," Gil announced, "the tavern. Sets and places, please." The players dashed into the wings, coming out with boxes, a table. All of them except Percy took up lounging positions, Caroline asleep on the table with one arm dangling. "Lights . . . on your cues, ladies and gentlemen."

Jesse slashed her hands crosswise to douse the house lights. She pushed her palms down, with a jabbed finger here and there, reducing the stage lighting to a few red-gold shafts. Then, with a twist of her upper body, she brought up a flickering fireglow from deep at the back of the stage. Matt watched her work, knowing perfectly well he wasn't supposed to. He had watched Rubylaser, pitching their game, x-hundred times, but Ruby worked all with fingers and voxing and blink-switches. Jess was something else again.

Percy came on, walking heavily, bent forward.

"A little tireder, mine host," Gil said. "Remember when I showed you Brian Ahearne doing David Garrick doing the innkeeper?"

"You are welcome, gentlemen," Percy said, as Clem the taverner. "What wine will you drink? Claret, metheglin or muscadine? Cider, or perry to make you merry? Aragoose, or peter-see-peter-see-me. Canary or charnic*oooooops*!" He took a tumble in midair. Caroline had tripped him.

"Half his first speech, and he's scrimmed out already," Caroline said. It was an explanation, not an excuse or an apology.

"Look through the text, Peej," Gil said gently.

"Sorry. It's a lot of wine to keep track of."

Scrimming out was unfortunately a lot easier when you gamed a lot (Matt knew that Percy was in a group Jesse pitched to; they were a planetary exploration team, opening *new* new worlds). In the game, you were *supposed* to see the image and not the reality behind it.

The tavern scene ended in a duel, to wake the audience up and get one of the plots in motion; the hero, having killed a fellow over his sweetheart's virtue, must flee England, pursued by the sweetheart, who runs afoul of pirates and becomes a pretty fair buccaneer herself . . . and so on.

They worked for two hours, stop-and-replay, start-again, getting maybe a third of the way through the play. Finally Gil called time, measuring out his usual congratulations and thanks as if there were no hundred-hour (ninety-eight, now) deadline ahead of them. He folded the Manager's Vest over his arm and slipped away into the depths of backstage.

P.J. said "So should we—"

"We're not supposed to, right?" Caroline said.

"We can talk," Matt said. "There's other things to talk about."

So they went over to Sir Bernard Lovell Plaza, a three-deck hexagonal space with oak trees on a grassy slope. They sat on the grass, tugging off shoes, letting rehearsal sweat dry in the still air and reflected sun, and talked: about the text, about lights and props and the right angles for swordplay on the deck of a pitching pirate ship, about the game teams they were in and whether the new vue on the New Worlds was any good or not.

Phil had turned his head to look at something, and faded out of the conversation. Gradually the others noticed, and turned as well, and stopped.

There were four Slammer kids sitting around a table, just off the edge of the grass. You couldn't miss them. They were dressed like Slammers, in weed fabrics of odd weaves and cuts, they had an average of one-and-a-half shopping bags each—what was the Slammer urge to buy bags and bags full of stuff? Was the whole Earth weighted down with purchases at six times the gravity?

And they all had drinks and snacks, and they were *throwing the drinks in the air.* Tossing handfuls of fluid up, watching them come down, shattering droplets apart and poking them together as they fell, arguing about whose waste would hit the ground first.

Jess looked furious and Matt felt furious, but it was Caroline who exploded, like vacuum busting into still air: in one second she was on her feet, and in the next she was in the air, twisting and waving her arms so that she hovered above the wasters' table, screaming "Slammers! Stupid sookin' Slammers! It's *not* your vackin' *water!* You want to piss, piss on your own dirty planet!"

The voice, the sudden violence, the way she hung there in the air and somehow didn't fall, pick one or all of them; the blueballers fled. They tumbled over each other, they crashed into the floor and the walls and everything else in the vector envelope until they were out of the plaza, leaving zero-point-seven-five shopping bag each behind.

Caroline dropped to the grass, her arms stretched limp, shaking, sobbing.

Matt stared like everyone else, having no more idea than any of them what to say or do or think. Then, in another flash, Lafayette Lonestar was there with him. Lonestar stood him up strong and sent him to Caroline's side. It was Lonestar who picked her up, brushed the grass from her clothes, hugged her.

It was everyone else in the plaza, everyone, even the shopfolks and the security people who had looked in to see what in deep dust was happening, who clapped and cheered and bravoed, just as if they had been on stage, just as if they had been playing for real.

They sat there until it stopped. What else could they do? Take curtain calls? Caroline was still as dust in the bottom of a crater; she had gotten them all hot to glowing and she knew it. Matt knew that he and the others would gladly have forgiven her if they could, if they *could,* but dragging attention in on someone else's cool was not something you forgave, only let pass. Even Lonestar could only stand at a distance from Matt, looking on with cryostatic eyes.

They tried to pick up the pieces of the conversation again, but it was impossible. Phil left first, then Caroline, then P.J.; they went by different ways, and doubtless none started in the direction that actually led to his or her coldspot.

Matt went next. He left Jesse alone, grass held between her fingers and toes, looking up at the top of a tree. Then he turned a corner and the plaza was behind him.

Something cool stirred against his side. He reached into his shirt and caught it: a thin, splayed little lizard, smaller than his palm, black as the sky with thin stripes of electric red. It wrapped a red tongue around his thumb.

Matt carefully put the lizard on the floor, and it ran off, back toward Lovell. Was the green patch cool for the lizard, Matt suddenly wondered, or just home?

And then he knew where to go next, as from a hint dropped in Ruby's game; if not a way closer to the goal, at least one to put off death another moment.

A quarter-hour's walk through the Hub and a lift down to Transit level brought him to a square room, six or seven meters across. The walls were of a rough-finished ceramic, in a mottled finish of tans and greens, covered with what at first looked like a geometric engraving. Seen closer, it was paneled with tiles, each tile an identical four-footed lizard; they interlocked to cover the surface without a gap.

In the center of the room was a statue of a dragon, in glazed pottery of browns and golds, its head on a long arched neck that nearly reached the ceiling. Its eyes were faceted crystals the size of Matt's fist that shone with flickering light from within. After a minute, they blazed, and blue fire shot from the dragon's nostrils.

Behind the statue was a sidewise passage, lined in burnstone, that led to a downward ramp. Matt followed it, through a spinney and past a row of firefoam nozzles, down into misty air, full of moisture and smell. The ceiling was low, scalloped with torchmarks; a drop grid held rows of long tubular lamps, coils of piping. The space from Matt's knee height to chest was filled with greenery: row upon row of planters filled with masses of broad-leafed vines. The way between them was narrow and twisted wildly. Here and there was the most un-Lunar sight of brownish water dripping of its own volition into puddles on the floor.

The planters were laid out in a maximum-edge

fractal shape called a dragon curve. The vines took in sewage and carbon dioxide, breathed back clean water and oxygen, metabolized waste into celluloses and sugars and alcohols for Lunar production. The dragon stretched on and on, covering hundreds of square meters below the city.

There were plants like this on ships; wyverns, they were called, turning spent air and waste back into fresh air and feedstocks. Mostly, Matt had read, they were cased away, green boxes that breathed in as the crew breathed out. It was difficult to imagine a working ship having a place that felt like this, dripped, tangled and smelled like this.

Something rustled the plants a distance away; Matt turned, then turned again as a pair of hands shot out from below the dragon not five meters from him.

A woman pulled herself into the aisleway. She was wearing a jacket and shorts of some slick, waxed fabric, black rubber sandals, all stained with dirt and chlorophyll; the jacket had a hood drawn tight around her face. There was a coil of soft black tubing around her upper body, and a couple of pouch belts around her waist. Matt was reminded of Stringer after a hard session laying Maze, but Jack never picked up more than a little dust.

"Hello," she said. "You lost?"

"No," Matt said. "Are you a dragonmaster?"

"Just a rider. You want a master? There should be one around someplace. The Lord's up with Ellegon." She looked at the masses of green. "Kazul's got a touch of indigestion, and I've gotta go flush his guts."

"Kazul's . . . this dragon?"

The dragonrider giggled. "Sure as borosilicate isn't the Dragonlord. So, you Copernican?" The question was a little too sudden, too offhand.

"Over under sideways down, we're the pole the sun goes round."

"Okay, okay, I didn't mean anything. Kazul's the baby here. Most of his stock's from Ellegon, the oldest. But he's special, is my malachite Kazzy. You see this?" She reached into the green body, pulled out a nearly black leaf the size of a spread hand. "We crossed with Fafnir, the Martian oldest. Faf concentrates water like you wouldn't believe." She let the leaf go. "I think he'll fly."

Matt nodded, half wishing she would talk more about the dragons and half wanting her to go away.

She looked around. "I know I left a pipe flanger around here somewhere. Have you seen a tool like—" She made a bizarre gesture.

Matt saw it hanging from a planter. "There it is."

"Aha. Thanks. 'Scuse me now, back to the coils. Watch out for shoggoths." She bent down and vanished beneath the racks of dragon. Matt went to where she had gone, bent down, but he couldn't see anything, and the smell of soil and rot stopped even the thought of following.

Something clattered and rustled overhead. A shoggoth came into view, clambering along the ceiling grid. Its body was a geodesic cage half a meter across, stuffed with actuators and sensors and logic; eight thin arms, jointed shoulder-elbow-wrist, extended from the vertices of the cage, each ending in a three-fingered hand. The roby crawled along the grid with four arms, pausing now and then to poke at the dragon with one or more of the others. One hand unreeled a cable from within the body and stuck a probe into the soil trays, or maybe the roots.

Matt walked on. He heard conversation some way off; after a moment's thought, he went that way. It took a while; the fractal curve had plenty of strange bendings and blind ends. Finally he could hear the dragonfolk clearly, see them less so, through coils of green and panels of wet cellufilm.

There were three of them, one the woman he had seen before.

"—but we're still coming up short on electrolytes and rot products," she was saying. "We need a body, that's all."

"Popul Vuh doesn't owe us one for a while," said another woman. "You know what the Lord said."

The third man said "How about a couple of Angos?"

The first woman said, in an amused voice, "You wanna rustle Angos? Yippee ti-yi yo and all that?"

"Rustle?" said the other woman.

"Steal. Sorry. Earth will tell."

And she had asked if *Matt* were Lunar-local, he thought.

The man said "Angos die like anything else." Hastily he added, "Except dragons, of course."

"Yes," the second woman said, "and they get eaten like everything else, including dragons. But except people."

They fed people to the dragons? Matt wanted to open his slate and scan facts right then and there, but this was the wrong then and definitely the wrong there.

The woman from Earth said "Doesn't leave us very many options, does it." She turned her head. "There was a kid down here just a little while ago. I wonder if anybody'd miss him."

Matt started to walk away, lightly and quietly, careful not to disturb the dragon as he wound about it. He knew perfectly well that they were making some kind of dragonrider joke, and he kept on walking, taking the occasional look back.

He nearly collided with a tall man in a long green coat who came suddenly out of the plantmass.

"You're not going anywhere, you know," the man said.

He was old, with a square gray beard, gray hair that poked out from under the hood of his coat . . .

or robe, or whatever it was. His face was a deep brown, his eyes black and bright. He was wearing large squarish eyeglasses that mounted an assortment of accessory lenses and spray displays. He was leaning slightly on a glass staff as high as his shoulder.

The dragonmaster pointed a finger. His hands were rather grubby. "This is Ellegon's J talon," he said, very mildly. "You've got fifty meters to walk, and nothing but more dragon when you get there."

"Oh."

"I'm Holly St. Antoine," the man said. "I've been known to get lost here too."

It was another of the founding Names; Hollis St. Antoine was the Dragonlord, the chief botanist and keeper of these plants for all of Copernicus. "Matthias Ronay."

"You'd be Albin's son, then."

"Yessir."

St. Antoine nodded. "Welcome to the lairs. Are you down here often? Can I 'voke you a spell of direction?" He rubbed his fingers on his staff, and there was a star of light in his right eye as a display went active.

"No, it's all right. I haven't been. Here. Often."

"Are you looking for treasure?"

"What?"

"Long ago, the tale goes, there was an old dragon who crouched on his treasure for so long that it armored him against intruders. It's nice and dark down here . . . in the sense of not letting eyes look in."

"I'm not—hiding."

"No? Well, *I* am. So, if there's nothing else I can do for you . . ."

"I met a woman earlier," Matt said suddenly.

"Romance under the whispering nightshade?" St. Antoine shook his head. "No, wait. Height somewhere between you and me? Spends a lot of time tangled in the root system? Just a bit *intense*?"

Matt looked at St. Antoine's eyes. How old must he be? Were there Coran chips bracing his old brain's speech centers? With extreme caution, Matt said "I think she was from Earth."

The Dragonlord started to scratch his beard, then looked at his fingers and stopped. "That would be Livia. Grand-niece of mine. Was she polite? You have to know, so much of Earth smells like dragonloam, they don't learn any manners."

"She was talking about bodies. Dead people . . . to fertilize the dragon, I guess?"

The Dragonlord chanted:

> *"Up the dragon, down the green,*
> *Bact and Air work sight unseen;*
> *Bact's the diner, Air's the host,*
> *Meth and Ox from sweet compost.*
> *Down the chutes and up the vents,*
> *Bact and Air pay recompense;*
> *Biomass and nitrogen,*
> *Praise ye compost, sing amen."*

St. Antoine stopped. Matt didn't say anything. "Yes, we fertilize with bodies," the Dragonlord said finally.

"For the water?"

"No, no. Though I'm sure you hear a great deal about water. No, that's not our problem. Do we seem dry?" He waved a hand through the misty air. "Lunars can't wait to give us their water. Once they've done with it, I mean. Done *in* it, enriched it with salts and organics. It's an indolent life the green kings live, being watered constantly." A shoggoth went racketing by in the middle distance. St. Antoine tucked his staff in the crook of his elbow and shoved both hands into the dragonmass; it spread and curled away from him. "Bit of sensitive plant in this; bred towards wyvern. Guards itself from acceleration and the MIRAGE snap. Livia's tropism is toward wyvern, you know. She couldn't wait to get here from Earth, can't wait to get off here and on a ship, and then will she put a root down? No, it'll be this hybrid to balance a breathing mixture, that one to fix nitrogen, another to house the wild Somebody's Bird on Somebody Else's World. One of these days I swear she'll breed the Great Black Daisy of Gaia."

She wanted those things—? Matt felt guilty with himself, for what he had thought of Livia.

And he knew what it was time for him to do.

"I should go home now," he said. "How do I get to a Transport station?"

"To the rear, left, twenty meters—no, we might as well be dropping breadcrumbs. There's a better way." St. Antoine manipulated his staff, and a shoggoth clambered over to them. "Now, let her get your scent." The roby stretched two arms toward Matt, sized him up. "That's it. Now, follow her."

"Thank you, sir."

"And do be welcome again, young Ronay. With husbandry, our treasure is not diminished by use."

The shoggoth led Matt through the dragon paths, pausing patiently for him when he stopped or stumbled in the wet or just had to think. He didn't see anyone else; there must be eyes down here, there were always eyes, but how far could they see through the thickness?

The shoggoth pointed to a spiral stairway. Matt went up. It was surely his imagination that the roby waved goodbye. At the top of the stairs was a narrow flush door, with a peephole and an OPEN SLOWLY sign; Matt looked through and saw the Tran station beyond.

He went home, really actually home. He needed to spend some time there, over these next three calendar days, to balance the trip to come. Things had to be kept cool, cold, icy. Stable orbit, low signature.

He thought about the incident in Lovell Plaza, hoped that it wasn't already blown.

The house was quiet. The door to His office was open; there was light from within. Matt paused. He wondered if he should say something, about the dragonfolk, about bodies to feed the dragons. Would it help matters, if Matt showed an interest in His business, something that was Lunar and not ships? Would it turn His thinking away from Lovell (which He surely knew about, surely had screened once or twice or six times, might be watching right now on the huge display).

But they had said it was Popul business, not Water. If he brought up the wrong committee's business, he would only be told that he *did not understand how these things worked,* with no trace of a clue where to find out how they did.

Matt walked lightly past the door and into his room.

In the study, Ronay had one small square of the display open. He had come home, sat down to work with the Goldberg Variations in his ear and drifted imperceptibly into sleep. Then he woke, cold and damp, with the foul aftertaste of a forgotten dream. He was alone, Sonya was still at work. He pinged Tycho, and now sat facing Lawrence Duveen, just the two of them, eye to eye and neither bigger nor smaller than life.

Ronay said "VACOR is planning something."

"Ballantine *said* this?"

"He communicated it. He kept hinting—"

"Ballantine's always hinting. Cheapest gambit on the board when you don't have anything real to play. You of all people should—"

"He had me sit in on a company conference—"

"During which they said—"

"They spoke in tongues. Lynch suggested we buy the conferencing system."

"From VACOR?"

"He wasn't specific."

"Polite of him. And not a bad idea, actually. Sometimes SELENA makes my teeth itch."

"We use SELENA for very—"

"Specific reasons, yes."

"What is it you want to say, Larry?"

Duveen's eyebrows went up. "Are you changing the subject, Albin?"

"No."

"Pity."

Ronay turned his head.

"What is it, Albin?"

"Matt's door . . . I didn't hear him come in."

"How *is* Matt, Albin?"

"Gil Vela wants him for the theatre." Ronay's eyes lost focus as counterpoints rattled against each other in his mind. "Lynch talked about Gil—"

"Cryptically?"

"Maybe."

Duveen laughed.

Ronay said with intent, "I don't think Ballantine would put Matt into any plans. I wouldn't like to be wrong about that."

There was a pause. Duveen said "Explain that last statement to me in a way that doesn't sound clinically paranoid."

"Do you know about Matt's closest friends?"

"Not much. He's close to Sam Rincon's girl, isn't he? She's supposed to be some kind of mechanical genius."

"She's fourteen and holds two patents for chip design. Sam says she'll pass him by in a couple of years."

"I see. And Sam Rincon's one of our most important exports."

"But they're all special. Phys-Plant showed me a vue of this jumping gym they built; they hand out engineering degrees for less."

"They all did this? Rincon's daughter—"

"That isn't the point, Larry. There's this group of brilliant, brilliant kids, and *none* of them are anything like any of the others: there's Rincon, and a goldminder, and an artist—Natsu Okuda's girl, Sonya knows her. One of them was born on the Big Bad Blue Thing, and the others don't seem to care. Can you imagine that? Can you imagine *us* not caring?"

Duveen looked down, and his face went into shadow. Almost inaudibly, he said "Not us but you."

Ronay said *"Something* holds them together—"

"You think it's Matt."

"You think I'm projecting."

"I *know* you're projecting, Albin," Duveen said gently. "That doesn't mean I think you're wrong. . . . By the way, does Lynch Ballantine reenter this story anytime soon?"

"You know that Ballantine's trapped here."

"Not something I cared to know. What do you mean, 'trapped'?"

"Some time back, he did something to offend The Vacuum Corporation."

"There's light in the darkest corners."

"They put him on Luna for whatever it was. He'll never get transferred. Certainly never back to Earth."

"That only leaves five or six dozen other planets, and the occasional Frame. Some people even like living on ships, I hear."

Ronay stared. Duveen said, very softly, "Sorry, Albin. Go on."

"I don't know any more details."

"Did Ballantine tell you this?"

"Yes. He wasn't sober when he did."

"You really are friends," Duveen said, in an odd, opaque tone. "But then, he's quite theatrical, isn't he?" Lightly: "Maybe that's what he wanted with Vela?"

Ronay said firmly, "He's in a cage—exile, if you

like—and he's angry." He did want to change the subject, almost desperately so, but the theme had hold of him. "I think he'd like to do something really terrible, just to dare everyone, us and VACOR, to find a way to punish him."

"Hmm. Kind of makes you sorry Execution Lock is just a legend." Duveen tilted his head. "It *is* a legend, right, Albin? The Ronays haven't really been keeping—"

"Larry."

"Well, if that's the case, the worst thing we've got is . . ." There was a flare of recognition. "Kicking him off Luna for good."

"For good and all. But it's like Waterhole: the person with the best view won't be reporting back. What might he do . . ." Ronay said, across a widening distance, "what might anyone do, who wanted to escape badly enough . . ."

"Does Matt want to escape, Albin?"

Ronay put a hand to his eyes. "A touch, Larry. We were talking about Lynch."

"That's so. Albin, do you remember when you decided to go roving for water?"

"What? When?" Roving for water meant taking a vehicle out in search of the native Lunar ice that one or two people still thought must exist somewhere. Three or four generations back it had been a popular sport; since then, it was considered a socially proper method of suicide, especially if you didn't take an excess of supplies and parked the rover where it could be easily recovered.

"Oh, I think we were both about eight years old. You were planning to do it on your seventy-thousandth hour."

"Really . . ."

"You *knew* you were going to hit frost. I knew you were right too. That's why I was going with you."

"I don't . . . truly don't remember."

"No? I'd call that a waste of a dedicated obses-
siveness, then. But I suppose you found something
else to do with it."

Ronay nodded. He got the joke. He might, if
things were different, have laughed at it, at himself.
If things were different.

Duveen said "You said Matt was home?"

"I heard his door close."

"Go talk to him, Albin."

Ronay looked up.

"I mean it. Go tell Matt you love him. *Now.*"

"Larry—"

"Not me, *him.* I mean it. Now."

"His door's closed. You know better than—"

"Knock. Later, Albin."

The pane irised shut.

Ronay pushed himself out of the chair, went
from the bright room into the dark hall. Matt's door
was only a few steps to the right. He still did not remember a plan to go ice picking, years ago, but he
didn't doubt Duveen. He was absolutely certain that
back then, when Ronay's father had always been
struggling with some issue of resource law, back
when Albin had hated him—

He was certain now that he had been certain
then, that he could bring in water single-handed.

Ronay knocked.

"Yes?"

"May I come in, Matt?"

"Jussamoment." Matt opened the door. Ronay
looked straight at him, suppressing the impulse to
scan the room.

"Yes?" Matt said.

"How was your day?"

"Oh. Well . . . I guess you know."

Ronay started to say that no, he didn't, but
stopped; he wasn't here to pry. "I wanted your opinion on something."

"Yes?"

"I suppose I spend a lot of time talking about water."

Matt tensed up, and Ronay could feel the temperature drop. Before things could freeze, he said "Okay, *all* the time."

Matt smiled faintly. "It's your job."

"You know that it's important. That sometimes, we do things that other people don't understand—because it does matter so much."

"Yeah, I see that." Matt was warming up, Ronay could feel, with a sudden shock of joy; Matt seemed pleased—relieved, somehow. If Ronay pressed on, explained that, yes, sometimes what they did for the sake of water, no matter how important, was too much, went too far—

No. He broke the stare, allowed himself to look around the room, at the remarkable clutter of books and prints, toys and models, clothing arranged as if decompression had hit the laundry. He was sure that Matt could locate anything here instantly. Except possibly for the clothes.

"Is that an Escrimat?" Ronay pointed at a gadget piled among half a dozen others, between Matt's slate and desk console.

"Uh—oh, yeah. They call it an Esparco, though. Now."

"May I?" He stood in the doorway as Matt brought it over: a handgrip within a smoothly curved guard, about ten centimeters of weighted rod standing in for the sword blade. A limp fiberline connected it to a fingerless harness for two fingers and a thumb, like a bowshooter's glove.

Ronay almost laughed at that comparison: there were no archers on Luna. Just as there were very, very few real fencers. He tested the feel of the grip: it was lightly padded over a solid core. The rod gave it the feel of a meter of rapier; a gyroscopic core could feed back the mass of an even larger blade. "Do you have another one of these?"

Matt looked up sharply, then said "I'll play from the slate. That's what I do at— what I'm used to. Do you want the goggles?"

"I don't figure to fight blindfolded."

Matt brought him a pair of bulbous, silvery eyeglasses. Ronay put them on, saw the room heavily darkened. He poked audio plugs into his ears. Matt helped him with the maingauche glove.

"Okay?" Matt said, muffled.

"C'est si bon."

Through the murky glass, Ronay saw Matt open the slate, crouch on the floor with it. Light from its screen splashed Matt's face.

Without warning, Ronay was standing in the village tavern of a thousand costumed swashbucklers. Afternoon light filtered through tiny lozenge-paned windows. Pewter tankards sat on wooden tables whose only finish was age and smoke, spilled drinks and battering. A rickety-looking stairway led up to a balcony, just the right height for a dying fall, or a leap to the hanging chandelier.

"Do you spurn me, sir, that you turn your back so readily?" It was Matt's voice, straight, not voked up. Ronay pressed the maingauche against his hip, flexed slightly, and the tavern rotated around him.

He saw Matt: taller, older, but still recognizably Matt, his blond hair that flowed past his lace collar, his stance in the velvet doublet and high riding boots. He held a partly full wineglass idly in one long-fingered hand.

"I do not turn my back on you, sir," Ronay said, "but I do turn my back, sir."

"A nice distinction. And whose back is it that turns so?"

Ronay thought a moment. "Chalons. Simon de Chalons. Which gives you the advantage of me."

"Laf—" Matt paused, tapped his fingers on his sword hilt. "Le Fou, let us say."

The Fool? Ronay thought, and waited.

Matt's image said "That does not inspire you to comment?"

Ronay smiled. He wasn't sure if the goggles could pick up a smile, so he toggled the glove for a half-bow. "I dare say such an obvious thing is not worth commenting on."

"You dare say. Dare you anything else?"

"Oh, this and that." Ronay clutched the sword hilt. "And all." He drew, seeing the blade measure the space between them, hearing offstage sounds of chairs being shoved back and bystanders ducking for cover. "On your guard."

"I am on my guard, sir," Matt said, and tossed his wineglass. Ronay took an involuntary step and batted it out of the air with his blade, hearing the glass shatter, feeling a shock as the gyros spun.

Matt used the moment to draw, and cut the air barely past Ronay's sword arm. "You are slow, sir."

That was right enough. Matt had a clear advantage in body control; whatever he was doing at his slate gave him full freedom of movement, while Ronay struggled to remember the left-hand action codes. There was no such difficulty with his sword; his right hand knew exactly what it was doing, keeping Matt's blade always a span from disaster, leading an easy three-beat andante with the steel baton.

That was it. Ronay's left hand fell suddenly to its natural work. Tempo a little higher, please. Around the table, dodge the flung tankard, yes, you, the oboe, if the nice composer hadn't wanted to hear you we'd have sold your chair to a paying customer.

He had Matt backing up the stairs now, trading position for pressure, using his image's large plumed hat (indoors?) for defense and distraction and the sheer hell of waving it around. Matt grabbed a lamp, threw it—"I cannot get used to this fighting with furniture. Wherever do you learn it?" Step, step, pace, pace, bloody harpist, you can strum like that when you've got wings and a halo too. Korngold fanfares roared and echoed in Ronay's mind.

Matt was fighting with vigor, grace, but his style wasn't right for rapier; he thought he was swinging more mass and less length, and kept missing chances. Ronay saw where his opportunity would come . . . just about the center of the balcony.

A caesura in the music: did he want to take the kill?

He slowed his drive, legato. The sword was beginning to weigh in his hand, the gyros putting on synthetic fatigue, as if this were real. More real. Not a game. Whatever.

They traded blows at a standstill for a minute, two, without room to maneuver on the narrow balcony. Ronay had a perverse urge to walk through the railing, just to see what would happen.

They locked blades, hilt against hilt. Ronay felt the pressure. Matt looked him directly in the eyes. There was a gleam of understanding there, of recognition. Was it the operator or the code between them?

Ronay was suddenly inclined to buy Duveen his new conference filters, and we'd see then whose teeth itched—

Belowstairs, the door burst in, and armed men flooded onto the tavern floor.

"City guards, I dare say," Ronay said. Bravo, Matt, he thought.

"I dare that as well. May I note a certain lack of fighting room up here?" Matt nodded toward the flimsy railing, the chandelier rope. "After you, my dear de Chalons."

"No, I insist, after you, my dear le Fou." Ronay saluted and leapt down the staircase. He turned to watch as Matt vaulted the rail and dove for the chandelier, his swing carrying him squarely into a guardsman.

Ronay's sword was lighter now; second wind or different rules. He disarmed a guard with an effort-

less circular blow, whacked him on the backside with
the flat of his sword and sent him howling into the
street.

There must have been at least half a dozen
guards, maybe a full dozen; it didn't matter. They
were the heroes, they were going to win, and end up
arm in arm through the streets of Paris, looking for
an intact tavern to dine in. . . .

"I promised your mother orange chicken for
dinner," Ronay said softly to the boy beside him.
"And there's almost enough time to make it. Think
you can cover for me if she's early?"

For a moment he felt Matt's shoulders tighten, a
cold breath pass by. "Sure," he said.

Ronay paused in the door. "I love you, son."

Matt gave something like a nod, and then sat
very still. Ronay went out, down the hall, into the
kitchen.

He took the chicken from the cooler, sliced it
apart and arranged the pieces in a cooking tray. A
half-liter of orange juice concentrate and water sub-
merged them; he lit the oven, put them in to start
cooking while he looked around for a couple of live
oranges. He found them, turned them over in his
hands, thinking about the water the forcing houses
needed. It was gray water, of course, but in the end
the hydrogen budget came out the same.

Matt came in. That and the act of cooking reminded Ronay of something. "The Wassersteins have
asked us to dinner in a couple of days. Think you can
take it?"

"A couple?"

"We agreed to three nights from now. You have
another engagement?"

"I—yeah, we do."

"Yes?"

"We'll be over at Ruby's place."

"We?"

"All of us. You know."

"I guess I do. All right. You'll be there through dinner?"

Matt didn't speak. Ronay said "All night?"

"A couple of nights."

"I know I started it, Matt, but this 'couple' thing isn't working out too well. Two nights?"

Another silence; then, in a little flute voice, "Seven."

Ronay tried not to laugh, but one chuckle got out. "You're all going to be at the Rincons' for seven straight nights?"

"Pretty much."

"It must be quite a party."

"It *isn't a party*."

"A game?"

"Yeah. We've got to . . . stay together."

"I assume you plan on eating and sleeping during this ordeal."

"That's part of it. It's all live time, you know? So you can only eat when you're really eating, and sleep when you really sleep."

Ronay knew the sound of a brilliant improvisation, but he let it pass unremarked. "Will Sam be there?"

Pause. "No. He's coming back from a job. On a Frame."

"And this is happening in—"

"Two more days. We didn't know that long ago— we had to change it. Because Ruby's dad was coming back, and—we didn't want to be in his way."

"Very considerate of you," Ronay said, he hoped not too dryly.

Matt nodded. Ronay believed he'd gotten the point and did not push it. "Will you be close enough to reality that you can answer a ping? I mean, just in case the dome busts, or something."

"Sure. I'll have my slate, sure."

"Okay. Here. Peel some oranges."

Matt took the fruit. "Do oranges come off of dragons?"

"No, from orange trees. There's a grove room—they call it a 'forcing house'—over on the edge of Verne, by the Ango ranch. It isn't very big, though. Tycho has bigger ones, and Serenity City. Those are probably from Serenity."

Matt looked hard at the two oranges. Ronay said "Aren't you going to ask how I know?"

"Okay."

"Because most of Tycho's are juice oranges. They squeeze them, concentrate the juice, take most of the water out."

"Oh."

"I promise, I won't say another word about water tonight. If your mother brings it up, tell her I promised."

Sonya came in shortly after that, and she did not bring up the subject of water. She didn't say much at all through dinner, and as soon as the table was cleared she and Matt both went back to their bedrooms. Ronay stood in the door to the music room for a moment, thinking of—nothing, really—and went back as well.

Sonya was sitting up in bed, under a reading light that cast a precise cone of white light in the dark room. There was a thin drape of Frame silk, pale green—Earthlight green, it was called—over her shoulders, and her fine red hair, which had to be short for the sake of exosurgery, was brushed out. She had a book open in her lap, a tasset, open and lit, balanced on one knee. She waved a hand. Ronay raised his hand, then saw that she was working, entering data; there was a cordless inductor pickup on her wrist.

"Hello," she said, looking up.

"Hello." He sat down on the edge of the bed. "Kto shto, krasnya?"

"Tout doux, chéri."

"Shall I leave you alone a little longer?"

"Not another moment. Just let me shut down here. Want some light?"

"No." He touched her ankle, through the thin wool bedspread. "I remember where everything is."

He undressed, wrapped on a thin robe and got into bed. Sonya touched off the light, then pressed another key; on the dark ceiling, stars came out, and the Copernicus ringwall rose into view, washing the room with an ivory cast of reflected sunlight.

"If you were working . . ."

"No. One of the wire jobs, day after tomorrow, has some major reconstruct work. Requires a little more advance planning."

"What was the old surgery for?"

"Not so old. She was in that tracklaying crew, out from Archimedes, that got caught in the flare—remember?"

"Yes." Those tracks led out to the site for the Waterhole reservoir. One of the crew had died. It was different, of course; it had not been anyone's deliberate act.

"So there's a silver thyroid, and the remnants of an old part-wiring . . . planning, that's all." She leaned against his shoulder. Her cheek was cool against his. "Now tell me what you're brooding on, so we're even."

"Matt won't be at Sol and Louise's dinner. He and his revolutionary council are going to be in session at Sam Rincon's. For at least seven days, though I wouldn't be surprised if it runs into overtime."

"Ah."

"I sense great depths in that 'ah.' "

She said something sibilant into his ear, either "Spasiba" or " 'S'possible."

When it was apparent she wasn't going to say any more, Ronay said "I was thinking about what Sol said, about crazy stunts. Sometimes I try to imagine you and Sol as kids. . . ."

"Is it that hard?"

"You and Sol . . . and, hm, Kim Guptal, and which one of the Wynants? C.C. or his sister?"

"F.C. Fi. 'Fidelity to the Cause.' I wonder sometimes if I understand the Wynants."

"They're Names. They have more important things to do than be understood."

"Stop that," she said sharply. Then, "I suppose half of what we did is past understanding now. I was sure I'd . . ."

"What?"

"Ne vazhna. Tell me something you did when you were little."

Ronay thought. Not Duveen's story of roaring off for water. "I never thought I'd live in one of the Chartered Cities. I thought I'd have a shelter, somewhere on Farside, just books and a datalink and a dragon in a greenhouse."

"All alone through the long skynight?"

"Mhm."

"Why is that, Albin? Luna is so empty, there are so few of us, and when we're young we all want to be so alone."

"Just a fantasy. We all want to find the secret ice lode, or the Native Lunars, or at least their lost city . . . we all want to hitch on a ship and see the New Worlds. We all start out . . . weightless, floating."

"Wakarimasu."

"Matt *could* be wired, correct? He's not too young."

She pushed herself a little more upright. "Once again, it can be done. Opyat, there must be compensations made for growth and development, and corrective operations will be necessary later in life."

"Corrective op . . ." Ronay's mind swam.

"Everyone with the nervnya net requires work from time to time. But it can be done. What is desired enough can be done. If what is done is desired enough."

"I want Matt to . . . have what he wants."

"I know that."

"But it needs to be . . . something . . . worthy. And I don't *know* what he wants. And I don't think he knows either."

"Y'panyimayu."

"I *was* that age once. I really was."

"Yes. Paslutshyie myina, syertsina. What shall I do? Shall I put the glass in him, the cardiac assist? He has asked, and I have said no, because . . . it did not seem as if it would solve anything."

"I don't believe that it would."

"Very well then."

She put her fingertips against his chest, her hand arched so that the inductor did not touch his skin. He grasped her wrist and pressed it close; the metal was not cold at all.

Looking backward, it was possible to see how things became so complicated. It was like the evolution of cosmology: world-centered to Sun-centered to island galaxies. You began with the thought that anything was possible, if you could only get *alone* enough; then other bodies perturbed yours, and anything could be done in the glow of that perfect bright companion.

Beyond that, though, there were so *many* stars, so much obscuring dust. Decades ago, Jacob Gold had been trying to solve a multiple-bodies equation, at the same time his wife Hannah was exploring the capacities of the latest generation of computers, and their young friend Leon Avakian thought he had found the secret to infinite energy in a disk of shadow matter coupled to the galaxy. All three of them had been wrong, come wildly short of the reality; what they had gotten was in fact the machine that traveled to the New Worlds.

If Ronay could actually show his son how wonderfully complex the human equations were, how much could be done and how much might be discov-

ered—would Matt see? Or would he turn away, in
fear and anger and disgust?

"Sonya, mon tresor rouge," he said, and held
her for perhaps a quarter of an hour, until her
breathing slowed to the piano largo of sleep; he eased
her body level, her head on the pillow. He rolled onto
his side to lie with his hand touching hers; he smelled
the chemistry of hospital and warm skin and hair,
and against all expectations was asleep in moments.

He woke before she did, a little after nine, pulled
on his robe and a pair of slippers, made a cup of hot
black tea. The watchboard said Matt was still in his
room. He supposed Matt would stay around the house
until his adventure began, buying time away with
time in; it was what Ronay would have done. What he
had done.

He went into the music room, closed the door.
He put down the teacup, picked up the breath control-
ler, a thick rod half a meter long with a mouthpiece
at one end and finger levers and touchspots along its
length. Ronay fired up the central unit, jacked in the
tinwhistle, put his lips to the mouthpiece and blew a
long low note. Water in the midst of dryness, he
thought, had to be woodwind music, with perhaps an
overlay of white noise. And slow, precise, crisp percussion; he dialed that into the console and played a
bit of melody as it came to him. On the wall in front of
him, notes flashed onto the time-grid; Ronay toggled
the left-hand switches to harmonatique accompani-
ment, and clusters of backing instruments, strings,
glasswinds, more percussion, appeared in their
places. It was only good for sketching, like filling in a
still page with blots of color or copyblocks. Later the
instruments would be tuned, given their own proper
voices.

After two or three hours, he had something
worth saving—it hardly deserved the name of a
rough draft, but something that could with sufficient
labor be turned into music. He threw the board into

orchestrion mode, and the composed and drone
themes shuffled themselves into their proper locations on the display. Ronay put down the music con-
troller and picked up a baton. Slowly, carefully, he
pointed it at the woodwind section, eased the point
toward percussion. The water drop he had been imag-
ining all this time fell through space and shattered
into dust. He conducted a few more minutes, then
stopped, abruptly at the end of the creative thread.

Yes. It could be made to work.

He left the music room, closing the door silently, checked the board. Sonya had gone; Matt was
still in his room.

Ronay showered in noiseless sound and fluid
dust, dressed for performance in a dark jacket and
white scarf.

When he opened up SELENA, Champion of the
Cause Wynant and Jason Olivetti were already on.
"Open exchange," Wynant was saying, quietly but
with venom, "is a fine thing."

"You *will* understand," Olivetti said.

"Or I can go jump and see if I can grab Earth?
Hello, Albin."

"Hello, Cham, Jason. What will we understand?"

"It'll wait," Olivetti said. Wynant looked
thoughtful, then nodded and said nothing.

Tracy Sorensen linked in, looking short of
sleep, then an unusually expansive Lawrence Duveen. Anton Sobieski offered greetings; Vargas from
Popul arrived wearing a jacket with work insignia,
an office silent and distant in the background. Finally Gus Felton appeared, a less than sharp view
from a picsel, with a dull sinus echo in his voice; he
was on a train, connected through pocket trix and
ear wire.

Olivetti said "Vargas has some data—"

Duveen said "The first order of business, I believe, is the continued business from last session. De-
fer to the Chairman?"

"I've spoken to Ballantine," Ronay said. "He agrees to another study on Waterhole, on two conditions: we pay a percentage of the cost—a token percentage, I should say now—and we immediately go back to work getting Archimedes ready for the water."

Felton said "No real problem on the construction. We've got plenty of rail in inventory, and Plant says they can put in a hardline all the way to the site, any time."

Karinovna said "I take it that means we won't lose any more crews." Her voice was perhaps excessively grim.

Vargas said "Population Services is satisfied."

"Oh, *good*," Olivetti put in.

"Good enough," Ronay said firmly.

Duveen said "How large is the token payment?"

"Thirty thousand Keplers if we pay up front, twenty thousand NA dollars if we wait until the study's complete in six months."

Sobieski said "NA dollars specifically? Not just any Terrestrial currency?"

"Correct."

"That doesn't sound like VACOR," Duveen said. "Did Ballantine offer any explanation?"

Ronay felt slightly amused. He had discussed this with Duveen yesterday, but the intonations of spontaneity were perfectly pitched. "The implication he left was that the dollar is going to be worth a lot more relative to the Kepler by then. But I don't know for certain."

Tracy Sorensen said "Either way, that can't be more than about a tenth of the study cost."

"Fifteen percent."

Olivetti said "I don't mind spending their money."

Sorensen made a displeased noise.

Sobieski said quietly, "The money is not the issue. A top VACOR executive spends more in a year on haircuts. It's a question of perception on Earth. If they pay for a study, it is their study. If we pay some of the cost, while they cover most of it, they are charitably subsidizing Luna."

Olivetti said "No one here is likely to see it that way."

"Possibly not," said Sobieski, "but it doesn't matter."

Ronay said "The question for the Board is whether we want the study on the terms offered."

Duveen said, in that light tone that always concealed a thunderbolt, "If we refuse the terms, we're back where we started, correct?"

"Ballantine says VACOR will publicly state we're stalling and obstructing the project."

"We *are*. So what about this: Forget the study. Restart the reservoir construction; we can fill it wherever the water comes from, or put something else in if not water. Take the ball back into their end of the court."

Everyone was quiet. Finally Sorensen spoke, with a faded and whispery exhaustion. "Well. Why don't we do that."

Olivetti had a shocked look that melted into a suppressed eagerness; the student who has just figured out that three notes played together like *that* sound pretty good. He didn't speak, though Ronay knew he was only waiting for the moment.

Karinovna said, in her lovely chiming contralto, "Someone said to me on a train, just yesterday, 'Councillor, when are you going to fill that damned hole with water? What does the Earth want for it, anyway?' I want to hear them answer that." She moved her eyes. "What are you thinking, Cham?"

Wynant's look was somewhere below the line of pickup. He looked up, said "State the proposition, and I'll vote on it."

Duveen said "Motion seconded."

After a few minutes of discussion, Ronay said

"The motion before the Board is as follows: the request for a new technical study on Project Waterhole will be withdrawn, and Physical Plant will be instructed to resume construction on the Archimedes Reservoir as soon as possible."

It was almost unanimous; Olivetti abstained. Ronay found himself perversely wanting to vote against, perhaps only for the sake of the record they were leaving, but he went along.

Olivetti said "I have some information I would like to introduce."

Ronay said "Go ahead."

A new panel sprang open in the display, lapping Olivetti's face. It was a monitor-pickup vue of a Point of Entry station, over the shoulder of the Customs officer and the person she was serving. In the background, a wall sign read WELCOME TO THE CITIES OF DA VINCI AND CRISIUM. The databurn over the picture showed it had been taken about thirty hours ago.

Ronay looked at Sobieski, whose face had frozen.

Olivetti's hands moved. The vue stilled and closed in on the man entering Customs. He was of average height, hair thin on top and swept out at the temples, a square face and rectilinear mustache. Another pane opened: the standard docs offload, with the standard awful picture. The man's name was Robert Ostrow, he was an American citizen alien-resident in Montreal. In an emergency, the local authorities were asked to contact The Vacuum Corporation Central Headquarters.

"Jason," Sobieski said in a determinedly even voice, "on whose authority did you obtain this?"

"Mine as a Board member. Look at this: he's declared that he's here as a tourist."

"It happens," Sorensen said.

"But he's traveling on a company account. First

cabin from Earth, and a suite at the Conforte DVC, all on VACOR's dollars."

"Well, they're Luna's dollars now," Ronay said, and most of the Board at least smiled; Duveen and even Sobieski laughed.

Olivetti said "I didn't exceed my authority."

"No," Wynant said, "but in my opinion you've misused it. That's for the record."

Ronay moved in. "So noted. Jason, before we return to business, is there anything further you want to say about this man?"

Olivetti thought for a moment. "He's an information economist, according to his docs. I've looked at publication citations for TECHNET going back five years, and I can't find his name."

"Maybe he's not very good at it," Karinovna said, and this time they all laughed except Olivetti, who looked down and pulled the data off the board.

Wynant moved to adjourn, which passed unanimously. One by one, the members left the conference space, until Ronay was alone with a blank screen.

When he left the study, Matt was in the kitchen with a glass of juice and a book; not a bound library volume but a nonce-book, quickly printed from a master-text store, to be recycled back into pulp (or exchanged for a permanent edition) once read. Ronay tilted his head, and Matt showed the title page: *The Star Fox*. Ronay smiled. "I've got to go out for a while, son. You okay?"

"Sure, Dad. Oh—Dad?"

"Yes?"

Matt held up the book again. "Did they really believe, back then, that there were going to be aliens —you know, people on the New Worlds?"

"Some people did. But in stories . . . well, the aliens are really about how people see each other, when they think or act in different ways."

Matt nodded. "And this was before there were really any New Worlds."

"That's right."

Matt said, slowly, clearly trying to solidify the idea in his mind as he spoke it, "When a ship holes out . . . and it isn't going where they know there's a world already . . . a lot of them don't ever come back. Almost half of them."

"Yes."

"Do you think they could be . . . could have found—you know—"

"There are people who think that," Ronay said seriously.

"What do *you* think?"

"I think there's something about the MIRAGE drive that we don't understand yet, that wrecks ships sometimes. I *hope* that nothing is deliberately killing our crews. I hope that they're all alive and well somewhere, and will eventually come home. But I don't know, son. Maybe you'll know someday." The last words came out through an almost intolerable flash of sadness, and Ronay quickly said "Goodbye, son," and left the apartment.

Just outside the door he stopped and looked over the balcony rail, drawn by a whirling splash of color below in November Place.

The Church of the Binding Disk was out on the floor, dancing. Perhaps a hundred people in vividly dyed clothes, wools and shiny novylon and glass, orange and purple, cadmium red and acid green, were arranged in a solid circle, turning counterclockwise. All were linked, hand to hand, elbow to wrist, ankle to knee—some of them weren't touching the floor at all, entirely suspended on their neighbors' limbs. All were singing—or at least, happily making noise; not many had a key or a note in common, and the words seemed to ripple to and fro across the circle like the shock of exploding stars in the great indifferent galaxy.

The Diskers didn't believe the galaxy was indifferent. They held that the Avakian Disk was God. Or a god, since by Avakian-Gold theory every object of galactic mass had its own Disk, and there might even be a metaDisk for the universe as a whole. Disker theology was not settled yet. Indeed, there were Diskers of the Heisenberg school, who held that not only was the nature of God unknowable, any attempt to perceive the nature of God inevitably changed that nature. The Localists held (or also held, because nothing prevented one from being a Localist and a Heisenbergian at once) that what was true for the Milky Way's rapidly rotating Deity might not apply to the Andromedan, or M31's, or the Lesser Magellanic Cloud's. Local Groupists said that members of a galactic cluster must be doctrinally similar, but there was still room for variation in the observable universe.

A fraction thought that if there was a vast black hole at the center of this (or that, or any) galaxy, swallowing down mass and light, it must therefore be the Adversary of God. And was not Lucifer a morning star fallen from brightness? Collapsed past the radius of grace, here defined as 2MG over c squared—was that not the Pit, from whose event horizon all hope abandon?

There was, however, no darkness in this dance. Lunars and tourists looked on; the Diskers reached out free hands to them, and some accepted, accreted. Ronay was no dancer, and certainly no Disker, but he found watching them, their pleasure, pleasurable. It was hardly any wonder that people had begun to worship the Disk; it promised some order in the galaxy they had so often been told was chaotic, offered a way to reach new worlds and make mortal sense of them. To make matter out of sterile theory: was that not the purpose of God?

He watched as long as he felt he could, and then moved on to the Transport station, toward Old Landing.

"Why, hello, Mr. Ronay," Jori said. The VACOR

receptionist was a slightly built young woman, with
a pale oval face and clear blue eyes. Her blond hair
was wrapped up in a band of cloth of the same Corporation light blue as her closely cut dress. Her voice
ran up and down scales with a remarkable trill. Jori
was Lunar-born, from one of the outpost towns,
Ronay had forgotten which. He wondered who her
friends were, what they thought of her job.

"Hello, Jori. Is Lynch available?"

"I'll see." She touched a key, looked at a concealed display. "Mr. Ballantine, Mr. Ronay is here to
see you. . . . Yes, sir, of course." Her eyes came up.
"He'll be right out, Mr. Ronay."

"Thank you."

Ballantine appeared. He was wearing a thin
leather jacket over a gold silk shirt, sharply creased
trousers of slubbed brown silk, and no shoes. His hair
was tied back with a fine gold chain. "Come in, Albin.
Jori, I do regret I can't send you home today. . . ."

"I have plenty to do, Mr. Ballantine."

Ballantine made a noise of acknowledgment and
gestured to Ronay. They went straight back to the
warm wood-paneled den. Stacks of papers and two
active slates were out on a table. "Tea?"

"Thank you."

Ballantine sat on the arm of one of the fat
chairs. "What may I do for you and for Luna?"

Ronay told him about the Board vote. There was
no particular reaction. "Well. I shall report, of course.
And if there's anything we can do to assist with the
reservoir construction, let me know."

Ronay nodded. "I'm sorry I just shoved in on
you."

"Had I wanted to be alone, I could have easily
said so; had I not wanted to say so, Jori does it with
taste and style."

"Are you expecting someone, Lynch?"

"Should I be?"

Ronay waited a moment. He had not properly

rehearsed how to do this; he had argued with himself all the way over whether to do it at all. "Do you know a man named Robert Ostrow?"

For just a moment, Ballantine's face twisted horribly; then it was back to a flat smile. "Yes." He picked up a glass from the work table and held it out. "Here's to him. Your tea should be ready. How do you happen to hear of him?"

Ronay moved deliberately to get the tea mug, using the time for analysis. He pointed to the table, the slates. "May I use one of those?"

Ballantine touched a keyblock; the Store light flashed and the screen went white.

Ronay took the unit, lined into the public affairs net, pulled the record of the Water Board meeting just concluded. He riffed through it until he found Olivetti's still of Ostrow at Customs, filled the screen with it. Then he handed the slate to Ballantine.

Ballantine read it carefully; the faces, the WELCOME sign, the dateline. "I didn't know he was here, Albin. That *is* the truth."

"I didn't imagine it wasn't."

"Would you tell me how this datum . . . came up?"

"One of the Board members doesn't like the Corporation very much. It's on the record."

"*One*, Albin?" He waved a hand. "Forget I said that."

"Who is Ostrow?"

"A catastrophist. Do you know about catastrophe mathematics, Albin?"

"Not a great deal."

"Neither do I. It involves curves that close off abruptly—surfaces that create or destroy themselves, or both. They're marvelous to look at on a screen." He put the slate down, slid into the chair seat, waved Albin to the facing chair. "Sometime when your troubles are few, get into NORDINET and look up the Aldine Project. That's where Bobby Ostrow used to work, though you won't find his name. When the government decided to open up all those black boxes, he decided to leave."

"And went to VACOR?"

"Where else indeed. He's answerable only to the Directors, and I suspect that if he wanted to, he could tell Karl Burton to walk into a lion cage dressed as a rump roast. His being here is bad news, Albin."

"He claims to be on vacation."

"Then I suppose there's hope, isn't there."

"You called him a catastrophist. I take it I should read more than mathematical theory into that."

Ballantine took a long drink from his glass, which Ronay was sure did not contain tea. "This water that we're going to sell you, Albin . . . why do you want it? Why, really?"

Ronay said "I'm listening, Lynch."

"Societies are kept going by images, and complexes of images. Religions, philosophies, advertising campaigns . . . One must have something to live toward, correct, Albin? And as the fulfillment of desire becomes less and less a matter of labor and more and more one of setting controls, of simply *having* the desire for the production network to fulfill—so the question is no longer, 'how shall I get what I want?' but 'what of these infinite riches shall I choose?' "

"Baudrillation," Ronay said, wondering if the extraordinary bitterness he so suddenly felt was the product of sympathy or contagion.

"Not many people know that term."

"My great-grandfather coined it, as I'm sure you know," Ronay said.

"Yes. I know. He writes about it with great passion. 'Ce qui nous craignons—' "

"What we fear," Ronay said, in Claude François Ronay's French, *"is the fully baudrillated society; in which the tyranny of materials is replaced by the tyr-*

anny of images; where a man is not starved by being denied bread, but starves for believing bread is out of fashion."

"Pain pas la mode," Ballantine repeated. "La peine du pain, I've always liked that." He quoted on: *"What fashion shall we set, in such a mutual Hell, to make our neighbors crowd together against us, and force us out and into Paradise?"*

"It did terrify him," Ronay said. "Toward the end of his life, he became convinced that he could do nothing to stop it."

"Like death," Ballantine said, with a sort of gentleness.

"Like that. He died before I was born, of course. The books and vues are what I really know. And family gossip, but you know what that counts for."

"I can imagine it."

Ronay paused to register that, looked at the table with the papers and slates. "There was a proposal to construct a response database containing the core Revolutionary Council—that proves how long ago it was—"

" 'Independence' sounds kinder."

"Hannah Gold herself was to compose the system. Claude François fought it, of course, until he died. The Golds had both passed on by then."

"So he won." Ballantine took a glass of plain water from the cabinet by his chair. "Or, seen differently, he contributed materially to the baudrillation of Lunar society, by creating the myth of the man who kept his mind his own."

Ballantine had a perfect instinct for certain things, Ronay thought. "What does the water mean to *you*, Lynch? No—what does VACOR mean to you?"

"Your great-grandfather was right about desire," Ballantine said. "Desire really is the only commodity. With no fashion to follow, one might as well be dead." He took a gulp of water, stood up. "Which is why I must get back to work. Always pleasant to see you, Albin."

Ronay finished his tea and started to leave, then stopped in the doorway. "If there's something I can do for you, Lynch . . ."

"The place isn't on the Moon and the people are dead," Ballantine said with a quite terrible clarity, "and it is always in front of me and they are always a step behind. But thank you for your kindness."

Ronay nodded, started to turn away. Ballantine stopped him with a suddenly raised finger.

"Be careful of Bobby Ostrow," Ballantine said. "He knows his fashion intimately, and wears it well."

Ronay went home. It was a difficult trip, because every shopfront he passed, every advertisement that glared from a bulletin board or news sheet, every shirt or jacket or cap with the insignia of a Skyhook team, even the ubiquitous symbols of Transport and Phys-Plant and Pop Serve, were loud and dissonant notes, scrapings on a bared nerve, promotions for the law of desire. He ended up walking home, through the pedestrian tube of the transit tunnel, alone. Partway along, he saw a handbill taped to the tunnel wall. Without thinking, or even reading it, he tore it down, crumpled it, stuck it deep in a pocket.

When he came out at the Verne station, he looked for a while at the pylons of Names, then went home, surprising Matt on his way back to his room with a load of food and drink.

"You're going away tomorrow?" Ronay said quietly.

"Yes."

"Maybe you could have dinner with us tonight, then."

"Oh. Yeah."

"I'll knock when it's time. Anything special you'd like?"

"No. Anything."

Ronay nodded, and Matt disappeared.

Ronay went into the music room, sat down on the conductor's stand and thought. He tapped the wall phone. A woman's face appeared.

"Copernicus City Sym—*oh*! Hello, Albin."

"Hello, May. Next date's in about half a sky, isn't it?"

"That's right."

"Do you think you could make room for one more gun?"

"Oh, wow." Light from a data screen splashed her face. "Yeah, that's a pops concert. Steven will be glad of the company. Did you have anything in mind?"

"Is Erika on the card?"

"No, but she might be available."

"Okay, if she's willing, let's do *Rhapsody in Blue*. If not, oh, you think of something."

"You've worked with Nino Lyon, haven't you? He's been wanting a crack at front piano."

"Never worked. But I've heard him. He'll be fine."

May nodded, made a note. "Uh, Albin . . . does this mean you're coming back? Honest and for true?"

"I doubt it, May. But thank you for sounding so hopeful."

"Yeah. Well. You *will* be able to rehearse? Or is that why you picked the Gershwin?"

"I'll be available. Thanks, May."

May spread her hands. Ronay rang off. He stood up, touched keys for the main library, selected a baton. The room struck up the *Rhapsody*.

More than a hundred and seventy years before, George Gershwin had composed it with the sounds of the New York City subway in his mind. Ronay wondered if the New York trains had really been so gorgeous and exhilarating as the music painted them. Could they have been . . .

By the time the great piano lead was in full swing, Ronay knew what the fourth movement of his hypothetical antithetical symphony must be about. But not now, not now; he had made a commitment with some of the time that he had not had to commit in the first place. Only so many orchestras could be led at a time.

He was still playing when Sonya got home, with nothing ready for dinner. Sonya just shook her head and called out for a pizza; Ango cheese and sausage, green dragon peppers and mushrooms.

The door chimed in less than fifteen minutes. Sonya opened it on a skinny young woman in a novylon halter and shorts, wearing roller-bearing sandals that had little gilt wings on the heels. She collected the payment and tip, folded the insulated delivery box and clipped it to her shoulders and was gone like a phosphene from the corner of the eye.

Matt brightened a little when Sonya set the pie on the table. She waited for him to say something. He slid a quarter of the pizza clear, levitating it on his fingertips, and what he said was "Thanks. G'night." Then he was away, gone down the hall.

Sonya looked at Albin, but he was silent as well. She could make him talk easily enough—there he was nothing like Matt—but she knew from seeing the state of the house that the talk would be about either the current state of the Board, which would stretch him tight enough to ruin his dinner, or else about the music he was trying to write, which would cut him with guilt that he was letting the world go ungoverned.

No Wynant had ever written a symphony. No Havilland could lead an orchestra.

Seeing him on the pedestal, fifteen years ago, she had first begun to lust for him: the sweat radiating from his pale hair, the thrust and bend of his thin and powerful hands, his compact broad body like a controlled explosion, fusion moving the regolith.

He was friendly enough at once, kind enough soon after, but she understood that she would have to wait him out. She did, taking out her frustration on tumors and thrombi and willful adhesions, waiting through Mozart and Tchaikovsky and even Beethoven.

It was Stravinsky that finally did it. The *Rite of Spring*. Albin had insisted he could not have sex after Stravinsky, there would be no power left. Just as he had said over and over that he wanted a wife only to push the Name into another generation.

She allowed him to say all of that, because she already knew what would happen by the first note of the *Rite*, the story of a woman chosen as sacrifice for the next year's harvest. It was no more necessary to contradict him than to draw great red circles around the revelation once he found it.

No power left, ha.

And tonight, she thought, watching him methodically slicing and chewing his dinner, tonight, yes. But she would have to make him talk, after all, must relieve some of the pressure on the nerves and vitals. She moved her hands across the table, stroked the back of his, palpating the swollen veins, the muscles much too hard. She pressed her work-hardened fingertips against key points of tendon and nerve.

The day Matt was born, Albin came into the room where Sonya was cradling the baby; after a long speechless moment he began to weep, and he put his face in his hands. Then he held out his palms to her, and she held them just as she did now.

"Do you see?" he had said. "Water."

Ronay paused, feeling her touch unlocking his bones.

"Maybe I'd better quit early tonight," Sonya said, sounding slightly doubtful. "It's a long time in the pipe tomorrow."

"Maybe you should."

"Aren't you going to give me a chance to reconsider?"

He hugged her, then kissed her hard. "I knew

there was something about you," she said, "besides
Stravinsky."

Ronay felt himself laugh in genuine astonish-
ment.

And then, in the bedroom, she said "Tell me how
the day went," and from the way she said it he knew
he had given something away.

He told her, then, in a great rush, about the conversation with Ballantine. She sat quite still, listening, until he was done, and then said, in a voice
supernaturally still, "I don't think I've ever really understood before this why you're so close to that—
man."

"Close?"

"What else to call it?"

"And do you know now?"

"More than I did."

"How does it . . . make you feel?"

"No. No, no, no. What I feel about you is not a
symptom, to be changed by another change in metab-
olism. I love you, Albin, and all I know about you is
part of that. *All*. I love you, knowing that you would
leave me, and Matt, and life, for enough water. I love
you even for that."

How did Lynch do it? Ronay wondered. How did
a man of such basic decency make himself so hated,
when— "And if it's not—*me*—that pulls the switch?"

"I don't know how either of us would bear losing
our son, Albin. I know it would be no easier for you
than for me. And I also know that you've done all you
could to prevent it coming to that."

"I've done *nothing* to prevent it." Here he was,
hurting her, for what? Nothing; not even someone's
life, not even water, for the sake of a Baudrillard sim-
ulation of an ethical position. Never mind how it was
done: how did Lynch *endure* it? "There's nothing I
can do. If Matt ever thinks of bringing Waterhole in
as something he *ought* to do—he's young, and bold,

and he hasn't been compromising himself for twenty years—"

"Is that what you think you've been doing?" she said, suddenly angry. "Compromising yourself?"

"I—" The thought hung in space, bending back on itself. Was this the catastrophe surface, the point beyond which nothing could restore the old continuous curve? "Should I . . . just leave you alone for a while?"

"Not yet," she said, anger wasting into sickening pain, "don't leave me alone yet."

He closed the curve around her. And if it was true that baudrillation had not yet overtaken them, that they could still want and give more than a pattern demanded, then perhaps they truly did comfort one another.

When Ronay woke, Sonya was gone, at work according to the clock. He heard a bump from the hallway and dragged his robe on.

Matt was pulling a large shoulder bag toward the door. He was wearing a big-pocketed Beta jacket, a cap, walking boots. He almost jumped when he heard the voice behind him:

"When you get to Paris, son, give my best to the Monsieur de Treville."

Matt turned. "I shall."

He wouldn't stop the game. "Remember that courage is all you have to get ahead on; if you see your chance, take it ere it's lost."

"I will remember, Father," Matt said, cinched up his bag and his slate carrier and opened the door. As he went out he heard his father still quoting D'Artagnan's father: "I wish I had more to give you, my dear boy, but here's all I have. . . ." It was broken by a phlegmy cough, or perhaps just a yawn.

He used his tag to get to Sokoni, where he was supposed to be going, then ducked out, pocketed the tag and paid cash for another train to Old Landing. There were three ticket windows at the station, a long

desk of dark red glass divided by blocks of marbleized
burnstone. Matt put down his bag in front of the most
preoccupied-looking of the ticket agents.

There would be a pickup recording the transac-
tion; there was no way to avoid that. But Security was
not supposed to be watching for ordinary Lunars. It
just had to be done and gotten over, that was all.

"Hello," the ticket agent said. "What can I help
you with?"

"I have some tickets to pick up. Here's the reser-
vation code." Matt pushed a card across the counter.
The agent keyed in the letters and numbers.

"Six reduced fares, two compartments, here to
Tsiolkovsky and return, is that right?"

"Yes."

"On the . . . on today's train?"

"That's right."

"You know you cut this pretty close? Another
half-hour and you could have lost the reservations.
And you still need to get over to Hub to board."

"Yes, I know that."

"B'sayder." The agent touched another key, held
out his hand. "May I have your tag for the charge,
please?"

"No, this is cash."

"Oh?"

They had a story prepared for this, but Matt
waited a moment and the agent shrugged a shoulder
and said "Very well . . . in Lunar currency?"

"That's right."

"That will be six hundred forty-eight decimal
six-oh Keplers, then, please."

Matt pushed a pile of bills and two small stacks
of coins across the red glass. It was an awful lot of
money, and it had taken a terribly long time to accu-
mulate it. The agent counted it efficiently, but with
great precision, as if he knew just what it meant to
them. Then he whacked a key, and tickets dropped

from a printer slot. "Would you like these in six envelopes?"

"One will be all right. No—two, please. One for each compartment?"

"Wise man. Two it is." The agent dealt the tickets into cellufilm folders with Transport emblems on one side and a map of the TranCity system on the other. He held up the last ticket. "This is your eastbound ticket; it's a direct all the way to the end. The day you're coming back, there's a change and layover at Mendeleev City. It's a fairly long wait—"

"Ten hours," Matt said.

"Ri-i-ight. So this ticket's Tsio to Mendeleev, and this one is Mendeleev to Copernicus. You'll have to get off, and have your bags all packed, though the station crew can transfer the luggage, keep it locked up at the station, if you tell them. Do you see this number?"

"Yes."

"Store it on something separate from the ticket, so you can't lose them both at once. There's a different one on each ticket, so log them all. If you lose the tickets, or can't use them, we need this number to get you new tickets or your money back. That's because it's cash and not a tag account, so we can't identify you otherwise. Wakarimasu ka?"

"Ken, toda." They understood that part very well indeed.

"Bevakasha." The agent smiled, put the envelopes in Matt's hand. "Have a great trip."

Matt sealed the envelopes into his inner jacket pocket, along with his Transport tag; he dropped a coin at the gate and rode to Hub, then climbed two levels to the TranCity station. He put his gear down near the entrance. It would have been convenient to ping Ruby and the others, tell them that everything was running, but the network had an indelible memory, and there were enough traces they could not avoid leaving.

He was probably under a camera right now, and he tried to avoid fidgeting at the thought.

Ruby came out of the stairwell. She was wearing a heavy jacket of leather-reinforced wool. There was a mobile console built into it, controls and display connectors, a main deck in a slab of epoxy inside the back pouch—like the Stage Manager's Vest at the theatre, but with much more power on board. She carried a small bag of soft black leather.

Matt stood up. "I've got them, no problems."

Ruby nodded. Her shoulders sagged a little, with what Matt supposed was relief.

Tani Case and Cissa appeared then, from an upper level. They were managing the supplies; they had zippered novylon bags of wrapped and stacked sandwiches, cakes, breadsticks in tubes. Each had a backpack full of drink bottles, like old vues of what people thought vac gear would look like.

Raf and Stringjack made rendezvous then, bringing the main baggage; Stringer had two cases, Raf three, and they were handling them with formation-pilot precision, side by side. There was no more trace of difference between them. Matt felt a little bit proud of that; he had helped keep them together until the Mazerun. That was behind all of them now.

A clock chimed 1200. Two hours until the train rolled out, and when that happened, nothing could stop them.

Until they reached Serenity City station, at least. A ping could outrun any train.

Ciss said "When can we get aboard?"

Matt said "Another hour. We can give the crew the bags now, though, and they'll put them on the train. Then we can get some lunch."

Jack looked doubtful. Raf said "What if they check the names?"

"There isn't any reason why they should," Matt said. "It's not like we're going through an Entry port. They'll just tag them for our compartments and load them." He picked up his own suitcase. "We don't have to give them everything."

They had agreed that they would not decide which room was the boys', which the girls', until they were aboard, but Ruby insisted (as she had done all along) that there was *no difference* and they might as well stop carrying the stuff.

So they checked in the clothes and supplies; the man at the baggage desk made out tags with no special display of interest. Holding their tickets, they went up a level to the departure lounge, bought drinks and meals, and sat down to look at their train.

The TranCity station was built along the south edge of the hexagonal Hub complex. The second-level lounge had a long, curved glass wall overlooking the tracks, which were on a crete apron, out in vacuum. The train waited on the near track.

There were five cars, identical in shape. They were twenty-five meters long, five wide, three-and-a-half high. A narrow service walk ran the length of the roof at the centerline; the rest of the roof was the deep silvery indigo of photovolt panels, shot through with radstripper coils. The sides were white reinforced epoxy, with stripes and giant ID numbers of the service red below long dark windows.

At each end of the train there was some glass in the roof as well, tinted almost as dark as the solars; small panels at the front end for the crew, large ones, a third the length of the car, covering an observation lounge at the rear. The narrow gaps between the cars were bridged by flexible bellows of vac-proofed Beta. Two wide boarding tunnels of the same material were sealed to the second and fourth cars; they puffed in and out slightly as the supply and baggage handlers moved through them.

"Which car's ours?" Raf said.

Matt looked at his ticket. "Three-one-five. The one in the center. Let's riff." He opened his slate and lined into the Transport base. As the others crowded

around the screen, a car roster came up. "Yeah. See—
the first car's control, and the second one is from
Tycho. Then us, and a coach car—that means it has
seats and tables, not rooms—and the observation
car."

"People stay in the car from Tycho?"

Ruby said "They can when it runs through. Every third day, like today." She sounded impatient,
which didn't surprise Matt at all. "Tycho to Tsio is the
longest ride there is without changing trains. About
forty-two hundred kilometers."

Jack said "Let's see our car."

Matt found a model, and they floated through
the diagram view; it was called a "four-four-five
sleeper," because there were four big compartments
like the ones they would be in, four smaller rooms,
and five little compartments, two meters square,
where the bed folded up into the wall. Matt had ridden in one of those, once, on the trip back from
Tycho.

Tycho, 1100 km almost due south of Copernicus, was the farthest Matt could ever remember having been from home; his parents had taken him to a
concert at Da Vinci/Crisium once, but he had been
much too small to remember.

A boarding announcement scrolled up on the
lounge wall; a moment later, a voice began announc-
ing that compartment passengers for the 1400 Tran-
City were invited to come aboard through Gate Two
(coach seat passengers would please wait to board
shortly through Gate Four).

Tani said "Do people really sit in seats all the
way out?"

String said "It's not that bad. They lean back,
and you can sleep in 'em."

Ruby looked up. This was the first indication for
Matt that Stringer had ever been on anything but a
Copernicus train.

A young, black-haired man in a neat uniform

and cap was examining tickets at the boarding gate. He had an assortment of stripes and service pins on his jacket, along with the Transport and TranCity emblems, and a nameplate reading V. BARAT.

"All of you together?" he said as they showed their tickets. "Bedrooms A and C through to Tsio! Long trip we'll be having together. Through the tunnel, turn right, through the connecting door, and then the first two room doors on the left-hand side. Panyimayu?"

"Da, spasiba," Matt said.

"Prekrasna. I'll be by to see you just before the train leaves. I'll knock two-one"—he tapped the air with his knuckles—"and that'll be me. See you then."

They hustled through the Beta tunnel in a draft of warm dry air. The car entry was fascinatingly busy with indicators, displays, notice and instruction signs, but there were people following, no time to look now. To the left was the sleeper from Tycho, two people standing in the corridor, apparently trying to find their room. To the right were the mated end doors, a short metal-and-epoxy archway. A tall cylinder to one side of the passage was labeled EMERGENCY PRESSURE CURTAIN.

A corridor a little less than a meter wide ran down the center of the cars. There was soft short carpeting, Transport red again, walls of soft-finished epoxy trimmed with smooth metal and extruded glass.

Ruby stopped at the door to A. Raf touched her hand. "Careful of a trap," he said, and they laughed. Ruby opened the door.

She had been right: there was nothing to prefer in one room over the other. Both were four meters long by two across, with two long windows looking on the Lunar plain. At the aft end (of A—C was its mirror image) were two beds, one above the other, with a short ladder (they commented on that, wondering what sort of arch-Slammer would need a ladder to climb a meter and a half). There were two

chairs, a table fixed to the outside wall, a basic enter-
tainment deck and a wardrobe on the inboard side.
Every door and drawer latched tight, and there were
hold-downs and grab bars all over, as if gravity
might abandon them at any moment. Elaborately labeled panels controlled lights and window opacity. A
small door in the end past the beds opened on the
other compartment; one at the opposite end led to a
toilet and shower section, ship's built-ins just like in
Ruby's home.

The bags had been neatly placed under the tables. They began stowing gear; Ruby pointed out the
electric cooler compartments in the wardrobe, and
the drinks went into those.

Bang-bang. Bang.

Matt looked in through the connecting door as
Ruby opened her corridor door. It was the steward.
"Dobry den. Do you all want to come in, or shall I do
my act twice?"

The boys came in. They all sat or leaned.

"Khorosho. My name is Vladimir, or just Vlad if
you please, and I'm one of the stewards for your car.
The other is Hsien; one of us is always on call. Right
here." He showed the call controls on the wall panel.
"If we're both busy, one of the other stewards might
answer. Just to be careful, use the spyhole in the
door, here, and make sure you see the badge and
nameplate before you open up.

"I know you brought some food along. If you
want something hot, or just a change, we have a restaurant in the last car. You can charge to Transport
tags if you like.

"Keys now. Six? And shall I set both locks the
same?"

They agreed. Vladimir put a probe from his
slate into the locks of both rooms, then burned code
into six plastic slivers. "Safety now. There will be a
spravatchnye vue after we get away from the station,
on what to do if there's an accident, or a flare warn-

ing, or we must stop between stations. If you're too busy to watch it then, you can call it anytime from the panel, number nine-nine-nine. Now, who here has a suit license?"

They all did, and went for their cards. "No, I believe you. That makes you all emergency deputy crew, panyimayu? If we have to go for a walk, and oh please sister Diana let us not—" He pressed his hands together and looked at the ceiling, and they laughed. "—then you will have to help the people who don't know how. You know, from *up there* . . ." He jerked his thumb at the sky, and they laughed again.

"Oh-kay. We will make your beds once a day, if you want." He looked at the beds. "Do you plan to double up, or shall I bring two sleeping mats? And extra pillows?" There were nods to that. "Very well. And call if you need towels, or washroom supplies, or whatever. Any questions?"

Raf said "Can we get off when the train stops at stations?"

"Yes, sure. And leave your things locked up in your room. Just be sure to take your tickets along, and very sure to be back in plenty of time. Anything else? Okay, one last thing. This is a sleeping car, so remember, please, some people will be sleeping in it. I must go give another performance now. See you all later."

"Da skorava," Matt said. The door closed behind Vlad.

Ciss said "What shall we do first?"

Matt said "Just watch, I think. At least until we've gone away from the station."

"What about the observation car?" Raf said. "Wouldn't that be a good place to watch?"

"It's always crowded," Jack put in. "Especially with the—*up theres*."

Matt said "I think we can see all right from here. There's plenty of windows."

Ciss's hands tightened on the slate in her lap.

"Maybe we should have gotten rooms on opposite sides. Then we could have had views both ways."

Ruby said, a little bit irritated, "We talked about that, remember? We would have had to go out in the hall all the time. And we'll get the other side view on the way back anyway." She stood up, took off her deck coat and laid it out carefully on the lower bed, put her black bag next to it. "So let's get organized," she said, her voice quieter but still tightly wound.

"Wait a moment," Tani Case said. She had hardly spoken since they had come aboard. She went to the wall screen, found a menu page and keyed a number. The display showed a Lunarscape, train tracks making a white arrowhead from the base of the vue to zero at the center. The Hub rose up to the left. There was a dataframe around the image, bargraphs and numbers; one of the indicators read 0 KPH.

"This is from the front of the train," she said. "I think this number is where we are, a distance marker. And that's speed, and that's time. I don't know about the others."

Ruby looked. They all did. "That's a force cube," Ruby said. "Acceleration in all directions."

"All?" Jack said.

"We *do* go around curves. And up and down too."

A chime rang, and the panel spoke in a smooth female voice, probably a voder: "The 1400 TranCity *Farside Direct*, making all station stops to Tsiolkovsky Station, will depart Copernicus in five minutes. All passengers please board; all those leaving the train at Copernicus should do so now. Please call a steward if you require assistance."

Matt lined the C cabin's screen to the forward view (thinking of this as a starship was more than a temptation—it was irresistible) and the team took up positions along the windows. Old Landing was visible in the middle distance, and beyond it Luna, just Luna, on and on.

There was a vibration through the whole car. Dust blew out from somewhere underneath. The walls creaked, and the clothes hanging in the wardrobe made a hollow rattle.

They began to move. An arrow stretched out on the force-cube diagram. It was very slow, slower than the local trains started up; just a gentle push toward the rear, and a rumble and whine from below.

Matt realized he was holding his breath. They were going; they were really *away* from the station, the city.

5 KPH, the display said. The rails ahead, heavy, seamless glass, gleamed in sunlight. 10 KPH. 15.

Raf watched the forward view. Jack leaned against the bed ladder, feet braced as if for a Mazerun. Matt stood up, went forward. Ruby was staring out the window, her hands limp in her lap. Cissa had her fingertips pressed against the glass, tracing the line of southern horizon. Tani was folded up on the lower bed, laughing quietly into her hands.

Matt opened the cooler, took out a flask of citrus water. "Where are the cups?"

Tani rolled into the air. "There are glasses in the bathroom. I'll get ours."

Matt nodded and looked through the connecting door. "Raf! Glasses from the bathroom."

The glasses were flat-bottomed spheroids, etched with a simplified Lunar map and the TranCity lines. Matt poured for everyone, up to the center of Mare Orientale. They clicked them together and sipped; Jack drained his, held it between his palms, spun it hard and let go; he caught it again one-handed.

"Matt," Ruby said suddenly, "give me your slate."

Matt's stomach jumped. They had forgotten. If a ping had come in—"Did everybody else—"

"Everybody else did theirs at my place. Come on, Lonestar."

Feeling not at all like Lonestar, Matt opened his slate. It was cool, no messages hanging. Ruby took the controls and treed Matt's unit into hers. "All right," she said, "test message in ten minutes. Everybody relax."

Nobody did. They sat by Ruby's console for all ten of the minutes. It pinged. She touched a key. The screen lit with her own face.

"This is a preset test message," the picture said, "to be sent at 1420." The image was replaced by a datascreen, bouncing frequency graphs, a node chart, columns of codes; Matt couldn't decipher it, but Ruby just riffed through it and said "We're all set."

Jack leaned against the wall. Matt relaxed.

This had been Ruby's major effort for the trip; a message sent to any of their slates would go to Ruby's house (where they were supposed to be) then echo down the hardline relay that ran along the train tracks, into Ruby's mobile deck, and finally to the target unit. An overlay would put a loop-vue of the Rincons' living room behind whoever was on, and (theoretically) nothing short of a manual link-by-link trace would carry past the apartment systems.

Time lag was the insoluble problem; the farther they got from Copernicus, the longer the delay between send and receive. They would try to avoid two-way conversations if at all possible, and if not, would try to reply slowly, deliberately, distractedly, the others helping out by keeping up a stream of game conversation in the background.

Tani said "Could we set one of the screens to the rear view?"

"We know where we've been," Jack said, but he said it politely.

Matt said "I don't see why not. There's plenty of room for everybody to get the view they want."

So the rear cabin view was set to the rear car's

pickup: the same data lines, but the beam of rails was aimed at retreating Copernicus. The arch of Verne Center, the rectilinear jumble of the Hub, the lights and thin geometries of the Ports. Even Ruby came back to look at Sokoni Tower, looking close to spot the spherical window of her house. It all did look small now, against the ringwall, the plain, the sky.

"There's a ship," Raf said. Lights were descending toward the port area, though from here, without TECHNET, it was impossible to tell which port.

"It's just a Terrasite," Ruby said, "a three-day wonder."

"Canned Slammers," Raf said, but nobody had the energy to laugh. Matt flipped the screen back to the forward pickup. "Do you want to watch the spravatchnye now?"

They did that. It wasn't exciting. It mostly said that if anything happened, to stay in your cabin and wait for the crew to tell you what to do. It did show where the suit lockers were—in the corridor ceiling and at the car ends—but they were clearly labeled OPENABLE BY CREW ONLY, in three languages and Sympla symbols. There was a short vue of a single car rolling along, the voice explaining that all the cars had their own power system and could get to shelter independently.

That over, they went back to forward view—they were at 50 KPH now, the normal cruising speed—and the windows. Ruby pulled up to the top bed in her cabin, pulled curtains around it to nap. "She had to do a lot today," Tani said defensively, though no one had objected at all.

Where the ground was flat, the rails were laid on blocks of waterless concrete, tied together with thin glass rods. Obstacles had mostly been burned through with electron guns. Where there was a gap, or a ridge to climb, the track was supported on X-shaped trusses of the same structural glass as the rails. Occasionally there was a rainbow bridge, suspended on glass and carbon filaments webbed from glass towers. Sometimes the track split into two parallel lines, so trains could pass.

Every fifty meters a white epoxy column stood by the tracks, a handsbreadth across and three meters high. They had something to do with signaling and communications. At the base, they were connected to a hardline—a buried conduit fused by the force of shaped explosives into ceramic superconductor. Matt had seen vues of hardline firings: a signal would flash, and then a streak of dust, laser-straight horizon to horizon, would burst from the ground. It seemed to happen all in an instant, but slowed down you could see the front of the detonation, moving at a kilometer a second, a shockwave rippling the ground to either side.

The ride was smooth, and mostly quiet, though when the train took a curve or an upgrade, making the force lines peak on the display, a high-pitched whine would leak into the car; then after a moment it would settle down to a low rhythmic rumble.

Fifty kilometers out there was a sort of tunnel: a tube of crete-bonded regolith, almost a meter thick, surrounding the tracks. They were only a couple of hundred meters long, a sudden blackout for a quarter of a minute. They were flare shelters, long enough to park a train inside and ride out a sunstorm. According to a guidebook Matt found in a wardrobe drawer, there were stockpiles of supplies in each one.

What if there *was* a flare alert while they were out here? They hadn't really considered the possibility. Matt decided he wasn't going to consider it, either. They couldn't know before the Sunwatch stations did, couldn't do any more than they could to stop it. The best they could do would be to help out, like Vlad the steward had said. That would surely count for something.

Ruby woke up after a couple of hours. They

were expecting her to start the game run, but she just started looking through the sandwich supply.

"What have we got?" Raf said.

"Chicken, isn't this? I think this is chicken."

"There's chicken," Cissa said, "and some ham, and dragon-egg." That last was greens trimmed from soft dragonleaf chopped together with hard-cooked chicken eggs.

"There's some jam too," Tani said.

"Chicken's okay," Ruby said. "Jam for breakfast."

"But never jam today?" Tani said, smiling. Ruby just nodded.

They ate, watching Luna pass the windows. There was a knock at the door: the steward's knock, two-one. Matt checked through the peephole; Vlad was peeking out at him from behind a pile of linen. He came in, carrying two rolled-up slabs of foam, a sheet and light blanket for each, and four spare pillows. "Didn't mean to interrupt your dinner," he said. "Can you manage these? You understand, there is no examination on bed-making." He put the bedrolls down, juggled two of the pillows. "Well. Spakoyni nochi."

When Vlad had gone, Raf said "Are we going to start the run now?"

"I'm tired," Ruby said. "I'm going to bed."

Ciss said "We're supposed to get to Serenity about 0400. Do you want to be awake then?"

"I don't know. If you are, remember what the steward said about tickets and getting back." Ruby pulled a tightly packed bundle of crimson silk out of her bag, took it into the washroom and shut the door.

"I suppose we should get some rest," Tani said, sounding unconvinced. "It's going to be a long trip."

"Yeah," Matt said, looking at the closed bathroom door. "Everybody knows where their keys are?" The others affirmed so. "Okay. If you do go out . . ." No, he thought, he didn't need to do that.

Ruby came out again, wearing a short, tightly belted silk jacket over an ankle-length nightgown. She kicked at the floor and shot up to the upper bunk, sat there with her feet dangling.

Matt said "Run tomorrow, Rubylaser?"

"Si, bueno, mañana," she said, and she did sound tired. " 'Noche, Matt."

"Good night," Matt said, and he and Raf and Jack retreated aft. Tani closed the connecting door, and Matt heard it latch.

Matt sat down in one of the chairs, idly unbuttoning his shirt. A hand touched his shoulder. Raf, stripped to boxer shorts, said "Which bed do you want?"

"You and Jack decide," Matt said. "I'm going to sit up a while, so I'll take the floor tonight."

Raf nodded. He took the bottom bunk, Stringer the top.

Matt sat in the chair for a long while, watching the white pylons flash by, the parallax movement of near rocks rushing past against a distant, stationary horizon. It wasn't at all like a city train, where all you saw was the tube and the platforms.

There were crawler tracks all over, near the rails; there was nothing on Luna to wear them away. But Matt never saw a crawler or rover, a prospector's station. There was a small shelter, smaller than the cabin, with a Transport emblem, but it was gone before he could see what it was, whether it was inhabited. He thought about opening his slate and trying to find out, but he just sat, just watched.

He leaned back, looked up at the sky. *One hundred diameters to MIRAGE engagement, Captain,* he thought; *very well, Navigator, keep us informed.* A signal post went past. *Ninety-nine, Captain.*

Ninety-eight.

By ninety he couldn't stand it anymore. He finished undressing, rolled out the floor bed; he blacked the window and found his way under the sheet by touch. For a while he thought that the rumble and shake of the train would keep him awake, but in the end they sent him soundly asleep.

He woke to Raf coming in from the corridor, carrying some canisters of juice. There was a soft, cool blue light on in the compartment. Raf handed him a drink. "The observation car's pretty nice," he said. "The sky view's really something, although it always seems like you're going backwards. I guess you *are* going backwards, but—"

"I know what you mean. What time is it?"

"A little after three. We get to Serenity in an hour. Do you want to get off there?"

Matt didn't, really, but it was clear enough that Raf did. And as much effort as had gone into the trip, it seemed wrong to waste any of it. "I think we can look around some."

Jack's bed curtains were still drawn tight. Matt partly cleared the window. They were crossing the Sea of Vapors, broad and bare to the horizon.

He knocked lightly on the connecting door. Ruby's voice said "Yes?"

"Do you want to see Serenity?"

"Momento." The lock clicked and the door opened slightly. Ruby was still in her nightgown, but seemed wide awake. Past her, Cissa was asleep on the floor bed, curled up in ivory-colored cotton flannel and a Transport sheet. Tani was nowhere in sight, maybe in the closed bathroom.

"If you want to get off at Serenity," Matt said, "we should start getting ready."

"All right. Don't wake Ciss."

"Stringer's still out too. Raf's coming. Meet at the end corridor?"

She nodded and shut the door.

Raf had lit the forward view. "Is that it?"

"Yeah."

Serenity City was at the southeastern edge of the Sea of Serenity, where it met Vapors. There was a line of hills behind it, and a major crater ahead and to the right—that would be Menelaus, Matt thought.

The city was all barrel-roofed dugouts, like Verne Center six times in a radial circle, with an antenna tower at the center. The tracks were headed for the outer end of one of the vaults. Off to the left was the port, a small field mostly handling Lunar traffic.

Matt finished his juice. It was orange juice; he remembered what his father had said about oranges from Serenity, wondered where the orange plants were.

"Let's get ready," he said to Raf, and finished dressing and tossed some things into his slate bag. Then he stopped. Better not use the slate away from Ruby's relay. He put his ticket, a pencil and a little notebook into his jacket pocket, checked his pants pockets for money and the cabin key.

At the front end of the car, the corridor turned right and faced a door, red-edged, vacuum beyond.

Ruby and Tani came out, closing the cabin door gently. Matt said "The view from here's no good. Let's go on to the next door."

They reached it as the port went by. It was empty but for a couple of cargo rovers and a hopper. No starships.

A steward came aft down the corridor: not Vladimir. Her nameplate read S. SOLAN. "Good morning," she said, pleasantly, quietly. "Are you the group from the next car?"

"Yes."

"We're a little early, so you'll have an hour and a quarter here. Try to be back ten or fifteen minutes before that, if you would, please, so we don't have to worry? There aren't enough of us to go looking for anybody."

"All right."

"You can stay there just a minute more, while I go wake someone up," she said. "Then I'll have to get the door ready. The rear door in your car's not in use;

you can watch from there." She went forward to a compartment door, knocked sharply. "Mr. and Mrs. Dellefsen?" There was a muffled response. "We'll be arriving soon. Are your bags ready?"

The door opened. The steward reached in, came out with two large hard-sided suitcases. She brought them back, set them in the short doorway corridor.

"May we just stay clear of you and watch?" Ruby said.

"That's fine. I'm Selene, by the way." She gave it all three syllables. "Don't you hate it when people name kids that? Almost as bad as Diana. Or Loooooona."

Matt supposed Cissa Luna Okuda would have smiled at that, as she always did.

Selene unlocked a panel by the door. Inside were controls, pressure gauges, two manual valve knobs.

Light filled the window in the door. "On door two," the steward said to nobody visible.

They had already slowed considerably; now there was a slight lurch. Epoxy and crete and glass came into view beyond the door.

They stopped. "Okay, girls, bring it in," Selene said, and two people in softsuits pulled a pressure tunnel out to envelop the door. Selene touched a switch, and a band of red light appeared around the doorframe, a matching circle of indicators on the control board. The lights went green as the tunnel sealed in place, and the dials jumped as it filled with atmosphere. "Coupled, solid, and pumped," the steward said crisply, then "Better stand clear—I've got four passengers here set to skamble."

She unlocked a large metal lever, pulled it down. The door cycled open. Selene stood back, gestured at the doorway. "See ya later, terminator."

The station was decorated with glass mosaics, abstract patterns that suggested maps, or musical notes, or maybe letters of an unknown language.

Some were designed with angled stones that shifted the pattern as one passed by.

A dozen passengers had come out of the coach-car tunnel, and several more were following them out of the sleepers, along with the stewards guiding bags. The team slipped, quietly, nonchalantly—certainly not skambling—past clusters of little reunions, through a station hall not much different from the one at Copernicus, and into the city.

Matt had expected it to be like Verne, but the space was completely different: there were small decks at every possible altitude, long vines and tensioners connecting them vertically, rainbow bridges of glass filament leaping between. In the distance, a number of people were airborne on brightly colored wings. One had long red ribbons trailing from the flightframe, another blue—and they were looping around one another, close enough to touch—

"Look at that," Matt said, and Ruby gaped. Dogfighting, playing riptail, would get your license lifted at Copernicus, for a month to forever.

Matt had to look down. At their level, apparently the main deck, there were more trees than in Verne, though they were smaller. "The greenwood," Tani said, and she was among the trees in four airborne steps; she touched the bark, sprang to grab a branch and perch there. A large blue-and-white bird fluttered away, and another cawed furiously at her. "What's your trouble?" she said brightly.

Raf said "There might be a nest."

"Oh." She looked around, saw it. "Oh, yes." She looked, but moved no closer to it. "Sorry, momma." She dropped back down.

"You've brought good manners with you," a woman's voice said, "so welcome to Thoreau Place." The woman, in a long gray robe, stepped into view. She was slim, fair and sun-touched, like an older version of Tani. Matt saw the patch of a dragon tender on her sleeve.

"Excuse me, please," he said.

"Yes?"

"Where do you force the—grow the orange vines?"

"Orange trees," she said. "Those are two halls anticlockwise from here." She pointed. "Confucius Hall, toward the sea."

"How long would it take to get there?"

"Perhaps a quarter hour on the ring train. Or you can walk, through the dragoncore, but that's not quick. Are you in a hurry?"

"We don't have very much time."

"Not to have much time is a serious matter," she said. "Enjoy whatever of our trees you visit." She nodded and walked away.

"What was all that about?" Ruby said.

Matt said "I wanted to know. We can't ignore people."

She nodded.

"And there isn't time to worry about it anyway. What *do* you want to do? How about a bookstore?"

"We haven't started the run yet," Raf said.

"Books are a good idea," Ruby said.

There was a store just on the edge of the plaza, a wood-paneled place called Henry David's. Ruby got a couple of tech magazines, the Lunar edition of *New Scientist*. Tani got a dataclip of novels, and Raf, after some prompting from Matt, bought a nonce-copy of *Scaramouche*. Matt found a manual on intercity train operations, inexpensive because it was a standard Transport publication. At the counter there was a chip of images of the city that he got for Cissa.

Then they went up to the highest level they could figure out how to reach, looked the length of the vault—the "hall"—dense as a dragon and far less orderly.

"What do you suppose the other five are like?" Tani said.

Ruby said "Probably worse. With orange trees."

They picked up some fresh pastry and a few more liters of fluid on the way back, got out their tickets and reboarded the train.

Ciss had gone back to the observation car. Jack was sitting by the window, playing a game on his slate: it was DISPATCHER, a version of MOONGAME about building and operating transport systems. Matt hadn't even thought about it; he had the slide somewhere at home, of course.

The beds in both compartments had been made up, and the floor in A cabin was swept. The steward Hsien came by to check that they were all returned, the voder announced imminent departure and the train moved out, across the Sea of Tranquillity.

They ate some of the cakes. Ruby acknowledged the looks she was getting by saying "Let me get through one of the magazines, and we'll start."

Matt said "And I have my call to make."

"Yeah," Ruby said, "you're set up for that."

They left him alone in the C cabin. Feeling the skin on his hands tightening, he opened up his slate, touched out the number. Ping to Ruby ping to groundline ping ping Serenity Relay to Copernicus Relay ping ping ping to Gil Vela, wherever he was receiving.

He was in his office, one-armed. " 'Tardes, Matt."

"Hello, Gil. Am I . . ." He spoke slowly, hoping to cover the second or two of lag through the lines.

"Another rule I didn't tell you about. Nobody gets to hear what the others decided until later. I must be related to Portia's father, what do you think?"

"I . . ." There was no way to delay this, now that he was here; he had to decide. One way, or the other. "I'd like the job."

Gil seemed relieved. "Shall I put the docs through?"

"Yes." Matt touched keys to accept the contract.

Rubylaser had promised him that there would be no
evidence of distance on the docs.

"Done," Gil said. "There's a work schedule in
with the rest of it,"—breath held—"first session's in
ten days,"—breath out—"just when the next practice
would have been. So you have time to get your life in
order."

"Thank you for this, Gil."

"It is a nipping and an eager air," Gil said, and
Matt knew he was quoting but could not think what.
The screen went dark.

He closed the slate, opened the door. The others
looked up, apparently all waiting. "It went okay,"
Matt said, in as strong a voice as he could produce;
Lafayette Lonestar offered no help.

So they went off to their reading, or whatever.
Matt crossloaded DISPATCHER from Jack's slate to
his own; there was a competitive version that they
could play hardlinked without raising a ripple in the
observable lines, but Jack wasn't interested. Matt understood. None of them really wanted to play a game.
They wanted to get into Ruby's world and run.

About nine, Cissa leaned in at the connecting
door, caught Matt's eye and gestured toward the corridor. He pulled his boots on and went out; she was
standing in the little exit corridor at the front of the
car, watching the ground pass the window.

"Thank you for the pictures," she said.

"Oh, that's all right. We didn't want to wake you
up. . . ." He had almost said "Ruby said not to wake
you," but he thought it was better this way.

She kept looking out the window. Matt didn't
mind that. When she watched the scenery she didn't
stare at him. She said "I wonder why we don't go any
faster. My folks say that on Earth, trains between cities run almost ten times as fast as this."

"I was reading about that in the manual. It's
partly because of maintenance—it gets a lot more
complicated when the trains go faster. And the cars

are built so if we went right off the rails at fifty, we wouldn't bust vacuum. That'd be a lot harder, faster. M vee squared, you know."

"Yeah."

"I read that they can run an emergency train up to two hundred kph. But, you know, there's hoppers if you need to be somewhere really fast."

"I don't mind the time." She smiled. "It's what the trip's about, right? Spend the longest time out we can, cool as the middle of a crater." She turned then, and her eyes were on him. "My mother has a saying that it's better to journey hopefully than to arrive."

"Huh?"

She looked back out the window, to Matt's relief. "I don't think it's really about traveling. It's—oh, I don't know."

"Yeah. Do you want to go back to the observation car?"

"No. I'll just stay here a little while. The steward said it was okay. Let me know when Ruby's ready."

"Sure."

He saw her shut her eyes tight, still facing the window. He wondered what would happen if he held her hand, or touched her shoulder. Would the stewards pick that moment to come by, or the rest of the team appear to call them in for the run? Would Luna fall out of its orbit?

He remembered his father's quote from *The Three Musketeers,* about seizing the chance, and because it was his father speaking, any possibility of action was spoiled. He went back to the compartment.

A little after ten, Ruby finally granted audience. Slates and add-ins were unlimbered, the backfill discussion began. "Okay, Colin and Bowstring are taking Robert Vaux home, and unless the gods of old England have changed their ways drastically, into a trap of the Sheriff's."

"Theo saw there'd be trouble. She traded her night-eyes for that."

"Theo's clever. She'll find a way to get them back."

"But just now she's taking Lonestar back to the inn, to get the hole in his side crafted shut. Does that about cover it?"

"Where's Judith?"

"You left her at the inn," Cissa-about-to-be-Baroness-Huntingdon said, "smiling wistfully."

It seemed to get warm in the compartment with all six of them, so they propped the connecting door open with a bag, Jack hung a corner reflector in the doorway and Matt plugged the daisy pickup into his slate to check the link from all angles. Tani dimmed the lights in both cabins, turned the windows to black.

"K," Ruby said, perched on the upper bunk. Ciss sat at the table in A cabin, Matt in a chair against the wall, Tani on the floor as usual. Raf and Jack, who as Colin de Courcy and Bowstring were separated from the others, were in the C cabin. "The windup . . ." Virtual light began sparkling on screens, in eyes. "The *pitch*."

The inn was silent as Lonestar and Theo approached. Lonestar had cut a stick and was leaning on it, making him noisier in motion than he liked to be. Theo said "I'll go in."

Lonestar nodded, put himself behind a tree, got an arrow out for safety's sake and waited.

Theo was back in a moment. "It's well enough, I think. Judith's gone home."

"All right. Let's go in and think on our next move."

They sat down in the inn's common room. Lonestar leaned back, stiff with the bandage Theo had applied to his wounded flank. "The notion," Lonestar said, "was that I let myself be captured, and then one of you, pretending to have taken Vaux in exchange, would make a trade. Then Bowstring slipped herself into my place. We must assume the plan to be otherwise the same." He looked at the old witch, rocking away in the corner of the room, who would gladly tell him if that assumption were correct—provided he gave up something precious in exchange for the riddle of her reply.

"Who'll be taken," Theo said, "and who'll do the taking?"

"Colin's the logical one to give himself up. He's still a knight, of a good family, and Prince John can't ignore that. Colin might even be able to just walk into the castle and demand an amnesty."

"Which the Sheriff would never give him."

"No. But they'd have to have at least the pretense of a trial."

"And Sister Bowstring would be lucky to get as far as the Great Hall with her throat unslit. That makes sense."

Lonestar said "Which is just why I think they'll do it the other way round."

Theo put down the cords she had been braiding. "Oh?"

Lonestar stood up. His vision flickered to gray, and he sat down again.

Theo said "I told you—"

Lonestar shrugged. "At any rate, think about it: can you imagine Bowstring, faced with a choice like that, not wanting to do it the more dangerous way— and Colin not being chivalrous enough to agree?"

They both seemed to hear laughter from a great distance.

"Are you suggesting we go after them? Return String's double cross?"

"No. It's their play, and we mustn't sour it. But we ought to be . . . available. When the Sheriff tries his double double cross." He gestured. His vision blurred and reddened as he stretched his wounded side.

"Very well. Now go upstairs and lie down; you'll be no good at all until your side finishes mending.

Anyway, we have to give them a day to get *someone* properly captured."

Nottingham Castle stood on an imposing bluff above the town, square-fronted, high-towered, most defensible. *Not* impregnable, as Lonestar and his companions had proven time after time. But each time they raided the place, there were more defenses against entry, more traps in the way of escape. One of these days they would find all the ways closed off— unless John could be brought down first.

Lonestar and Theo, disguised as townspeople, sat at the edge of the town, in sight of the Castle approach, brushing the tangles from raw wool with large combs. It looked enough like work to pass the eyes of the passing soldiers.

Or it was supposed to. "'Ere!" an armed man said, walking over to them, trailing his short spear behind. "'Ere, 'ere, yoo!"

"Us, sir?"

"Wash yoo doo?" He sounded drunk, but then he smiled: a man missing that many teeth would sound like that under the best of circumstances.

"Carding the wool, Captain," Lonestar said.

"Yoo isn'ad."

Lonestar's sword was within a moment's reach, and the guard's weapon was not ready. But—"Of course we are, Captain sir."

The man leaned over. "Me muvver did 'at. Carra wool."

"And I'm sure she did well, sir."

The guard looked at Theo. "Yoo keep 'im doin' 'at?"

"Yes, my lord Captain."

"Muvver ne'er make Dad doo 'at." He turned and walked away, shaking his head. Lonestar rolled his eyes, and Theo swallowed a chuckle.

As they did, the soldier turned suddenly, his spear at once extremely ready for action. "Whaarnt—"

Lonestar's arm tensed. But the soldier wasn't looking at them.

Two men were coming up the main street. The first was Robert Vaux, looking somewhat ill-used. His clothes were dirty, his hands were tied behind his back and he was blindfolded. He made his way along guided by the prod of a sword in his back.

The man—if that was the right word—who held the sword wore marvelously rotten armor, scabbed with rust and caked with dirt; he might have crawled out of the grave in it. The sword he held to Vaux's back was stained and pitted, but it would doubtless kill a defenseless man. Maybe poison him as well.

A moldy cloth hid the man's face. On his shoulder, a heraldic badge had been gouged out, as by a beast's claws.

"Whaaaassis?" the guard said.

"Out of my way, lout," the man said, in a sort of spitting roar. "I've something to sell to your master, and he'll be quite annoyed with you if you lower its value."

"Hoo bee yoo?"

"Death," the apparition said. "Be you my herald to the Sheriff—or rather you join my kingdom?"

Snaggletooth took a step back, then turned and ran with a surprising spryness up the ramp to the Castle gate. "Death" gestured menacingly at the townspeople who had come out to look. He made an elaborate gesture at Lonestar and Theo, who hastily signed against evil; they had recognized Colin's hand signal for *All well so far.*

They watched as the two men entered the Castle.

Theo said "Do we wait?"

"No. At least, not here. Let's visit the baker's."

A third of an hour later, dusted with flour and smelling of warm bread, they were passed through the gateway (kindly offering the gate guards a basket of fresh soft rolls for their trouble) and made their way to the kitchen. A cook, a friend of the cause, let them in. They spoke only of baked goods: not everyone, even in the scullery, considered the Sheriff the worst of evils.

"Has the new bread been popular with his Lordship?"

"Oh," said the cook, "very much so. They were a little wary at first—you know how it is, with an unexpected taste—but now they only want more."

"I see."

"So I'm glad you've come: the first delivery is well nigh gone—only a crust left in the pantry."

That didn't sound good. "Tell us more."

"Ah, what more can I tell you? You know the state of our ovens."

They knew well enough where the Castle dungeons were. "We'll see what we can do, then, friend."

"That's all any can do," the cook said, and the glimmer of wit left her as Ruby-beyond moved her attention on to further plots; no more information here.

There were now only the three of them in the kitchen; the cook moved to one door while Lonestar and Theo went out the other, into the servants' passageways.

Theo said "Dungeon, or Great Hall?"

"We know they haven't killed Bowstring, and Colin's here; this isn't the time to change plans. But it would be good to know what kind of shape String's in: can you tell?"

Theo reached inside her overtunic, brought out a little glass heart, the size of her thumbnail, on a strand of silk. She cupped it in her palm. It began to pulse with deep amber light, slowly and regularly.

"I'd guess they haven't done too much. Probably haven't given her anything to eat or drink." Her face tightened. "I keep getting darkness: I hope that only means a dark cell."

"All right, nothing we can change there. Great

Hall, then. Let's see if we can make them bring her to us."

Theo trembled then. Her hand shook violently, and she clenched her fist on the glass heart.

"What's the matter?"

"I'm—I'll be all right. When this is over—let's get home as soon as . . . home to the greenwood, I mean."

Matt felt himself hovering inside Lonestar. Theo's magic was linked to the woods: out of them, and especially among all this man-cut stone and forged metal, she was weaker. But Matt had a certain feeling that it was Tani Case who had spoken just now. He looked up, thoughtful, but no sign came from Ruby-in-the-Sky.

"If it goes well," he made Lonestar say, "we'll be home with no worries."

They made their way to a rather plain door: access to the Great Hall from the kitchens and wine cellar. Gently, Lonestar slid open a peephole in the door. It was there because it wouldn't do to collide with an unexpected armed nobleman. Just so.

"It's an *interesting* offer, you must admit," the Sheriff of Nottingham was saying. His voice echoed in the three-story-high Hall.

"I don't like it," said Sir Guy of Gisborne, who paced into Lonestar's view. Gisborne was wearing a heavy black tunic, and his hand fiddled with a jeweled dagger.

"Gisborne, you never like anything unless it has a sword or a bolt safely through it." The Sheriff sounded almost merry. "Go and fetch our half of the bargain. Alive, please."

"You intend going through with this?"

"I intend getting Robert Vaux—who I will remind you is one of the few friends we can count on—and whoever this is holding him inside another or two of our thick Norman walls."

"Very well."

"A suggestion, my lord Sheriff." That was Eamon the mercenary. His presence complicated things.

"Of course."

"Bring the woman to that topmost balcony. The view is very good from there."

"And the floor's a long way off. Excellent idea. Do it, Gisborne."

Grumbling, Gisborne went out.

"Lonestar . . ."

"Wait."

The Sheriff said "Show the stranger and his guest in."

Lonestar moved as far as he could, then let Theo watch as Colin, still masked, pushed Vaux into the Hall. Eamon looked at Colin closely, but showed no sign of recognition.

"You know what I want," Colin said.

The Sheriff stepped into Lonestar's view then. He was a big, imposing man, handsome, and no fool at all, as they had learned many times. "You want to ransom one of your subjects, I believe."

"Today I am only interested in the living."

"Oh yes, yes, I was getting ahead of myself. Well, if you'll just be patient a moment . . . ah. There you are."

Lonestar couldn't see. He decided to chance opening the door; it should be oiled and quiet, out of sight and mind. It was.

The Hall was the full height of the Castle; the topmost balcony was a good twenty meters above a hard stone floor softened only by a few Moorish carpets. Gisborne was standing there, his knife to Bowstring's throat. She was still wearing her metal mask; Lonestar wondered how *that* had happened. Unless—

"Theo," he said, very softly, "read again: is that really String up there?"

"I . . . can't," she said, shaking again. "I'm too far away—"

"All right," Lonestar said, "all right." He held her hand.

"How do I know that's who I want?" Colin said.

The Sheriff shrugged. "She claimed there were horrors beneath the mask. It cost nothing to take her at her word, and it interfered not at all with the operation of the rack." He looked at Colin. "All this mask business—are you a part-time basilisk as well?"

"Look and see," Colin said, and pulled away the cloth covering his face.

The guards at the door took a step back. The Sheriff cursed. Gisborne lowered his dagger to sign against evil. Only Eamon stood absolutely still, looking at the raw, bloody, maggoty face with idle interest.

Bowstring grasped the moment: she jumped to the balcony rail, stepped off into space.

De Courcy shoved Robert Vaux into the Sheriff's arms, knocking them both into a sideboard. He grabbed the rope that held a chandelier suspended, slashed through it with one stroke. The huge chandelier came down, the rope whistling through its pulley. Colin went up.

He collided with Bowstring in midair, flinging his sword away to grab her. Their combined weight overbalanced the chandelier, and they started to descend.

While everyone else fumbled, Eamon was walking purposefully toward the landing site, sword drawn.

"Time we joined the party," Lonestar said. "Can you slow that man up?"

Theo nodded, put her hand on one of her bracelets, shut her eyes.

The carpet Eamon was crossing suddenly folded itself up around him. Lonestar ran into the room, sword raised to thrust through the cloth bag.

Eamon started to slash his way out as the chandelier spilled its passengers to the floor.

Lonestar caught Eamon's sword on his own, looked him in the eyes just as they had done days ago. Eamon was still mostly caught in the carpet. Lonestar beat his sword aside and punched him in the jaw. Eamon fell down.

The Sheriff yelled something. Vaux was doing his best to be inconvenient.

Lonestar and Theo helped String and Colin up. "Where to?" Colin said.

"Front door, I think, nothing too clever."

Colin showed his hideous face to the door guards, who recoiled again, and then they were through. There wasn't much resistance after that—in fact, the halls were suspiciously empty—until they plunged through the gate, taking care not to trip over the guards there. Those soldiers, having eaten well on Theo's drugged rolls, would sleep soundly for the rest of the day.

In a stable at the edge of town, Baroness Judith was waiting with new disguises and horses for everyone, and Robert Vaux's wife, who delayed them long enough to give kisses all around. Even Colin, once he had wiped the mask of rotten meat from his face.

"Remember," Judith said, "demand all the way into the Great Hall that the Sheriff do something to get your husband back. And then praise him a little when he produces Robert; we don't want Nottingham to become a bad loser."

And then they were off, into the safety and quiet of the greenwood. Judith of Huntingdon turned to look at Lonestar—

The scrimmagery of Old England faded out, and they were all back on Luna, in the eastbound train.

Jack came in from the aft cabin. "If I'd realized we were just going to *walk* out . . ."

"If you hadn't been so concerned with twitting the Sheriff," Ruby said, rather crossly, "you could have just let Robert Vaux walk home after you'd rescued him the *first* time."

"The witch said Colin and String had to be kept together," Tani said. "Was that because of . . . the business with the long fall?"

Matt was wondering about that: had it been something Raf and Stringer had arranged or improvised on the spot—or had Stringer forgotten he wasn't in Lunar gravity?

"Maybe," Ruby said. "Now, if you'll all excuse me." She pulled the bed curtains shut.

"Last performance today?" Tani Case said. Ruby didn't answer.

They started to split up for bed, as the night before. Matt caught Ciss looking at him with an odd and spooky directness; the kind of look that wouldn't have surprised him from Tani, but . . . "Good night," he said, and Cissa said "Good night," and Matt went into his cabin, shut and latched the connecting door.

It was only about 1900.

"We'll be at DVC pretty soon," Raf said. "Do you want to get off then?"

"No," Matt said, "let's do it on the way back."

"Okay. My turn on the floor, right?"

"Sure."

There was a reading light in the bunk that wouldn't bother the others with the curtains drawn. Matt read the introduction to the rail manual, looked at the diagrams of equipment. Then he slid it under his pillow and snapped off the light. He could hear Jack turn over above him, caught the whisper of pages and a little flash of light from Raf's bunk, where Raf was reading about the man born with a gift of laughter and a sense that the world was mad.

They weren't even halfway to Tsiolkovsky.

He thought he understood, now, why Ruby had put the run off and then cut it short: it was the one familiar thing they had together. She didn't want to use it up too soon.

Matt tried not to think about it. If he thought too hard about the distance, the time, the unfamiliarity, he would start to miss home. That would not do. He had seen little hints of it in the others, the way they looked out the windows, the way they looked back. Even Rubylaser was showing signs. They had to keep looking forward.

"Matt was set on this, whatever it is," Ronay said to Sol Wasserstein. They were clearing away the dinner things; Louise and Sonya were in the front room, talking. "Again, I'm sorry."

"Again don't be sorry," Wasserstein said. "You don't imagine how relieved Tess sounded when she heard she was off the hook." He scraped a plate. "I asked her if she was off to see a boyfriend. If looks could kill . . . Has Matt . . . ?"

"No."

"You sure about that?"

Ronay just let it be a joke.

Sol said "You'd think we would have run out of places for them to go by now. City's no bigger than it was when we were that age. Where did you go when your bones itched, Albin?"

"Sometimes to Old Landing top. That was before VACOR expanded."

Wasserstein said "Other side, Albin. 'As a man wipeth a dish, turning it over and upside down.' Or something like that." As he illustrated the technique, he said quietly, "Shut the door, will you, Albin?"

Ronay closed the kitchen door. The soft mumble of the women's conversation faded out. Wasserstein put the stack of plates away. He leaned against the counter.

Ronay said "What's the problem?"

Wasserstein sighed. "Yeah, quick way's good, I guess. There's been some discussion at the hospital of . . . asking Sonya to step down as Chief of Exo. *Not* to leave the staff, all right? Not one word is being said about her competence as a surgeon. She's the best we've got, and Bill Cunningham wouldn't have—"

"That's understood, Sol. What *is* the problem?"

Another sigh. "Chief is a staff job, administrative. And Sonya just doesn't *communicate* enough. She listens just fine, to everyone, but nothing feeds back. Things get done, they run on schedule, as much as they ever do, but nobody hears a suggestion, or a review.

"There was this conference—no, that's too confused. A while back, Wally Loh mentioned there was a shortage of TFE skin grommets. I put someone on it, and he comes back with 'what shortage?' So I have to play Mycroft Holmes to find out that Sonya's fixed the faulty order on her own time, no report. It needed doing, Albin, and she did it, but she didn't do it the right way, and I feel like an unholy heel for saying so."

"No," Ronay said. "You've talked to Sonya?"

"*Albin.* Of course I've talked to Sonya. And she listens, and she says she'll be glad to quit anytime. But that's not the right way either. I don't know what the right way is. I'm calling you in to consult on what the right way might be; I thought she might talk to you." It was some measure of Sol Wasserstein that he could say that without a trace of unkindness.

"Thank you for telling me, Sol."

Wasserstein gave a shrug that both summarized and ended the conversation. "I could have been a scientist," he said, easing a pumpkin pie out of the oven. "But no, I didn't want the responsibility. Tea's ready, Albin: would you pour?"

As the deep red fluid filled the cups, Ronay tried to order the current crisis into the great and constant flow; this was, after all, Luna, where there was a sea of them.

The Sea of Crises, like all the Lunar maria, was just a vast and static pan of dust; on the TranCity

Farside Direct, another long, empty haul after leaving Da Vinci/Crisium station. Then, during the third day out from Copernicus, there were three stops only a few hours apart: Hubble Station, then Möbius town, and then Lobachevsky Station. The stops there were less than half an hour, long enough to transfer a few passengers, freshen atmosphere, water and fuel. Carefully warned (again), Matt and some of the team got off to see Hubble and Möbius anyway.

The stations were not much more than that: a place to service the train, connected to some habitats and industrial projects. Möbius was a little larger, a few thousand people. It was on the line between the Near and Far sides and was the main relay point for data from Earth to Farside. It had originally been called Marginis, for the Mare Marginis nearby, but the people who lived there objected to being called "marginal" and changed it by unanimous vote.

Ruby was persuaded to pitch after Möbius and Lobachevsky, and it went well—good, contained little adventures where they rescued an abbot from one of Prince John's more aggressive barons, and stopped an attempt by a troop of drunken knights to disrupt a country fair.

They hit terminator just after Lobachevsky. The surface was mostly black already; every stone cast a shadow forever, the rest of the light was spilled horizontally across the plain.

Ruby wouldn't start the game until they were past the line. As they watched, she asked Raf about sunsets on Earth. They had vues and backgrounds, of course, and their lightselves had waited for the cover of sunset, or ridden away into it, any number of times.

Jack looked doubtful. Matt pointed out that practically all the New Worlds had Earthlike atmospheres, and therefore Earthlike sunsets, which seemed to settle the problem.

So Raf talked about the red haze of nightfall, the

redness of the Sun itself, as it was supposed to turn when it aged and died at the end of things. He described sitting still by the shadow of a stone and watching the shadow crawl, of the blaze across half a hundred kilometers of open water. "There's supposed to be a green flash sometimes, just when it goes down."

"Green?" Ruby and Tani said almost as one.

"I've heard about it. But I never saw that. I always hurt my eyes trying."

Ciss shivered. "Well, *yeah*."

"No, no, it's not so bright at sunset, you can look right at it."

Ruby said "Why green . . . ?"

"I don't know. I suppose it's like rainbows." He seemed to think hard about the prospect of explaining rainbows, then said "In the islands, the sunlight's really straight, and the shadows are all sharp and black, like here. You burn up standing in the sun and get chills in the dark. Like here."

The train ran through a deep rock cut then—the windows actually brightened, the cabin lights through the windows reflecting from the burnstone —and then it was dark, and would stay dark until they passed this way again.

Ruby pitched then. Lady Judith insisted on wearing a disguise to the fair and staying near Lonestar, though she had the most to lose of any of them. Of course she did make herself important, distracting a constable with a yell of *Cutpurse!* when the man looked too carefully at Theo, then being all solemnity when the addled local priest begged heavenly indulgence for good King Richard while his dear brother John was away on the Crusade or whatever . . .

"Have you thought any more about Musketeers?" Raf said, as the session wound down.

"When we get back," Ruby said, a little short, but not so unhappy as she had sounded the day before. "I couldn't bring *everything* with me. . . . Be-

sides, you don't expect to end your days as English
outlaws just by knocking a Norman lout into a river
and kissing a pretty young boy, do you?"

That got them to the third midnight, ten hours
from Mendeleev, the last stop before Tsio. They
agreed that they would probably not get off at
Mendeleev, since they would be stuck there for half a
day coming back.

Matt slept well. When he woke, they were past
Mendeleev, southbound.

The darkness was amazing, with no Earthlight
at all. He had seen vues, and understood the albedo
calculation, and asked Raf to explain moonlight, but
the idea—one-eightieth as much as the same phase of
Earth? Could that be anything?

The view through the windows (there was
hardly any point in darkening them) might almost
have been Space, except for the periodic flash of the
signal posts, the complete darkness of the lower horizon, and the faint wobbly trace of the horizon. The
pale luminous band of the galactic equator arched
over, like one of Raf's rainbows.

Raf was still asleep. Stringer was out of the
cabin. Matt dressed and went back to the observation
car.

The back half of the car was all glass from waist
height up and over, big panes with a thin grid of
blackened aluminum strips between. The floor and
low walls were carpeted in dark red. The lights were
dim. There were chairs with gray fabric covering,
and tables of high-finished gray plycore on metal.
The furniture was loose, on solid ballasted bases.

There was only one passenger in the car, a
small dark-haired woman in a white suit, with a book
face down in her lap; she seemed to have fallen
asleep.

Matt passed her carefully, took a seat at the
back. Floodlights on the back of the car lit up the
rails for a hundred meters or so, and the signal posts

strobed in a chain of red specks. Otherwise the world outside was all dark, stardusted.

"Hello." It was Vlad. "Like some tomato juice?" Matt took the cup.

"I have an easy time of it from here on," Vlad said. "There's no one left in the car but your group and a man who got on at DVC, and he stays in even more than you do. Cheers."

"Nazdrovye."

"And tonight," Vlad said, "I will be at my parents' house. Where my mother will insist that she must make my bed, because I am not working."

"You're from Tsio?"

"I was born there. My real place is in Mende. At least, that's where my girlfriend lives, and I think that counts for something." He smiled meaningfully, and Matt nodded. Vlad said "You have to have something, between the cars and the service rooms. I saw you had a copy of Sermon One: did you read the part about crew apartments?"

"Sermon . . ."

"Services Manual One. The book that was under your pillow. We call them the Sermons. Because you must be doers, and not hearers only. Da?"

Matt said "Are your parents astronomers?"

"No, no, Transport. My family have always been Transport. My grandfather came to Luna when the long rail lines were building; he was a track engineer. But we go far back, with trains. A hundred fifty years ago, my however-many-greats-it-was grandfather and grandmother met on the Pioneer Railways. Do you know of those? Is your family from Earth?"

"No."

"They were trains run by young people. Some younger than you. You would start out with an oil can, or serving tea in the dining car, and work up, until you were a driver, or a car superintendent."

"Is that what you'll be?"

"Oh, maybe. It's not the same now, though. A

superintendent mostly works with a console, making sure there are enough linens in the cars. I would not like to give up riding the trains—what would be the point? And you see that Hsien and Selene and Ross and I are all pretty much alike. Nobody is boss, you just do your job well. That's why my grandfather left Earth: too many bosses, he always said.

"See, I haven't told you the great story of the Pioneers, back then. Do you know about the great war? In the middle of the century?"

"Some."

"Our country was invaded, you know. And the Pioneers were not going to just give their railway to the enemy. So everything they could pack up and carry away, they did. Tools! Dishes! Light bulbs! And what they could not carry, they *blew up!*"

Vlad put a finger to his lips and turned, but the sleeping woman had not stirred.

"So," he said, more softly, "when the war was over, and the invaders driven out, they brought everything back and rebuilt the railway. That is our . . . semya nasledstva . . ."

"Family heritage."

"Yes. So you see. What does your family do?"

That stopped Matt cold. He could not remember ever meeting an adult Lunar who did not know what his father did. He thought now that Vlad must be teasing him, but there was no sign of that in his look.

"My mother's a doctor. My father is a symphony conductor."

"Ah?" Vlad hummed the "Ode to Joy," and again Matt thought it was a joke, and again decided not. "That's right," he said.

"And a doctor. What kind?"

"Exosurgery."

"That's the kind with wires inside?" He tapped his ear, put a fist to his chest. "Or cutting open?"

"Wires. Are you all wired?"

"Oh, no. Just hearing, and the jack for, you

know, blood oxygen. I have a cousin, though, Stefan. He works on a starship, and he has the whole nervnya net, and the Apparat Syertse. That's a good story too. When Stefan got the job—he was just old enough, and he came home to tell us. His parents were there, and mine, and our grandparents. Stefan said—he was young, remember, and all excited—'Father, I am going out to space, but they say I must have a Russian heart.' There was a little quiet, and then my grandfather started to laugh, and his sons laughed, and in a moment we were all laughing, Stefan hardest of all. A Russian heart."

Vlad finished his juice. "Well. Would you like to see the driving compartment?"

"Sure." He stood up. "Would it be all right if my friends came too?"

"Of course. You're a nice fellow to think about them."

They stopped in the sleeper to collect the others, and then went forward, through the first sleeping car, to the door marked CREW ONLY. Vlad opened it; it didn't seem to have been locked.

The corridor turned right, ran along the side of the car, windows looking out on the surface. There were doors along the inside. "This is the mail and special-freight room. Crew room—someone may be asleep in there, don't go in—mechanicals room." He unlocked that door, said "Don't go in, but look." It was just a narrow, noisy room, with displays and monitors along one side, a workbench with racked tools. The door at the far end was an airlock. Ruby crouched in the doorway so the others could see over her; Matt saw her eyes tracing out the room, the bench, burning them into storage.

Vlad closed the door and they went on forward into the cabin.

It was a large, open room, lined with trix and controls. The nose was glass, like the observation dome but not as long. Selene the steward and another crewman were playing cards at a table. Someone else was watching a Skyhook game. "Who's winning?" Vlad said.

"Orients. Like usual."

At the very front were two large chairs facing a console. Displays on the board showed graphics of the track ahead, top and profile and forward views, like a game. The headlights lit up the tracks farther than the rear lights had, but they were still just a finger into the dark. A crewman sat in the right-hand chair, reading. She turned, saw the team, and straightened up in her chair and smiled. "Hello."

"All okay, Kim?" Vlad said.

"There's a freight meet at two-five-oh, and then it's green ribbon to Tsio."

Stringer said "Are you . . . driving?"

Kim said "The system is." She pointed to a set of hand controls within easy reach, and a small panel running a set of medical traces. "I can use these if I have to, and that board knows I'm alive and awake enough to do it. But most of the time, the rails know where we're going, and the signal system gets us there."

"Tick-tock," Ruby said.

"That's right," said the driver. "Track Integrity and Continuity, Train Operation and Control." She shrugged. "Pretty dull, huh?"

Matt watched Ruby watching the controls. The look on her face had nothing to do with dullness.

There was a sound from the sports-channel screen. A player in Tycho gold threw himself at the side wall of the stadium, bounced off the glass ceiling and shoved the ball through the hoop for two points. An Orientale player threw a punch at the air, catching a stern gesture from the referee. "How about that," said the crewman watching the game, as the screen played the muffled roar of the live crowd. "Might beat the spread after all."

Vlad said to Matt and the team, "That's really all there is to see here."

"Thank you," Matt said. They started toward the corridor.

"May I stay a while?" Ruby said abruptly.

"As long as you like," Vlad said. "And all of you; I was not ejecting you."

But the rest of them went back, Vlad opening the door for them. He made a small gesture to Matt, just in the doorway, and Matt waited until the others had gone on down the passage.

"We're not really supposed to let people in here, you know," Vlad said quietly. "It's a rule. You can read about it in the Sermon."

"We won't tell anyone. Thank you again."

"Nye za shto, and I did not think you would. I just wanted you to know that we will not tell anyone we saw you here, either."

Matt held still, not knowing what to think or say.

Vlad held up his palms. "You have tickets back, so you are not running away. But this is not for any training or business, and you have no family there to visit—even for the short time you will be there. You are just adventuring. You will have a different crew going back, so I wanted to tell you, it is all right with us. Wakarimasu ka?"

"Ya panyimayu, spasiba."

"Khorosho. Now, I will be riding back to Mende in two days, and be on the cars west two days after that. Will I see you either trip?"

"No . . . we're coming back on the next train." It was easy enough to say; Vlad could have easily checked their tickets if he had some particular reason for wanting to know.

"So soon? Well, enjoy your time anyway. You will be seeing the Gold Prospect? And the Linden Circle? Or do you have someplace special to go?"

He was just asking, Matt thought, he was just being kind. "We're going to see those for sure."

"You should have a meal at Siri Semyonovna's. It's called Restoran Rassvet. On Gagarin Avenue, just out of the Core. It doesn't look like much—don't say I said that—but it's very good."

"Thank you."

"Eh! Siri does my family favors, what can I do? Say, 'Next time you leave here, be sure and take the trains'?" Vlad grinned and shut the door.

Matt went back to the compartment. No one asked what he and Vlad had talked about, which was a relief. He got back into the bunk and stared at the dark windows until the train motion put him to sleep again.

Raf woke him about an hour out from Tsiolkovsky. He cleaned and sponged up in the bathroom and packed his stuff for arrival.

The wall unit made the announcement: the right-side doors on the second and fourth cars would open at Tsiolkovsky Station.

They went forward to wait near the door. Matt said "I'll go back, just to check if we left anything."

The rooms seemed clear. As he came out, he saw a man standing in the passage to the forward door. The man carried a leather shoulder bag and a small metal suitcase with spacecraft handling labels.

Matt waited. The man's suit was definitely Terrestrial, a dark blue-gray with a faint geometric pattern. His face was very blocky, with a flange of hair swept out at each temple. His eyes were dark and shadowed, as if he hadn't been sleeping, and his mustache was just the shape of Groucho Marx's—maybe not quite so large, and not so black.

He stood still, ignoring or not seeing Matt for several seconds, then turned abruptly and said "Hello."

"Hello, sir. I, uh, don't think this door will open. When we arrive."

"I know it won't. I just wanted the view. Your group is watching from the next car, I believe?"

"Yes."

The man bent his knees slightly for a better view. Some of the long tunnels and outer structures of Tsio were spotlighted in the dark, others suggested by pinpoint marker lights. "Only you Lunars know what darkness is," he said, pronouncing it with a short *u* as a real Lunar would.

"Are you an astronomer?"

"No. I am visiting old friends. We have a few important things to discuss."

"Oh."

"You might know them? Hannah and Jacob Gold."

Matt felt uneasy. There were living people who had known the Golds, back in the time of Independence, the birth of the MIRAGE drive (they were the G, as Leon Avakian had been the A) but—"Sir, the Golds have been dead for a long time."

"Yes. It's a late visit, I know, very late. But I'm told Hannah was a patient woman; perhaps she will still tell me what I need to know." He turned, smiling. "Or perhaps not. Experiments are like that." He held out a hand. "My name is Robert Ostrow."

"Matthias Ronay."

There was a little pause just before they shook hands, like some mechanical register turning inside the man. Matt wondered if he was Coran-wired; if he had known the Golds, he must be.

The end door opened. Vlad said "About that time. Bring your bag, Mr. Ostrow?"

"Ne vazhmyiti, spasiba."

"Pozhalasta. Gospodin Ronay?"

"Nyet, spasiba."

Vlad saluted and went on back, into the next car.

Matt said "I'd better go along."

"I hope your trip is productive."

"Thank you. And yours."

The train was slowing as he rejoined the team. Just as before, the tunnels came out from the station, were locked and sealed to the train; the door rolled aside.

It was strangely dark on the platform. All the others had been brilliantly lit; Tsio had soft indirect lamps and glowing panels in the floor guiding the way out. The platform lounge had small tables, each in its own defined cone of light.

Things were a little brighter in the station proper. "Lightspill," Cissa said then. "Nothing shines out on the observatories."

They found a baggage desk. Matt said "We'd like these checked onto the Mendeleev train? At seven?"

"Are you in compartments? I can't accept coach check-ins until five."

"No, compartments." They presented tickets. The agent looked vaguely at the doors the team had just entered through, but just said "How many bags?"

"Six."

"I can only check through to Mendeleev. You'll have to take them off and recheck there for the trip to Copernicus, b'sayder?"

"Yes, thank you." They handed the baggage over.

"Where first?" Raf said.

Tani said "How about something to eat that isn't a sandwich?"

"Vlad told me about a restaurant," Matt said. "Then I can try to ping the man I met on the train— Yuri Korolev—and see if he can show us something where he works."

Stringer said, rather sharply, "He may not even remember you."

"Well, then, he'll say so, and we won't be any different than if I hadn't asked. Same with the restaurant: we don't have to eat there, but we could look."

Jack nodded.

Ciss said "I want to take a walk, while we're on Farside."

Matt said "That's a good idea. But we can save that for last—we can still do it at Mende, hai?"

"Right."

Tsiolkovsky had been planned in what the early Lunars called "ray-crater" design: a circular core development, with cut-and-covered trenches, "avenues," extending outward in six directions. According to the plan, everything was supposed to be rigidly geometric, with ring tunnels intersecting the avenues at precise intervals, clusters of habimods and standard structural blocks set up at the crossings to a predetermined number and size. Matt had seen an old, pre-Independence vue, gliding over a digital model of the expanding city, as a voice said that all the modular stuff would "speed and regulate the construction, enabling this city of science to shelter its workers and thinkers in greater comfort, at less cost, than has ever been imagined for the Moon."

It hadn't worked out like that.

The designers hadn't realized how fast electron torches would burn rock in vacuum; they supposed that their tunnels would be major construction jobs, when really you could, and did, bore and line wherever you wanted. They knew about crete ("waterless concrete," the old vues always called it—Matt wondered what "watery concrete" might be) but hadn't thought about glass except in windows. Slammers still had trouble with the idea of structural glass.

So what had really happened was that the central core had been built, but in pieces and irregularly, with plazas for the trees and grass that those old planners didn't seem to think were important, and only four of the six avenues were bored, but for more than twice the proposed distance. Seen in a sky view, Tsio was a splatter on the Lunarscape, still sort of radial but organic rather than mechanical.

Starships did not land here. There had been a big hopper port at one time, but now most of it was paved with solar cells; a hopper or two was kept ready for emergencies, but people took the train.

And once arrived, they had a bit of trouble finding their way around. After half an irreplaceable hour of following likely-looking corridors, Matt insisted they stop at a spravatchnye kiosk, where they got a map and, for five Keplers, a black epoxy disk the information agent called a tumblebug.

"It works like this," she said. "You want to go to the Rassvet—good place too—you see, that's here on the map, AC275 on the list. Press the buttons. Go ahead. A, C, two, seven, five."

Matt did. A green arrow lit up on the top surface of the device.

"Now watch," the woman said, and spun the disk on the countertop. As it whirled, the arrow kept pointing in the same direction. "Now, this only points straight lines, you still want the map to get around corners." She stopped it with a finger. "If you don't want to keep it, when you go, turn it in at any kiosk and they'll give you four K deposit back. Enjoy your stay."

The map and the disk led them back to Avenue Gagarin, a broad double walkway with a strip of modest greenery down the center—grass, some bushes, a few small neat trees. A few people were strolling, but there was no one resting on the grass, and—

"There's no sound," Tani said. "It's like the place up in Hub, where they built those offices nobody wanted. You can hear the leaves rustle. . . ."

They found the restaurant in minutes. "If we'd kept going this way . . ." Jack said, but there was no force in it.

The place didn't look like much. Some tables with white cotton drapes, pictures of buildings on Earth with weird flattened domes on top. There were three other customers who looked up and smiled and waved when the team came in.

Siri Semyonovna turned out to be an enormous, grinning woman in a flowered apron. Of course she knew Vlad Barat! Of course she had breakfast for them—"Or any meal you want! When it's dark on Tsio, people work until they notice they're asleep and half-starved at the telescopes! Sit down, sit down!"

They did. Matt and Stringer helped translate the menu for the others; Matt, smelling wonderful things from the kitchen and feeling suddenly very hungry for real unwrapped food, ordered blinis with applesauce and sour cream, and eggs chopped with horseradish from a Serenity dome. It was all wonderful, the blinis delicate, the applesauce gloriously lumpy, the egg salad sharp almost to painful. Cissa, who was having a pityi soup with Ango meat, asked for a taste and gaped. Matt didn't mind. His mother could cook like this, when there was time.

"We ought to have ikra," Siri said. "But you know, caviar—" She pointed at the sky, and they understood. "Sometimes, when the scientists come back from over there, they bring caviar, or fish, sealed up, you know? Then we have solyanka. Oh, don't stare at the menu; I make solyanka with the tank sturgeons that won't kill you, but the Black Sea fishes—there's a difference, that's all. For that we wait for daytime, so there's at least an excuse to waste time here. But I am wasting your time."

They spent over an hour at the restaurant, eating, watching other people (all of them regular customers, it seemed) enter and order without even looking at a menu, in Russian and Chinese and Japanese and English, all of which Siri registered without a blink.

"You are going at seven?" she said. "You will not be back? Okay, I tell you: come by here at six. There will be something for you, better than railway food. Six. Plenty of time to get your train." She looked casually at the pile of Keplers on the bill, said "No, we don't tip friends," and handed a good fourth of the money back. "And here, you had the horseradish, and you had the onions, and *you*—bozhemoi!—had the radishes *and* onions." She dealt out mints to everybody. "Six. Remember. It'll be all ready."

"Shest' chyisov, bolshoi spasiba," Matt said.

Moving slowly, uncertain of their mass, they left the restaurant. They found a public terminal, and Matt riffed up Yuri Korolev's name. There was a home address and a work number at the Astrophysical Center.

"Work first," Ruby said.

"Yes, I know." Matt keyed it in.

The screen lit with a symbol, stars, calipers, an equation and a stylized spectral pattern; it said YOU HAVE REACHED THE TSIOLKOVSKY ASTROPHYS-ICAL INSTITUTE in four languages. A voice said "Korolev here."

"Dr. Korolev? Could I see you, please?"

"Moment." Korolev appeared on the screen. Behind him was a work room, a large display table in the center. Someone else was running fingers over the tabletop, moving data. "Yes? Who am I addressing?"

"My name is Matt Ronay. We met on the Transport platform—in Copernicus a few days ago—"

"Oh, yes. But— Is there something I can do for you?"

"Well, we're here, sir. In Tsiolkovsky. I was wondering if you'd have some time to talk to us."

"You . . ." Korolev looked around, behind Matt. "There are a number of you? This is a school trip?"

"Not really. There are six of us. We're just . . . interested. We won't keep you long, we're only here for a little while. And if you're busy, it's quite all right."

"Moment." He turned around, said something to the other person in view, got a shrug, turned back.

"It's no problem. And we are doing something interesting, I think. Can you find us here?"

Matt got instructions and the tumblebug code for the Institute. They went down a level; the lower avenue level had lightweight, open carriages suspended from an overhead guideway. They rattled softly and swayed in a very odd fashion.

Rubylaser watched the overhead supports flick by. "It's to isolate vibration," she said. "No shaking 'scopes or antennas."

Korolev was waiting for them at the Institute lobby, a low room with plain white epoxy furniture and an all-glass ceiling. He shook everyone's hand, offered fresh glasses of tea—"You see, Matt, I have learned your manners—" and led them through a maze of plycore cubicles. Some were occupied, some empty, one housing a man in a white coat curled up asleep on the carpet.

Finally they came to the room Matt had seen on the public screen. The other man was still there, and a woman as well, seated at a desk console out of view of the wall screen.

"Luise Fischer," Korolev said, "and Daniel ben-Yair." They completed the introductions. Matt could tell that the Lunar scientists recognized his name, but nothing was said.

"So, are we ready to show this to a skeptical audience?" Korolev said happily.

Fischer nodded. Ben-Yair said "If they don't intend to publish first."

"Khorosho. Matt: you said you had been reading my papers on Avakian shock. Do the others know what that is?"

Ciss had perched on a chair. "Matt?"

"When a MIRAGE-drive ship holes in or out," Matt said carefully, "there's a pulse of . . . energy." He couldn't remember any more precisely than that, and could have kicked himself for not reviewing the work on TECHNET.

But Korolev went right along. "That's right. And, being Lunar, you all know how old the Avakian-Gold Equations are, just as old as your Independence, and the interstellar voyages just about sixty years old." He touched the desktop, which lit with a map and control points; Korolev touched and traced, and the screen showed a ragged ovoid of light, surrounded by distorted globs of objects, data annotations on them all. "This is an optical image of New Helvetia, the fifteenth New World located but the nearest to Earth in space, fifty-one light-years." He pointed. "The star, the planet. The arrival of the starship *Spring of Hope* in the system. You can see the Avakian shockwave; it's not optical, of course, we've converted it."

Ruby said "Fifty lights? Is it that faint?"

Ben-Yair said "Yes, unfortunately. There's also another wavefront distorting the image; it may be a gas front from a very dim star, but we're not sure."

Matt looked at the splat of light, and looked at it, trying to imagine: it was a starship holing in, more than fifty years ago. Who had they been? New Helvetia. *Spring of Hope.* TECHNET would know.

Fischer tapped fingers nervously on her console, which was not active. "We haven't the resolution we had fifty years ago, when we started waiting for that image. Atmosphere."

"Oh, atmosphere," Korolev said, trying to make it a joke, but not really succeeding.

Raf said "Atmosphere?" The rest of them were quiet.

Ben-Yair said, in a very calm voice, "All the habitations and most of the work done on Luna release some oxygen, some water vapor. Our gravity holds some of it; not much, it will never be more than a . . . haze, but it does degrade viewing."

Korolev said "But there should be nothing significant for fifty, perhaps a hundred years."

"Yes," ben-Yair said, "at the current rate of formation. If that doesn't change." He looked at Matt; Matt supposed the man could not help that, and didn't blame him. "At any rate, it doesn't bear talking about right now."

They had tea, and the scientists showed the team around the Institute, apologizing that it was mostly data machines, not real telescopes; a big window looked out on one of the medium-sized radio telescopes (the largest one was inside Tsiolkovsky crater itself), though in the Farside night it was just some colored marker lights against the blacked-out ground, below the stars.

It was still beautiful.

They left a little after 0400. Ciss asked about a walk again, but they hadn't been to the First Hole yet, and Dr. Fischer had said that was fenced off from outside access, should be seen from Gold Prospect.

Gold Prospect turned out to be a large crescent-shaped chamber with a high ceiling, wrapped part of the way around the Hole, which was illuminated by spotlights. The inner curve was all glass, with display cabinets and historical vues at a touch. The interior had seats, a few trees, expanses of novylon carpet; in Copernicus or Tycho or Serenity it would have been all green, but they understood now about stray water vapor. The air had in fact come to feel papery dry. Tani walked the length of the inside glass, pausing only momentarily at the displays, then sat by a tree, leaning against it, quiet.

Matt looked out at the Hole. It was a rough crater, about fifteen meters across, its edge crisscrossed with rover tracks and footprints—"Old ones, from when they were gathering the stuff," Matt said to reassure Ciss.

There was matter inside matter, that was how it worked; a wheel inside a wheel.

The Golds were on Luna—the Moon, then— when it had happened, Jacob having contributed the theoretical mathematics and Hannah the applied;

Leon Avakian, the physicist, was still on Earth, building what he thought was a power source.

Avakian supposed that the unaccounted mass of the Universe was in vast disks of "shadow matter," a little like tachyons, a little like neutrinos, a little like nothing else, that existed alongside and within galaxies, making up for their lack of solidity by an incredible rotational speed—vastly faster than light. (In this display case, a projected 3-D vue of the idea, Avakian Disk inside Milky Way.) With the right apparatus, Avakian thought he could couple real space to the disk, just enough to draw off energy.

He was partly right.

The apparatus consisted of hundreds of thousands of particle traps, cryogenic coils the size of a finger bone (here were two on display, one clean and new, one in reassembled pieces), each of them holding a particular particle at a particular energy state. Because energy and position are never both knowable (here a still of Werner Heisenberg), Jacob's primary equations calculated the "envelope" of likely locations, Hannah's machine-intelligence execution shaped the envelope in the right fashion.

When the power was applied, at a laboratory in the North American desert, the whole test rig had imploded, vanished, leaving sheared-off conduits, broken walls and a rush of air to fill the vacuum. (Stills and a model of the ruined lab.) Also gone were parts of two offices and a technician named Lochert, who had been on the wrong side of a safety line, apparently making coffee.

The Terrestrial project ended there. Leon Avakian eventually went to newly free Luna, where his old friends the Golds had a surprise for him on Farside.

The experimental rig had arrived here, blasting this crater into the regolith barely a thousand meters from the Tsiolkovsky core. No one on Earth had seen it, of course; Luna kept the secret, and sifted through the debris, trying to reassemble it. (Here was most of the coffee machine. Most of Lochert was outside, under a stone monument.)

"If we're going to go out," Ciss said, "we ought to do it now."

Matt nodded, turned. He saw something at the far end of the room that made him stop. It was the man from the train, Ostrow, sitting next to a bent old man in a tracked chair. Ostrow was talking, gesturing. The old man just sat.

Matt could not hear what was being said, and certainly was not going to try and eavesdrop. He watched for five, perhaps ten minutes; Ostrow kept talking, more and more intensely, and the old man just sat, with an occasional slight motion of his head. Possibly he was wired, subvocalizing his answers, or using spare nerve capacity to toggle a voder. He certainly wasn't touching keys or pads.

Finally Ostrow stood up. He leaned over the other man, near his face in what might have been a whisper but looked entirely like a kiss, then slung his shoulder bag and walked away. Matt turned away compulsively.

Cissa said "What's the matter?"

"Nothing. I—just give me a minute. All right?"

She stepped away at once. Matt started to walk toward the old man in the chair, who had not moved at all. It was acceptable to do this, he told himself, because the man might need help; if he did not, and he was Lunar (surely he was) he would make that known, and Matt would withdraw at once. It was not wrong, when someone might need help. . . .

"Sir?" Matt said.

The man raised his head slowly. He was wearing a robe of deep violet velvet, very soft-looking stuff, and a matching beret that flopped down the right side of his head. Matt supposed it covered a bank of Coran chips, shoring up lost neurons. No hair at all showed from beneath the hat. A picsel display was clipped to his robe at the left shoulder.

The man was *ancient*. Wherever his face was not all creases, it was tight over bone. His hands, little and brown and curled and lumpy, lay idly in his lap. His shoulders moved, just slightly, and there was a hiss, oxygen being fed through some unseen coupling.

His eyes were narrow and brown; they looked tired, but not filmy or distant.

"Day, day," he said, "good day," and Matt nearly jumped.

The man did have Coran support, Matt thought. The Cortex Analog trix were looking for words, pattern matches, that was all. Though they should not have been so slow, with an ordinary greeting; maybe the system was bad, or the conversation with Ostrow had loaded it up.

Matt said "Good day to you, sir."

"Do you wish . . . to . . . talk, talk to, talk to me? Five or three or three people are come to talk to me. Are you one . . . one more?"

"I'd be glad to talk to you, sir."

"You are a . . . young man."

"That's right, sir."

"Were you born?" The phrase came out without hesitation, and Matt paused, not knowing how to answer; then he realized that the old man was searching for the rest of the thought. ". . . knowing. Knowing, language . . . competent . . . military effectiveness coefficient upper percentile?"

"I'm not—military, sir."

"No, of course," came the answer, smooth as weightless bearings. "That was the answer being avoided from the first. Surely you don't expect it to appear now, in the form that you hoped for when we were all naïve."

Matt looked into the man's eyes and saw the sparkle of wit: he thought, then, that he understood.

The old man had been compiling this response, selecting his words and lining them up, like Rubylaser setting her fielders in the game. Something Matt had said, or done, had triggered the reaction.

Or perhaps this was the answer that the other man, Ostrow, had been trying to get, but hadn't been patient enough. Matt wondered if he should go after Ostrow, bring him back.

There was, he thought, another possibility: that the old man in the chair had saved the words up because he *did not* want the Earthman to hear them, that this databurst was the same as Matt's holding in anger at—whatever—until he was cold and alone, and then blasting it at the walls, the ceiling, the Earth beyond the high window.

Matt held still. If he was not supposed to hear this, it didn't matter—he was no one and would never repeat it; but he had a strange feeling that he was meant to listen.

"She always feared it would be born killing," the old man went on. "But you know this. What do you think all that work was for, why the money came, and the energy and the effort? But that's the difference between goal orientation and process. Anyone with two cells and nine months can make a human. The trick is to do better. Classic Frankenstein. Classic. She knew the life of Mary Shelley day by day, and it was her haunt and humor."

She? Matt thought he must know who that meant, but—

"MIRAR was her child, hers alone: Jacob, whom she loved, brought the bones together, but in her mind it would have stood, run, played without bones nor flesh to cover them."

He was talking about Hannah Gold. MIRAR was the Mass Inertial Referent Algorithm, the mathematics that controlled the MIRAGE system.

"It died . . . and it died, and died, because we kept killing it, until we understood about the mass distortion, which took much too long; I think we were all cross with Hannah's child, he would not do the trick the way we wanted. . . . She had turned away, long before. And he never spoke to her. *Never.* Her son goes to the stars and back, but never speaks of where he has been. And you will not break him for the facts, because he has died too often to break under pain. But he may tell you. When he wishes. In the way he wishes.

"That is your answer. I hope it is not what you want. I hope to God, who is no particulate disk, that it makes you angry enough to go away and do something sufficiently disgraceful to yourself."

Matt stared. His neck ached from tension. This was—there was only one person he *could* be—

The old man stopped talking. His eyes closed, and his head tipped forward. The display at his shoulder lit with the words ALL SYSTEMS OK, and then scrolled up

I am sleeping.

I do not require assistance.

Thank you for your concern.

Matt took a step away. The others were waiting for him at a comfortably cool distance.

"Who is that?" Ruby said. "What was he talking to you about?"

Matt knew he could not answer, because if he said who, he would have to explain how he knew; even if he pointed at a still, claimed it was a simple pattern match, matters would come around to what the old man had said, and Matt could not repeat that. Not even to the team. It would have to stay frozen inside him. At least, at the very least, until he understood it better himself.

"He's just a man who's lived here a long time," Matt said. "He's too old to work now, and he wanted to talk. I think he's probably pretty lonely. . . . We've still got an hour to walk, Ciss."

They accepted this and moved out. Matt took one last look back at Leon Avakian, alone in the plaza.

No one else, it suddenly seemed, wanted to go for a walk. Raf and Stringer felt the need for Maze time; Tani Case wanted to visit the Linden Circle, apparently the closest thing to greenwood in Tsio; Rubylaser said she wanted to find a bookstore. That committed Matt, since nobody could go walking solo. They agreed to meet at the restaurant at exactly six, promising further to ask directions if it looked like missing the deadline. Tani, who was going farthest from the Core, got the tumblebug.

The excursion point was a short way to the southeast of Core, on Tereshkova Avenue. An attendant with an inexplicably sour manner checked their licenses and ran them through the quiz booth; Matt's questions were on the meaning of the leftmost helmet indicator (faceplate reflectivity), leg inflation adjustment (left side chest module) and the location of the buddy hose to share air between two suits (top center back module). The questions were supposed to come up at random, but Matt seemed to see the buddy hose a lot; he suspected there was some kind of hidden weight in the system.

They were given partial plate: cloth leggings and sleeves and a hard plastic chest unit. It was a little more awkward than full mail, but quicker in and out. The attendant checked seals and ran diagnostics from the chest jack. "You've got two hours' air, and you're clocked for fifty minutes. Single tone alarm at forty, triple tone at forty-five. At fifty someone has to go get you, but that isn't going to happen, is it?

"This isn't the big city, and we've got exterior

lighting rules. So you stay inside the red strips, and suit lights are on at *all* times. Everybody wants to know, so *no*, you can't go see the MIRAGE Crater. It's fenced. Climbing the fence pulls your license for a thousand hours. *Jumping* the fence pulls it for a year to forever, depending on the kind of mood the review panel's in."

They put on helmets. "Time check," the attendant said. "Zero mark."

"Zero mark," Matt and Cissa said.

"Okay," the attendant said, suddenly mild, "door one. Enjoy yourselves."

The way out was just a cylindoor, like at home, a four-paneled door of thick glass that pivoted at the center; a puff of air escaped when it turned, but the design was simple and nearly failproof, and air was cheap.

LIGHTS ON PLEASE, a sign said, and Matt and Cissa switched on helmet and knee spots. At least the sign had said please. They unreeled phone lines from their chest modules and connected the plugs. "Hello hello," Matt said.

"Zero noise." Ciss hefted her slate and they began to walk along the well-traveled ground, picking their feet up, neither shuffling nor skipping. Nobody could hear them talk, as long as they stayed on phone, but they could be certain someone was at least generally watching. That Outside was cold was a Slammer conceit.

The area was divided into lanes and squares by waist-high lighting strips. The nearby ones were white; in the distance, seventy-five or eighty meters away, were red lines marking the limit. The strips kept the ground clearly lit without dazzle; they also prevented cross-country runs. Matt had seen a vue of a puzzle layout at Tycho, a flat maze.

"So where to?" Matt said.

"Over there. The boulder, left ahead."

The rock in question was a dozen decs or so

across, in the center of a light-ringed open area. It was quite smooth; someone must have decided to leave it for interest, but buff all the possible snags away. Cissa leaned over it, looking into the distance, walked around it. "Do you mind sitting for a moment?"

"Of course not." Matt pushed himself up, sat down on the stone. The thing was here in the excursion zone; there were no warnings against climbing it.

Ciss said "I need some distance." They disconnected the phone lines, and she moved back several steps. She opened her slate partway. "Now," she said on FM, "look a little to the left, please. Toward the, uh, antenna there. Yes." Matt could no longer see what she was doing. "A little farther left . . . *there*. Hold steady. That's great."

She came into view again; her slate was shut.

Matt said "Can I see?"

"Not yet. It's just a stillvue now. I want to work on it." They reconnected the phone lines and began walking again.

Almost to the red lights, Ciss stopped so abruptly that Matt turned to scan her back module; everything seemed all right. "I wish we had longer out here," she said.

Matt looked around. "It's really not that big."

"No, I mean on Farside."

"You know we talked about it. We're kind of stretching the time as it is, and if we'd had to get hotel rooms, it would have gotten . . . complicated. You remember."

"I know. And it's been a . . . good trip." She touched the phone line. "But you're leaving, and I don't know what to say."

"Leaving?" Matt said, bewildered.

"For the theatre. You told the director you were taking his job."

"But that's not leaving. The Company's in Copernicus—they do a few performances in other cities, but that only takes up a skyday or so out of the season. I'm not going anywhere," he said, with far less force than he felt.

"Oh," Cissa said, almost softer than breathing. "But you won't—be—*around* as much—"

"I don't know. It's a *job*. Gil keeps telling us how hard we'll be working, but I think he's exaggerating, to be sure we're all serious, don't think it's a . . . game." Was that it? he thought. "I'll still need to, you know, *see* people. Run and play."

"Oh, well . . . sure," she said.

"I'll be right—"

"Okay. Okay, okay."

"Ciss, I just—"

"Call me Judith," she said, quietly and precisely clear, "just once, not playing."

He understood: he knew how Judith of Huntingdon felt about Lafayette Lonestar, what they could do that Ciss and Matt couldn't. "I'm right here, Judith," he said, "and I am not leaving." He put an arm around her shoulders, a clumsy and meaningless gesture in suits. That is, he knew it was clumsy —she was a cm *taller* than he was—and he hoped it was . . . he didn't know what.

How *did* Lonestar feel, right now? Matt touched helmets with Cissa, hearing the buzz of her breath and her suitworks: this was the secret way to talk, no phone, no radio; in stories from before there really were suits, the characters clicked glass to talk one to only one.

But there wasn't anything to say now. So Matt listened. Maybe that was more important.

After a full two minutes by the helmet clock, Ciss said "I'm all right now," the words distorted helmet to helmet.

"Come on. Let's beat the bells back." They reached the cylindoor just as the ten-minute warning sounded.

Everyone got to the Restoran Rassvet just on time: Raf and Jack clean and flushed from gym showers, Tani looking more than usually distant, a few leaves caught in her hair, Ruby holding a permanent book on Renaissance France and a couple of dataclips. She looked in a questioning way at Cissa, but there was no discussion.

Siri Semyonovna clapped her hands as they came in and brought out a neat white bag that smelled of garlic and onions and warm Angolamb. "Yes, there is probably a little too much," she said, "but you aren't wasters, I can see that. You'll share it. Be sure to save a Kievski cutlet for Vlad Barat if he's aboard. He loves those."

She took thirty Keplers for the bag, about what they would have paid for the same volume of cafeteria sandwiches.

On the way to the station, Tani brought out the tumblebug and said "Should we return this?"

Ruby took it, tucked it away in her coat. "I'll keep it. I owe you all a Kay for it."

Was it an appropriate souvenir? Matt thought, and knew the others were thinking the same. But Rubylaser had all sorts of mex and trix; she could come up with a reasonable origin, should anyone ever ask where the device had come from.

The sleeping-car steward at the entryway was a woman named Delancey, rather older than Vlad had been. "Oh, *boy*," she said as the bag of food went by, and breathed deep. "I know where *you've* been. First car, turn left and all the way forward, compartments A and C. I'll be in to visit you just after departure."

They went aboard. Same type of car, same bags in the same place, same drill. They started to unpack the meal, gave Delancey almost a third of it for the crew—"I'll tell Siri you did that," she said, "but I think she knows. She knows how people are"—and still were stuffed on kasha with minced Ango, chicken soup with piroshkies, butter-stuffed chicken rolls (Vlad's favorite) and jam blinis.

They needed to sleep then. It was ten hours to Mendeleev, where they would have to keep awake and busy for ten hours until the train home. Matt took the floor pad, because he was certain he would not sleep, and indeed he fought it for almost an hour, thinking alternately of Leon Avakian and Cissa, like hopping from one foot to the other.

Then he rolled on his side, burped chicken and butter, and was under.

"Wake up, Matt."

"What is it, Raf?" The car was dark but for the cool blue nightlights.

"There's a Snail outside. Come look."

Matt wrapped himself in the crisp Transport bedsheet and went to the window. There, indeed, only a couple of hundred meters away, a Snail was working, bathed in its own lights.

A Snail was a huge mobile factory, a hundred twenty meters long and eighty wide, containing all the equipment to fabricate and lay and wire neomorphous solar cells. It crawled across an expanse of cleared ground, grinding regolith as part of its raw material, doing the final grading and surface prep— the front end contained a movable electron torch for stubborn rocks—leaving behind a half-meter an hour of power collectors.

They worked by night, allowing time to check continuity and lock out faulty sections before the Sun lit the work up. Some crews stayed with the same machine, half a skyday laying cells, a day or two shaking down the working installation, the rest of the time till dawn off at the town or city of service. Others chased the dark west, hopper or train to the next Snail. That was the closest thing on Luna to being starship crew, always in motion by night.

Not close enough, though, and entirely too near.

Matt said "How long to Mende?"

"Forty minutes."

They hadn't done much unpacking, so it was only a few minutes' job to get everything back into the bags and ready to go. They had breakfast on the rest of the fruit blinis and some juice from the rear car, then sat by the windows to watch Mendeleev approach.

Mende was three square stacks, four levels above ground. At the corners, six-level towers, like Sokoni at home, connected them.

They were passing the port now, the only Farside starport and the second busiest on Luna; there were at least ten ships parked, piperackers, blockframes, disks, a couple of small air-faired vessels. Nothing much seemed to be moving.

The train line ran between two of the city blocks, tunneling under a tower, emerging in a valley of crete and epoxy. They thanked the steward and deboarded.

"—passengers, all passengers," a voice said from overhead, "please check with Information for the latest details on the transportation situation. Hopper and starship passengers are especially urged to stay in contact with Transport—"

"What's *that* about?" Ruby said.

Matt said "I guess we'd better find out. Bags first?"

"No, this first."

The information agent explained (patiently, and obviously for the hundredth or so time) that there had been a minor accident at Port Leonov, the starport, and it was affecting some schedules, but they were fine, train service was not affected at all. Also, if they were spending their layover sightseeing, there were hazard advisories around the port. Thank you for asking and enjoy your stay.

Matt said "I can probably get more off TECHNET."

Ruby touched her datacoat. "Yeah. Let's do it."

It riffed up easily. The ship was the *Duke of Lancaster,* a blockframe registered in Trieste. She had been manifested with some dry chemicals and sapphire tool parts, nothing hazardous, but apparently one of the containers had a fast oxidizer in it. Matt pulled down a newsclip. One Lunar handler had been badly burned, and another had broken bones. An investigation was under way as to the cargo labeling—

"Okay," Matt said, "now we know."

They left the bags with Transport. It was now 1930; they could board at 0300 tomorrow for a departure at 4.

Ruby said "What do you want to do now?" Matt had the impression she hadn't slept much on the way from Tsio.

"Dividing up was okay," Tani said, tentatively.

" 'S true," Jack said. "We're all on Ruby's line if we need to get together for anything."

Raf said "Matt?"

Matt thought. "How about if we decide on someplace to meet in four or five hours—2400, say—and then get something to eat? If someone has an idea to do together, there'll still be time then."

Ruby said "That'll do. Yeah. Where?"

"Passenger entrance to the starport?"

Jack said "Won't that be a little warm?"

Matt said "Shouldn't be; we won't go *in* the port. By then somebody will have seen a restaurant, too."

"2400, then."

Tani vanished. Ciss looked at Matt for a moment, then smiled and left with Raf and Stringjack. Ruby said "You going to the port, Lonestar?"

"I might. I won't cross any red lines."

"No. See you, then."

"Later, Laser."

"Later, Loner."

She left him by himself.

There was a Museum of Farside History, beginning with the first photograph taken by Luna 3 more than 120 years ago: a faint round smudge, less detailed than Dr. Korolev's picture of a starship holing in fifty light-years away.

Glass cases displayed souvenirs of the first Farside landing, by the Aeneas 4 mission: cameras, film packs, dry O_2 bottles, the foil seals from sampling containers. A glass cube showed one of the earliest holovues, the landing team working and waving to the camera, the image grainy and sparkling, shattering into primary colors. They seemed to be having fun, skipping and jumping in their bulky old-style suits; four of them linked arms and danced a hora for the camera.

The largest hall was about the Tsiolkovsky observatories. It was much more detailed than anything Matt had seen at Tsio. He supposed the astronomers there preferred it this way.

The last hall was the history of Mendeleev City, as it was built block by block. There was a live terminal for visitors to enter their opinions on where Four Block should be built, possible new architectures for it, and what it should be named. The first three were properly Chandrasekhar, Feynman and Hawking, but Matt had scarcely ever heard those names in use.

The place used up a little more than an hour of Matt's time.

He found a planetarium nearby; the sky show seemed more to orient visitors than interest Lunars (there was, Matt noticed, a different show during daylight), but it was another pleasant half hour.

A public information terminal told him that Three Block had a theatre, which would be performing *The Miser* at midnight; it would last until three, just boarding time. The screen put up the seating diagram: there were six available together almost anywhere they might want. He canceled without buying. They probably wouldn't all want to go. Matt didn't know the play, but Molière was supposed to be very funny. Cissa might like that. Ruby seemed to need a good laugh.

And then again, Ciss might not want to go to a theatre. Not if she still felt bad about Matt and Gil's company.

The local Skyhook team was out of town, but only Raf and Tani really liked to watch Skyhook. Matt wondered if the others had looked around a dragon lately; he found an entrance to the One Block dragon, not far from the meeting point.

He wouldn't push their doing anything as a group. They still had a long time together in the car ahead.

Like Ciss, he wished they could be here longer, where everything was different, new; he also wanted to be home, and was certain they all did. That was the problem with the Mende layover: it was neither here nor there.

It was 2150. There was no point in putting it off any longer: Matt went to the starport.

The port was busy. There were plenty of vehicles in motion, inside and out. People in Transport red and Population blue and Economic Services silver were at work, as at any port. But there was a tension Matt sensed as soon as he entered the area. The people were too quiet. There wasn't any of the side conversation, the jokes, the talk about sports and food and after-work stuff that there *always* was. Maybe Mendeleevitches were quieter than Copernicans—but not this quiet, or this kind of quiet.

Matt sat down on a bench with a good view of offloading operations. A couple of Transport people were nearby, slates open and working. Nobody paid any attention to Matt.

Ordinarily, Matt would have opened up himself and lined into VACOR TECHNET. He should have been in plenty of range of Ruby to do so without more trouble than a second's lag. But he didn't want any more trouble at all. He sat by the window and watched the red-and-yellow rovers roll.

"Hey," someone said in his ear. Matt twitched around. It was one of the Transport team. "What'cha doing here?"

"Just watching."

The man looked him over. "You from Mende?"

"Copernicus."

"Uhm? Where? What block?"

"We don't have blocks. I live in Verne Center." Matt swallowed, trying not to let it show. "Where are you from?"

The man relaxed a little. "Two Block here. Verne —that's the one with all the glass on top, right?"

"Yes."

"Yeah. Sorry to've bothered you. Be careful around here, daijobu?"

"Sure."

The other worker had come over. "Something wrong here, Stew?"

"No. Just a Lunar minding his own business. Tov, toda, friend."

"Ohaiyo gosaimasu."

The two workers went back to their slates. Matt thought about leaving right away, but if people were really suspicious of him, he wasn't going to reward it. After twenty minutes he went out, deciding to look for a likely place to eat nearby.

As he wandered, he passed a Disker chapel, with a circular dance floor tiled in glass mosaic. No one was dancing, though. Brightly dressed people sat around, apparently meditating in silence and solitude, something Matt had never seen Diskers do. But it wasn't his business, and he passed on.

Finally he found what he was looking for; and when he described it, the others agreed to follow.

It was called The Hanging Gardens, and it took up the whole above-ground height of One Block on the side facing the port. That wall was glass, almost obscured by flowering vines that trailed down in masses from the ceiling grid; they covered the grid too, a green canopy.

There were grassy slopes to either side, each with two tall elm trees, and a second deck halfway up in the center, paved and connected by rainbow bridges of refractive glass. There were lyrebirds perched in one of the elm trees, and a half-dozen little round ibises with long curved bills pecking at something in the grass. In one corner, behind a barely visible glassweb, two small Angos were cropping grass, looking with their heads down just like mounds of waving, silky long hair.

Tani Case was transported at once, of course; so was Raf, somewhat to Matt's surprise—and even more so, Jack went at once to one of the trees, looking for the most elegant way up it.

Ruby sat down on the grass, looking at her crossed ankles, hands in her lap. Matt thought she looked horribly close to crying. Then he thought he knew: it was too much like Sokoni, like home. He gestured quickly to Cissa, and they sat down flanking Ruby. "Look at this," Cissa said, and pulled her slate open.

It had the still she had taken at Tsio, of Matt sitting on the rock, looking into the distance, but she had worked on it. The background was still photoprecise, but the sitting figure in the suit now seemed to have been done with sharp diagonal strokes of paint on a palette knife, in glaring silvers and a red that might be visible without lights, bits of the darkness showing between the color.

Looking closer, Matt saw that Cissa had retouched the surface as well: there were phantom sparks of color in the surface, and a hint of gold in the boulder. There seemed to be something in the dark as well, black in black, but he couldn't quite discern what.

"I like it, Ciss," Ruby said, her voice firm.

There were food vendors all around the gardens. They got some duck-sausage casserole and strawberry fritters and warm rolls with plain and garlic and honey butters, and sat down by one of the elms to eat.

Not far away, at stools around a table, were three people Matt thought must be starship crew. They were wearing loop-and-tuck coveralls, with big and little sealable pockets and holding straps all over, and bright embroidered patches with the trademarks of component and service-chemical companies. One had a beat-up tasset computer strapped to the calf of her left leg, which made sense only out of gravity. They were *sitting* like crew, legs wrapping the chairs, hands always on the utensils, tucking them under their plates when they paused to sip a drink or gesture a point of conversation. The woman with the tasset was long-limbed, with straight black hair in bangs just to the tops of her ears, epicanthic folds, thin quick fingers. The other two were a massive dark man with curly hair cut short to his round head, and a woman with blond ringlets, very even features—Matt looked from her to Raf and back, and almost but not quite asked if anyone else saw the resemblance.

The black-haired woman leaned back, looked up into the heights of the tree behind her, reached out and stroked its bark with her fingertips.

Overhead, one of the lyrebirds screamed, a horrible sound that turned heads all over The Hanging Gardens. Then the bird fell from its perch, straight down in a streaming comet of colored feathers, and landed with a soft little thump a meter and a half away from the startled woman.

Everybody stared at it. The crew woman unlocked from her chair and knelt beside the body. She held out a hand, carefully, carefully, but the bird didn't move at all.

"Wha'd she *do* to it?" someone said.

Matt heard then—or thought he heard—a sort of low bass note, like a slowly bowed string. It came from no particular direction, and it oscillated, loud, soft, loud. "Do you hear that?" he said to Cissa, next to him, as softly as he could.

"Hear what?"

Tani said, just to their group, "She didn't do anything to the bird. They were just . . . sitting like us. . . ."

"Look at them just *sitting* there!" somebody shouted.

"—don't have to *live* anyplace—"

"—do what they please and then move on—"

"—move on *laughing* at us—"

The woman stood up. Someone—a Lunar in a Population Service blue jacket—came around the tree and shoved her, hard with both hands. She tumbled, tucking her feet up so that she didn't fall, but landed in a crouch with one arm in and one out.

Matt heard the thrumming rise in pitch, quicken its pulse. Another disturbance started up on the other side of the room, people jostling, shouting.

And then, abruptly, people—*Lunars*—were hitting each other, throwing loose objects, swinging fists and furniture with complete disregard of mass and force.

An alarm sounded, and everyone stopped who could stop: it was an undulating whine, the Fire alarm, not the insistent on-off scream of Decompression. Okay, Matt thought, he had been hearing the alarm, but he knew it wasn't so.

And after that moment the confusion started up again, worse than before. Smoke was rising from the far plot of grass. Nobody seemed to be paying attention. Matt looked around, trying to find some sense or explanation. He saw none, as the smoke rose and spread.

"We've got to move," he said to the others.

"Where?" Cissa said.

"Not as a bunch," Matt said, thoughts racing.
"Look, they're starting fights with groups. Scatter
and we'll all make it. Go like blueshift now, stop when
you're clear."

"But *where*?" Ciss said again, high-pitched, almost a scream.

"Train at three! Keep cool as you can till then,
but *train at three!*"

Ruby pulled at Cissa's arm, and they were gone.
Jack went up, shaking the tree. Tani disappeared like
a shadow in sunlight. Raf squeezed Matt's hand once,
let it go and skambled; Matt saw a droplet of molten
gold blaze through the crowd.

The blond crew was moving toward the other
woman; her face was calm and very determined. The
man was blocking interference around her. Someone
raised a length of hexrod in both hands and brought
it around in an arc with the blond woman's head as
endpoint; the dark man got his shoulder in the way,
grunted as the glass bounced off. Someone else aimed
a long leaping kick at the black-haired woman's
spine.

Matt leapt. The target woman half-turned, and
Matt caught her upper right arm; his momentum
took them both aerial, and the jumper plowed into
three more Lunars, all fall down.

Matt and the woman landed in the clear. "Come
on," Matt said, but the woman ignored him and
looked back. Her two companions were almost away
from the crowd, the blond woman nearly flying, the
man simply pistoning people aside with his thick
arms.

The blond woman made a gesture: Matt read it
as *Who's this?* and signaled back *This way urgent*.
They nodded. He turned and began skambling, terri-
fied to look back.

On the left, ahead, there was an opening. Matt
knew where it went. He hand-signaled for the turn,
not knowing if the right people were there to see and

awfully frightened the wrong ones were, then used
the hand to swing himself through the opening with
minimum loss of velocity.

Beyond were stairs down. He arched his back
and sailed down the passage without touching them;
at the bottom, he grabbed a ceiling strut and swung
off his speed, hearing himself gasp, nearly losing the
glass in sweaty hands. He turned. All three of the
crew were still with him, gliding and bouncing down
the stairway. From above, Matt could hear noise of
pursuit.

"Just a little farther," Matt said. "I don't think
they'll follow us far down here."

"I see what you mean," the blond woman said,
looking around at the masses of green dragonvine
surrounding them, the tables turning this way and
that by the obscure rules of the dragon fractal curve.

They rounded a corner, plunged on between the
planter tables. A distant shoggoth went clicketysnick, clicketysnick. Insects buzzed, and a pump began knocking.

The man said "There's no way out of this turn,"
and Matt saw he was right.

"Underneath," Matt said. "We just need to hide."
He slipped under the table, into the dark, damp tan-
gle of roots and plumbing. His shoe skidded in mud.
The others followed, the man last; he grimaced when
he used his left shoulder.

"Please be quiet," Matt said. His sinuses were
full of the stink of soil, and humidity touched his
skin with a revolting intimacy.

The blond woman said, calmly, "Yes, we'll do
that." She would be the captain, Matt thought, of
course.

He was trying to be Lafayette Lonestar, but it
just wasn't happening; Lonestar wouldn't say stupid
things like *be quiet,* and he wouldn't tremble.

Matt saw motion. He looked through the un-
dertangle, hoping desperately to see a Dragon-

master's gown, but he didn't: two, maybe three pairs of legs, a length of structural rod, a piece of a chair.

"They aren't here," one of the people said.

"I saw 'em come down here."

"You see anybody now?"

"Maybe they're trying to poison the plants."

"No!"

"Yeah!"

"Dirty vackers! Come-from-*noplace* vackers!"

"They think we'll buy our *air* from 'em too?"

"Toddywobbles think we'll sell 'em our *shit*?"

Matt turned as much as he dared. He tried to gesture what he was thinking, but couldn't; speaking low, he said "Have you got something I can throw?"

The man pulled a red metal spotlight out of a trouser loop, raising his eyebrows. Matt nodded and took it. It was thick as both his thumbs, filled his palm. He slipped back toward the edge of the table. Slowly, slowly, he looked over it.

The people from the restaurant—from the riot—were maybe ten meters away.

Matt threw the light, going for distance. It landed with a hiss and a plop in the dragonmass.

"What was that?"

"Over—"

Clickety*rack*. Clickety*raackraack*.

The shoggoths had noticed the disturbance, and two of them were rolling over to investigate, arms outstretched, tools ready. All they wanted to do was inspect and repair the plants, but as Matt had hoped, the people with the clubs didn't see them that way. "Lesget*outtahere*!" one said, and they retreated up the stairs.

Matt felt dizzy. The ship people helped him up. "Nice piece of work, fella," the man said. "You do this sort of thing often?"

"No," Matt said, and suddenly it seemed most important to make them understand—"We're not like that, really! We're—I don't *know* what happened—"

"It's all right," the black-haired woman said. "After what you've done, how could we blame you all?"

"It blew out fast, Hani," the blond crew said. She was looking warily through the dragoncoils. "You gather anything?"

"Only the mob throb," the black-haired woman said. "And that came very late. It was sudden."

"As the bird's death," the man said.

Matt said "Mob . . ."

The black-haired woman, Hani, said "A crowd of people under . . . a certain sort of stress tends to act like a single organism. When that happens, sometimes you can hear a low-pitched sound from them. Their breathing, their voices not quite speaking. It goes up and down, like a pulse."

"Like subsonics?" Matt said. "Subsonics make people upset, right?"

"Like that," the man said, sounding interested.

Hani said "We're traders. We're supposed to catch things like that before the trouble starts." She shut her eyes—eyes like Cissa's, Matt thought—for a moment. "At least, I am."

"Let that pass," said the blond woman.

Hani nodded, said to Matt, "How long should we stay down here, do you think?"

"Oh. Well, the dragon goes all over—" Matt suddenly wasn't certain if he still had his slate; he looked down, and there it was in its shoulder bag, and one of his hands was white-knuckled on it. "I can find another way out. Do you want to go to—your ship?"

"Perhaps not right away," the blond woman said. "By the way, I'm Diana Heraklios. Captain and Master of the *Fata Morgana*. To introduce Hani Lancaster, Accounts and Cultures." The black-haired woman nodded, said "No relation to the unfortunate vessel."

Matt remembered: the ship that had had the bad accident was the something *Lancaster*.

"And the Perfect Master of All Things Mechanical, Button Dutton."

"Really," the man said. "Really Button, I mean. If it were a nickname I could get rid of it."

"Matthias Ronay. Very pleased."

"That," Captain Heraklios said, "is mutual."

There was a pause. They all just stood there. Matt noticed the others were breathing just as hard as he was.

"I believe, Captain," Lancaster said, "that you are about to be in code violation unless . . ."

The Captain held up a hand. "I know. Mister—hoot, Hani, it is 'Mister'?"

"Yes, Captain."

"Mister Ronay, in recognition of your considerable service to myself and crew, what, within budget and inventory, may I do for you?"

Just like this? Matt thought, *just like this?*

And he couldn't. Could not. He had the team to get home, he had a promise to Gil—

But oh, he couldn't *not:* and He, *He Himself,* had said it, the morning Matt had left for the train. *Remember that courage is all you have to get ahead on; if you see your chance, take it ere it's lost.*

"Do you have," he said, bravely as he could (because it was still Matt, not Lonestar; Lonestar didn't need chances), "a job? For me, on your ship?"

Captain Heraklios put a hand to her forehead. Dutton broke into a broad grin. Lancaster whistled long and low.

The Captain took her hand away, looking at the mud on it, then peering up at her marked forehead. "I said it, didn't I?"

"You used the language," Dutton said, "as we must all stand witness."

The Captain said "Don't you live here? Have a family?"

Dutton said "He's not tradecrew. Yet. Tell him the backprint."

The Captain said "God in an n-body system."

Lancaster said "The Captain offered you, in formal trade language, any favor that was not impossible or ruinous financially. We have space for you. So we are obligated."

"You have the forms, Hani?"

"I do," Matt said, opened his slate and brought up the standard contract.

"No, wait," the Captain said. "Can we at least get this kackavine stuff off and sit down to tune this deal?"

Matt used the slate screen to find them an exit, and a public washroom, and then a small, deserted lounge on the side of One Block away from the port.

"You do have a family, correct?" the Captain said.

"Yes."

"What will they offer on this?"

"How will they feel, Matt?" Lancaster said. "Could we talk with them?"

"They're not here. They're at Copernicus." Matt realized he had said that too quickly.

"Long way off," Dutton said.

The Captain said "It will not valve off the tension here if we . . . abduct you, just after the *Duke of Lancaster* incident."

Matt nodded. So much for that.

Button Dutton said "It's no abduction, Diana, and if it doesn't valve it won't piston either. Word's been out for a perfectly long enough while that Terralune was going through an Us First phase, as who the blue doesn't. At least nobody shot at us here—"

Captain Heraklios made a small sharp gesture, and Dutton stopped.

Matt said, quite without thinking, "Someone shot at you?"

Hani Lancaster said "It was more a pointing of guns than a hail of fire. It is as old as are ships: those with a nation, we without."

Matt could feel sweat stand out on the back of his neck. All the times he had shouted *Slammer!* were hissing in his ears.

He said, in a voice that would not stay level, "If you don't want me aboard, I won't go. It doesn't matter what you said."

The Captain said "It *does* matter what I promise. And have any of us said we do not want you?"

Dutton said "Hani was born to thrust and no-g, but the Captain and m'self climbed on pretty much like you are." He began to pronounce each word distinctly and separately, as if he were quoting something: "It is a long free fall, and full of doubt each meter and second."

The Captain said "What can you do aboard?" She held up a finger, to delay Matt's answer. "I know you've got motors and metal. But what skills have you got? Hear me right on this: if you're useless to us, that's our deadfreight till your contract's up. But if you're useless to *you,* and you know it . . ."

"I can run data. TECHNET especially, but I know some of the trade models. I can do some first aid, like Button's shoulder—" Dutton nodded approvingly. "I know Sympla, and . . . and the rest you'll have to teach me, I guess."

"Will you do this?" Captain Heraklios said, and raised a finger again, this time to Lancaster. "I made a deal, I can still codicil it. We're due to be on Luna for about eight hundred more hours. Some goods coming from Mars on the roundabout. I'll sign your contract, if you'll go home, and talk to your family about it."

Matt said "You'll be here—"

"No loss in one orbit. We'll go to Copernicus after the Mars goods are aboard. That'll be about seven-fifty hours. If we do that, will you cube this square?"

"Yes," Matt said.

Captain Heraklios took Matt's slate and signed

with a fingertip. "That's done, then." She stood up. "We should go back to the ship now."

Matt looked at the time. 0214. It had all happened just like that. "I have to get back to my friends too."

Button Dutton said, word-by-word, as if finishing his earlier sentence, "And this long doubt's the only life there is."

Matt went straight down to the train terminal, sat down to wait. That was no good at all. Should he ping them? The train would leave in, what now, an hour-twenty-seven, if they needed help he mustn't wait until there was no time to give it. . . .

Tani would be somewhere green. Raf and Jack were probably in a Maze or a gym. Cissa—maybe somewhere with a fine view, or maybe looking for Matt, say at the theatre. Ruby . . .

As he paced, he saw that Ruby and Ciss were already in the waiting lounge, huddled over books and tea and pie; Ciss sprang up and hugged Matt, and the three of them reassured each other that it would be all right until that would hold no more air, and by mutual consent they pinged the others. All safe and breathing. All in the places Matt had guessed.

"Where did you end up?" Ruby said.

"I went down into the dragon space," he said. "They didn't follow."

And that was all he said about it.

They would see through it at once, of course: even if Matt boarded the ship at Copernicus, it would be easy as pinging TECHNET to find out where it had been before. And the contract was dated; it had to be, to be valid. After all the care they had taken to establish that they were together, Matt could hardly claim he had gone halfway around Luna *alone*.

If he got on the ship, he betrayed the trip and the whole team. There was no possible way around that.

And he *had* a work contract. He had made a deal with Gil Vela. Was he supposed to break that, and then demand that Captain Heraklios keep a promise she had made without thinking?

What was it the Captain had said, cursing to herself? *God in an n-body system.* There were too many forces acting on Matt, too many sudden masses in too many directions. He could not even tell the team what had happened, what was hidden in his slate's memory, because that would seem to push the decision on them.

It was a long trip back. They read, they slept, after passing terminator near Hubble they watched out the windows, the endless monochrome scope-tracing of mountains and sky.

Ruby pitched, between DVC and Serenity, but it all went wrong. Matt knew what she had intended: it was going to be the final ride of the greenwood rebels. Some of them might die the real lightdeath, nobly and valiantly of course, perhaps saving the returned King Richard from the last desperate ploy of his bad brother John. Colin de Courcy was going to die brilliantly; everyone could see that. Theo would disappear into her forests. Bowstring—who could tell? Lonestar supposed he was meant to survive, be rewarded by the rightful King with lands and titles, and then merge those lands with Baroness Judith's; *hieros gamos,* Raf called it through Colin (in self enough, Colin was an educated man). Eventually the two of them would—no, not die, not really. Fade into gold, into light, into sunset. "Bury us where this arrow shall land . . ."

It didn't play like that. They lurched from danger to danger, avoiding ridiculous, useless deaths by the continuous finger of Ruby-in-the-Sky; and the finger shook, as fielders forgot who they were supposed to be, what they were supposed to be doing. The returning Richard turned out to be an impostor, who died dangling in a noose dropped by Bowstring from

an oak bough. Nothing was resolved. It was a long
fifteen hours from Serenity City to home port.

At midnight, as they walked off the train, like
outfielders unlighted by wit, Ruby said "Well, we
made it," and that seemed to finish things as properly
as they could be done. Matt wanted to say something
to them all, to Cissa especially, but he had only one
small thought; and if he called her "Judith" now, it
would not be kind or pleasant but mean and small.

Matt nearly fell asleep on the local train. He
stumbled into the house, found it mercifully dark,
went to his room. He stripped, sponged, crawled na-
ked into his own bed. He had been afraid that the
room, the sounds and scent and textures, would seem
strange. But they were familiar. So maybe there was
hope after all. He slept.

Sonya Ronay came out of the bedroom, went
into the darkened study where Albin was sitting,
watching the house security display on the huge wall
screen, the three spots of life.

"He's home?" she said.

"The train was precisely on time," Ronay said.
"He came straight here, went right to bed. I can't say
I blame him."

"What are you going to do?" Sonya's voice had
never been musical, but its tone was always so perfect
—Handel's *Water Music*—that it often came near to
breaking Ronay's heart; he supposed that his heart
was no longer breakable, or it would have done so
now.

"I'm going to wait," he said, "and when he
comes out, I will ambush him, and ask what I have to
ask." He looked at her, a pale shape in the doorway.
"You're working tomorrow. You should sleep."

"I won't. Not without you. That's just a fact, Albin."

"Yes," he said, not sure himself what he meant
by it, and went into the bedroom with her hand tight
in his.

When Matt woke, he knew what to do. He would go to see Gil, and talk about the theatre, the Company; that would make him strong enough. Then, once he was strong, he would erase the contract from his slate, and it would be over. He would have to call the Captain, of course, but that would wait.

His father was sitting in the living room. A slate was open on the table, among a pile of nonce-books and reports. "Would you wait, Matt? Please."

"What is it?"

"Would you like some juice?"

"All right. Thank you."

"Would you sit down, please?"

Matt sat, feeling hollow inside.

Ronay handed him a sheet of paper, a picture. "Have you ever seen this man before, Matt?"

Matt's palms stung with sweat. It was the man from the train, from Tsiolkovsky: Robert Ostrow. His name was right there on the docs print. An instant after Matt registered that, his father said "Specifically, I have to know if you saw him at Mendeleev. Around The Hanging Gardens riot."

Matt's hands shook. He stared at the paper; he couldn't look up.

"I need to know, Matt, and I haven't any time. The vues of the riot have been gone over to the last micrometer, everyone who could possibly be identified has been. You were there, you all were. We know what train you came back on, and we're reasonably sure which ones you went out on."

Ronay's voice was calm, quiet. "I'm upset that you lied to me, Matt, about where you were going. But it's over, you're back, that just doesn't matter now. This *does* matter. Did you see that man anytime at Mendeleev?"

"No," Matt said. "He wasn't at Mendeleev."

"He wasn't?"

"He got on the train at DVC, and got off with us at Tsio. He didn't come back when we did—at least, not in the sleepers—and there weren't any other trains before the—thing happened."

"I see."

"Is that all—you want to know?"

"Wait. *Please.* I said I'd seen the vues. That means I saw what you did, for those crew people. I'm very proud of you for that, Matt. In fact, that's really the most important thing about any of this. I'd like to tell the crew that."

"May I use the printer, please?" Matt said.

"Of course."

Matt went into the study, linked his slate to the machine. It only took a moment. The contract was only a couple of pages, since there was little for it to specify in the way of duties or obligations. Matt brought the paper back and put it in his father's lap.

Ronay said "They gave you this as a reward for helping them?"

"Yes."

"The ship is still on Luna? This is only valid until it leaves our space."

"Yes, I know."

"What are you going to do with this, Matt?"

"Nothing."

He started for the door, but his father stopped him with a raised hand. Ronay took a pen out of his pocket, flipped to the last page of the contract, and countersigned it. He held it out to Matt. "What," he said slowly, "do you *want* to do with it?"

Matt took the paper, much too frightened to speak. He sat down, on the floor.

Ronay touched keys on the slate. A man in hospital uniform appeared on the screen. Ronay said "Can you put me through to Dr. Ronay, please? Yes, it is important. Thank you." Then it was Matt's mother's face. "Sonya . . ." Ronay drew a long breath. "Matt is going to need a wiring operation. For starcrew. Nervnya net i Apparat Syertse. Very quickly; can it be arranged? Yes, of course you will."

Matt felt his hands crumpling the contract. He stopped them. Somehow, it was happening the way *he* wanted after all; Matt didn't understand at all, but he could hear it in his father's voice. The sound of another triumph.

Matt thought that he should have known.

Ronay looked straight into the slate. He didn't dare look at Matt; he wondered how he dared face Sonya. It suddenly seemed inevitable that it would end like this, giving orders for work he could not do himself. He needed a committee action to split up his own family. He should have known.

Sonya Ronay absorbed what Albin was saying, standing quite still before the phone screen, her hands folded calmly on the buttons in her wrists. She would need two or three days, naturally. The procedure was routine enough, the components were always in stock, but OR time had to be reserved, as well as a patient room for the first few days' recovery. And it would be better if one of the endosurgeons, Rene Jarrell or Evan Augustine, put the heart booster in. She would assist. And the wiring, that would be hers. She would have to check the schedules on the assist teams. People would be available, when the word got out.

Albin took forever to finish. He was trying to say it all now, the explanation and the apology and the reassurance. She would have to let him negotiate it through. A year, perhaps, for the preliminaries, until he stopped haunting Matt's room, listening for music in the silence. She would find a way to make him work on the symphony he'd hinted at; a temporary kind of child, but it would help them.

She keyed a number, found the person in, though less than fully awake, explained the situation.

"Thank you for telling me, Sonya," Lawrence Duveen said.

"Albin would have told you himself."

"I'm certain he will. But I may have some idea of what to say now." He sighed. "I do so love to be spontaneously wise."

She said "I think you suspected something like this would happen. Sooner or later."

Duveen nodded. "With all love and respect to you, Sonya, Matt's a Ronay. No society can hold him, once it becomes a settled society. Albin lacks the advantage to understand that." Softly, he said "It took a generation too many for your sake. I'm sorry for that, Sonya."

"And for you."

"Oh no, not I. But thank you anyway. If I can ever—if my presence will ever solve more problems than it creates—"

"You are always welcome here, Larry."

He bowed his head politely, said "Gokuro-san," and broke the link.

Gokuro-san was not just "thank you"; it was "thank you for your effort beyond the call of duty."

She pinged the grocery then, asking them to assemble the components for chicken cutlets Kiev. She would pick them up on the way home, prepare them tonight.

It took three days, all told, to assemble the right team, unpack Matt's red cells from storage, plan the operations. Dr. Jarrell had deferred to Dr. Augustine, citing both the patient's youth and the complications of his new position as Chief of Exosurgery.

Dr. Augustine, who carefully and deliberately said "Matt" and not "the patient" in even the most technical discussions, asked that they do the heart first, wiring second. He said that this was to balance the recovery times, test Augustine's ideas on connecting the Syertse electrical outputs to the nervnya net, have more time to monitor thoracic healing, and other medically acceptable reasons. Sonya understood the real reason. All the surgical team did. Sonya was to be the last surgeon inside.

So, after another 125 hours, here she was, her eyes two filaments of glass, her feet microturbines, her hands a laser and a nanotool cable, laying glass conduit in the soft universe of Matt's body.

Cells were nudged aside to let her pass; erythrocytes swam by indifferently in plasma space, leukocytes pausing now and then to observe, inspect the visitor's credentials. Once in a while a T cell took exception to her presence and intruded; wind up the laser from illuminate to destroy then, and fragments of the overeager cell drifted away, plucked at by the tool head, devoured by the next soldier in line.

She could pick up sound through optical feedback; rustlings, blood flow, the drum of Matt's heart. Her own breathing and heart were there too; Bill Chamberlain had taught her that, quite contrary to what the standard text said. "You need to know when you're tired," he explained. "You need to know when you're excited, nervous. The *patient's* sedated, he's having a nice quiet time of it, and furthermore he has a very hard time messing up."

Sensor beads were strung along the lines: electrical, physical (temperature, pressure, stress and torsion), chemical in a dozen flavors: transmitters, enkephalins, pH . . . up the line were feedback triggers, stepping up the speed and efficiency of the body's response to its own condition.

Nerve bridges on major motor arcs, because photons in glass are faster than polarity change in natural nerve. MicrO$_2$ stores along primary muscles, for a last bit of stamina, an extra few minutes of survival in black vac.

And because Matt was still young, still growing, expansion helices throughout the system. In another hundred thousand hours, there would almost certainly have to be maintenance surgery, where the glass had worn, or been invaded by fibrins, or Matt's actual maturation had taken a different route than their predictions. A hundred thousand hours from now . . . she might well be alive, able enough. So much might happen.

At the medulla, at the solar plexus, at the main coupling to the sinoatrial node and Apparat Syertse drivers, she wound up the laser again, steering the microturbines to burn nanogrooves into biopoxy couplings: she started to write SRG, Sonya Ronay Gurdzhian, then stopped. Just SR.

There was a broad conduit by the left kidney, just a confluence of minor wires, a low-maintenance area. No one was ever likely to inspect this one. So that was where she cut in MATT I LOVE YOU, a long burn, frightening the leukocytes no end.

She was beginning to tire; she could hear it in her breathing, feel the somatic alarm as the control wire hit the limits of safe motion. Pause. Rest. Recover.

She leaned back in the chair, reached out with her left thumb to spin the moral equivalent of a fader wheel. The stereo view dimmed, the operating room showed through. Above, in the gallery, Albin was watching. A boy and a girl were there with him.

From the gallery, Albin Ronay looked down at his wife and his son, both enveloped in glass and metal.

Cissa Luna Okuda and Raf Economou were with him. Ruby Rincon was still inconsolable; Sam Rincon said she came out of her room once in two or three days to stockpile food. Sam was letting Tatiana Casimirovna camp in the Rincons' living room, hoping for a glimpse of, a word to Ruby in passing. Weiszäcker, the one they called String, had disappeared completely; the train stations had been asked to report him if seen.

Ronay watched Economou and the Okuda girl; they were watching the online monitors with a care and intentness that amazed him. Oboe, he thought, and violin for her. Or perhaps she was an alto saxophone. From time to time they held hands, but it did not seem to be romantic affection. He tried to think of himself at that age, think which . . . or both . . . ? The boy might have stepped off a pedestal in Athens, the girl seemed to have that power of heart that, if a man could only find time to see it, he would prize above all other sorts of beauty.

Ronay caught himself wishing that these two would fall in love, and felt silly at the thought, and a little ashamed.

But what next, he wondered, what next for any of them?

Work, of course.

"Councillor Ronay?"

Ronay turned. It was the floor receptionist. "There's a message for you, Councillor. From Population Services. I told them you weren't to be disturbed, but they were *very* insistent."

"It's all right, Violet. Where can I take it?"

"Consulting room one. Just across the hall."

Ronay stood. At the door, he took a look back at the observation window, the wire's-eye monitors; at Okuda and Economou, who were watching him with a silent intensity that was not quite the same as curiosity. Ronay wondered if this was how they would remember him ever after: the man walking out on Matt because somebody wanted to talk about the interminable water crisis.

He crossed the hall, went into the consulting room. It had a table, a few chairs, a large wall display. He touched his receive point into a block on the table.

He could not help what the kids thought of it, just as he could not help what he did. He was contributing nothing to the surgery; Matt could not see him and Sonya was occupied. Still, if this could be put off . . .

The screen lit up. For a moment Ronay thought he was in the wrong room, was seeing a vue on emergency medicine. Then someone in Popsy blue, with a Security ribbon and Mendeleev badge, moved into

view, and Ronay registered who the mess on the floor
had been.

The person explained the particulars to Ronay,
who banked, thanked, and blanked. He sat for a moment, stood up; he felt suddenly nauseated. He stumbled to the door. A message. It had been a message,
sent by one of their own, in that singularly theatrical
fashion that the Wynants kept for special occasions.

But what was the message saying?

Ronay tried to think of something else, before
he should frankly throw up on the hospital floor. He
paused at the gallery door, but there was no explanation to be made. At least, not yet. Soon, perhaps. He
left the pass tag and a message with the receptionist
and left the hospital.

He took a train to Old Landing, walked up from
Transport level and turned down a corridor that was
quiet even for the Landing. After passing through a
couple of spinneys, he was in a small annex that had,
a generation before he was born, been Lunar Customs
and Immigration. The whole place was smaller than
the Ronays' home; it was curious to think that it had
once been sufficient for the whole world. Now there
were just a couple of empty pallets and a crate, a
stack of construction rods, scraps of cel and plycore.
Here and there short square pylons stuck up a few
decs from the floor: dataline couplings, where the service counters had stood.

A long window, chest to head height, showed
Lunar horizon and some of the grounding area. The
room was actually on sub-one level; the window was a
periscope, two Lunarcast front-surface mirrors with
a vacuum chamber between. But the view was blurred
and smudgy. Air must have gotten into the space between the mirrors. Air and moisture, clouding the
illusion.

He had played here, irredeemable years ago,
Ronay and his Musketeer Company, his Revolutionary Council, his happy few. Here they had touched

the soil of new worlds, saved France from conspiracy and Luna from reconquest by the alien armies of Earth.

They had held grave trials, seated on the datapipes like King Lear passing judgment on furniture, and sentenced the beaten Heavies to Execution Lock, conveniently to hand.

And now here he was, a heavy man himself.

Humanity, Ronay thought with the philosophy of desperation, had always fought gravity. Leaps, climbs, flight, Luna, Mars, the deep beyond; there were already people who lived innocent of weight, and one could hear talk of a generation after that, with bones only for convenience, with all limbs equal, humans fully three-dimensional.

Those children's parents would know, with all the wondrous testability of scientific proof, that while the nature of matter is universally to draw together, the tendency of the universe is to fly apart; and the knowledge would do nothing, nothing, nothing at all to soften the pain when their children drifted away. They would suppose that it was for some purpose, had some eventual meaning, for there is a certain providence in quantum observation; but again they would know that uncertainty is in the fabric of all things, and the purpose and the meaning might never be known, were in some sense never knowable.

Their tears would float as weightless spheres, crystalline, perfect. Perhaps, because of that, they would find it easier to accept that children are weightless both by nature and tendency.

Ronay doubted it very much.

He had to go home now. Work.

Ronay stood in front of his study screen, using it in touch mode, moving docs and stills around on the big display with his fingertips. It was like working a puzzle, with too many of the pieces missing and no clear idea of the final picture. He did not even know if time counted.

Here was The Vacuum Corporation's offer for a bizarre discount on a Waterhole study, with its half-hidden hint that the Kepler's value was about to go into freefall. Ronay slid and linked that to a MOON-GAME run, testing the effects of a starcrews' boycott of cargo-clumsy, violence-prone Luna.

Here were Robert Ostrow's docs, tied to a reconstruction of his movements, and Matt's comments on his behavior at Tsiolkovsky. Also a paper on population-group dynamics in small, relatively stable nations, with no authors named but produced by the Aldine Project on Earth. Lynch Ballantine said that Ostrow had been part of Aldine.

Here, Ronay's notes on Ballantine's recent activities, movements, statements. He pushed those to one side, with the report on Leon Avakian. Everyone Ronay had contacted was surprised to hear that Avakian was still alive. Avakian would not be questioned. He was too old, too frail, too unreal: the A of MIRAGE, an historical abstraction.

Lunar etiquette: Avakian was disqualified; Wynant had disqualified himself; Ostrow would be on his way home and wet in thirty hours, unless Ronay could find some qualification for him. Missing pieces.

Over here, the TECHNET listing of *Duke of Lancaster*'s cargo, the crew's deposition that they had declared accurately and had no idea where the warning signs had gotten to. And here, the statements by the Captain and Cargomaster of *Fata Morgana* that they had no contact with *Lancaster* or her crew, and had never met or heard of Matthias Ronay before their meeting in Mendeleev.

Down here, the forensic report on C. C. Wynant, the knife, the patterns of arterial spray across the room. A note that while Ostrow had never provably been at Mendeleev City, the train carrying him (and Matt) to Tsiolkovsky had stopped there for one hour;

and none of Matt's company had gotten off to witness anything.

A lot could happen in an hour. A great deal of data could pass.

Ronay sketched in connecting lines, traced notes. Suppose you wanted the Lunar economy to—not fail, but come under pressure. Or that you wanted it to learn self-reliance, stop depending on offworld trade. Suppose you wanted to discredit VACOR TECHNET, or to frame someone else for the attempt, or to show how a less respected, new datanet could be brought down.

Desire was a commodity. Choose a reality, the circumstances would rush to fit it. Ronay understood that with time, possibly with more evidence, he might know what had happened: but now he was only simulating, playing, baudrillating.

He had done nothing of any real use in the heavy world, but it had given him something: the fourth movement of the symphony he couldn't write.

Dry water, loud silence, speechless voices. Then for the fourth movement, turn the first three into a fugue; tumble them over each other until the sounds refracted, like facets and striations in a rainbow glass bridge.

He tapped the picture of C. C. Wynant's apartment, and it blinked out with a green afterflash. He filed another page, another. He had to put all this away now. Very soon, Sonya would be home from surgery, and (though she would not enter the study) he must not be doing this when she arrived.

When she did, he thought, he would be in the front room, playing his old black clarinet. Gershwin, Glenn Miller. *Blue Moon.*

There were still more people to talk to. Ronay reached to the pad.

Matt heard a knock at the door, reached out to the bedside panel. It had been several days since the surgery; he was no longer immobilized, but was sup-

posed to stay in bed, and there were still metal-and-
glass frames caging his arms and legs, a thick plastic
device strapped over his chest. His arm got hung up
on the bedrail as he touched a key. He wondered if Gil
Vela ever felt like this, when his plastic parts were
on.

The screen showed his parents waiting outside
the door. "Come in," he said.

The door opened. Matt's mother went directly to
the monitor boards on the wall, out of Matt's line of
sight; his father stood at the foot of the bed.

"I know you will be uncomfortable," Sonya
Ronay said, "but is there pain?"

"No. It feels . . . kind of hot."

Sonya checked a display. "That's normal. We
can't use anesthetic current and restructure current
at the same time. It doesn't keep you awake?"

"No." Nothing seemed to keep him awake for
more than an hour or two. He had actually fallen
asleep while Cissa was visiting. There hadn't been
much said, really, and she had been afraid to touch
him. Stringer had wanted to touch everything, feel
the wires in the skin, but a nurse had finally warned
him off.

Raf had brought him a book, an actual hard-
covered paper book printed on Earth; it was a history
of the Trojan War, with beautiful color stills of
Greece. It was clearly too precious to accept—and for
just that reason too generous to refuse.

Ruby hadn't come to visit at all. Sam Rincon
came by, and they talked about structural glass and
biopoxy, and Sam was clearly trying to explain about
Ruby, and failing.

Albin Ronay said "You'll be out of here in fifty
hours. They'll want you in a chair for a few days after
that, though."

Sonya said "And you'll *stay* in it."

Ronay said "Captain Heraklios is looking forward to having you aboard. And the Engineer, Dutton, says hello."

Matt nodded.

Ronay said "I suppose things will be busy, after you get home. You'll want to decide what you're taking along—the Engineer sent a pak on your cabin allowances."

"Could you put that through here, please?"

"If you want, son. As I say, there may be sort of a hurry on, once you're home, with so much that needs to be done . . . We may not get to talk much."

Matt tensed. He wasn't going anywhere at this moment, that was certain.

"You will have work to do," his mother said, "and I know that you will do it well. That—doing your work as well as you know it can be done, whatever less someone else may expect—that is what will keep you sound in yourself, Matt. That is what life is *for*."

Ronay said "I know . . . you haven't always been happy here."

You *know*? Matt thought, what do you *know*?

Ronay said "We want you to be happy. But you have to know that happiness is a made thing. You have to . . . pursue it, as the Charter says. And you must, *must*, make it for other people, to have any for yourself."

Matt said "The greatest good for the greatest number?" He said it from anger, meaning to hurt, with the sudden intense awareness that he *could* hurt them; but it came out not angry but uneven, in what Gil Vela would call broken meters.

"Yes, that's it," Ronay said, "that's just it," his own meter strained and creaking, "the greatest good for the greatest number. If you understand *that*, son —then there's nothing more I need to tell you." A moment's pause, and then a rush: "I'm proud of you, son —wonderfully proud of you. And I think I'm proudest of you for knowing that."

Matt couldn't speak. First he was shocked by the empty old phrase suddenly seeming to mean something; hard on that was the shock of his own eagerness to hurt, which seemed the ugliest, meanest thing he had ever encountered, in anyone, or anything, and in *himself*—

His bones and infiltrated nerves itched and burned; he wanted them to flash into fire, burn him away to nothing at once.

Of course it didn't happen. His mother just touched his father's arm, and checked the monitors again, and then they said goodbye and left the room.

"I will be along in a moment," Sonya said to Albin in the corridor. "I raised his heart to sixty-five, since he'll be upright soon. I should tell the floor team."

"I'll be in the lobby," Ronay said, and pulled her close enough to kiss.

When Ronay reached the lobby, Gil Vela was sitting on the arm of a chair; he had both legs on, but only his natural arm. Two small children crouched awed as Vela made his earring vanish and reappear with a snap of his fingers. Finally he tossed it into space and nothingness, said "All gone!" and the children ran across the room to a bemused adult, bubbling over.

Vela said "Did it go well?"

"Yes. That little scene—"

"Are you quoting?" Vela said lightly, kindly. "No matter. There are two kinds of people who laugh at Polonius advising his son: those who've played him and those who aren't yet aware they've played him."

"I owe you something, still. For the advice."

"You haven't got an actor to give me, and the Water Board doesn't fund the arts." After an awkward moment, he said merrily, "We're always appreciative of season-ticket buyers. And you and Sonya haven't been to the Earthlight Grand Cotillion in forever. Foolishly, I can't help saying it, I should like to see you dancing."

"Are *you* quoting?"

" 'S just my job." He started to rise, then said "Oh. I remember promising you I would tell you about the affair with Ballantine and VACOR."

"No. It isn't my business. As you say, I have nothing to do with arts funding."

"Different buckets at the same well," Vela said weightlessly.

"I suppose so. Thank you again, Gil."

Vela gave a one-armed shrug, shook Ronay's hand and went out whistling. Ronay turned away, shut him out; his head was too full of fragile music already, and he must not lose it. Not it too.

Half a skyday later, dressed in a black wool tailcoat, stiff white cotton shirt and a satin ascot, Ronay pressed the annunciator at VACOR's office door.

Lynch Ballantine answered the door himself; Jori was busy on the phone. "A formal visit, Albin?" he said, indicating Ronay's clothes. Ballantine himself was wearing a gold silk suit, no shirt, soft Angoleather slippers. "And after all this time with no sight of you at all? Do come in."

Ronay entered, returning Jori's wave. They went back to the wood-paneled room. Ronay said "I'm on my way to a concert. I have a ticket for you, if you'd care to come."

"Oh. Jori would probably appreciate it more."

"I have one for her as well."

"Us as a couple? Wouldn't that amuse the crowd! You're conducting—something of yours?"

Ronay handed Ballantine the tickets. Ballantine read "*Fourfold Antiphony*. This is, what, your sixth?"

"That's right."

"Regrets about C. C. Wynant."

"There are acceptable ways for Lunars to kill themselves," Ronay said. "Having it obviously *be* suicide is not among them, though I can respect his wanting the issue entirely clear."

"Who is the new Board member for Mendeleev?"

"Masina de Ruyter. She's second-generation. New to all this."

"She comes . . . unentangled, then."

"I hope so."

There was a pause.

Ballantine said "Do you know what a smoking gun is, Albin? No, of course you do. I've told you already that I don't know why Bobby Ostrow came to Luna, and I tell you now that if I could have given you a reason for holding him here I'd have done so. Even if the worst you could have done was send him home forever."

"You see the time," Ronay said. "Are you coming?"

"I'm thinking. Will Sonya and Matthias be there?"

"Sonya will. Matt . . . isn't on Luna any longer."

Ballantine stared, his light eyes wide. "Yes?"

"He was asked to join a starcrew."

"Albin, is this part of the same conversation?"

"He earned his way aboard. I had nothing to do with it."

"I'm genuinely pleased, Albin. No, truly: I am unambiguously happy for your son, and for you and Sonya."

"Thank you, Lynch."

"And yet, my spirit betrays all good will: Would you have made something like this happen, if it had not happened?"

"The Project is still an open question as far as I'm concerned. Though if it does come to that decision, I'm certain someone will be available to throw the switch."

Ballantine leaned against the wall of the corridor that led back to his private apartment. "You must have known that the Corporation could never have accepted a . . . young person in the Locker's seat. The plan, after all, is for many IMTs to come after—dozens, hundreds. Until it is as ordinary as dying. Eventually, I imagine, there will be determined children with appropriate illnesses. But not the first time out."

"Is that what you personally imagine? Or—"

Ballantine slipped his jacket off. His chest was hairless, muscular, the skin creased as a much older man's. His left flank was covered by a white starburst of scars, like the rays of Tycho crater. He stroked the marks absently. "I am in the always pleasant position of understanding two sides who will not ever understand each other. VACOR truly believes that everything off Earth is the frontier their ancestors ruined and lost; they are *convinced* that, being revolutionaries, frontier settlers, you find it easy to die for an idea. But you don't. Not even if it were your own idea."

"What don't we understand about VACOR?"

"Two things." His eyes were narrowed on Ronay, direct and—there was just no other word—evil. "One, you won't remember that Luna broke away not from the whole Earth, but from a specific circle of nations; those cut-up flags in Verne Center. VACOR's roots are planted elsewhere. Two, that the object—"

"Of power is power."

"No. The other thing that O'Brien explained. The object of torture is torture."

Ronay said "I must go."

"Just give me a moment to cover myself decently. Tell Jori she's going too; give my fellow Lunars full opportunity to imagine what wickednesses I commit on her innocence."

The Hub Auditorium was full. Ballantine and Jori took seats in the reserved box, along with Sonya and half a dozen others. Gil Vela was there, wearing all his limbs in a formal suit; he exchanged a quiet

word with Lynch Ballantine. Ballantine sat down, his
hand on Jori's, his expression that of a man beyond
the power of Life and Death.

Ronay shook hands with Vela and Jason
Olivetti, then went up on the platform. There was ap-
plause.

May Abberline, in a long blue dress of Frame
silk, stepped forward. "On behalf of the Symphony,
we'd like to thank you all for attending this performance of an experimental new work . . . and I'm
sure you join all of us in the hope that this repre-
sents, at the very least, a much more frequent return
to this stage for today's composer. Now, conducting
his newest work . . . Albin Ronay."

The baton came up, held for a long moment,
came down.

A drop of dust fell into a sea of dryness.

Matt watched, and listened, on the screen in his
cabin aboard *Fata Morgana*. They were almost to the
safe MIRAGE distance; the image and sound were almost four seconds out of date.

The things he had decided to bring were still
mostly packed. The cabin hardly seemed big enough
to hold it all, and he was still getting used to the need
to lock down absolutely *everything* in zero-g, no matter how short a time you meant to take your hand
off it.

In a clear plastic bin near the screen were Raf's
book and dataslides from the others. Cissa had given
him her drawings, naturally, including the one she
had begun at Tsiolkovsky. Jack's was the complete
works of Rafael Sabatini. Tani Case had taken a camera all over Copernicus, vueing everything.

He had saved Ruby's for last, a little nervous—
she had never come to see him, never sent a ping or a
pak. When he loaded the chip, it turned out to be all
her game data, and clips of them in the best of their
runs, right up to the last one before the Tsio trip.

After that ended, Ruby appeared, sitting on her

bed in her red silk robe. She had been crying before
she started the record, and broke down again and
again. She screamed at him, but it was worse when
she spoke quietly; then she was intense, Rubylaser-
light beaming feelings about herself, about him, that
Matt had never imagined she had or could have. Be-
trayal. Being alone—not cold but *alone*. Wanting to
touch.

Could he have known? If he had been looking,
would he have seen past the characters, past Ruby-in-
the-Sky, to this—was this really Ruby-in-Herself?

She wasn't playing, that was certain. She was
hurt. He had done it. Whether or not she ever stopped
hurting, he would always have done it.

It went on for almost an hour. She finished by
explaining that the chip was flash storage: he could
erase it all if he wanted, but not keep the game and
wipe her solo.

He was still trembling a little, thinking about it,
wondering if he had ever really known anything
about anyone's real thoughts. It was not fair, Matt
had thought often enough, that people expected him
to know what they knew—about rules, manners, bodies, the awful power of hidden feelings. For the first
time he saw that knowing could be just as unfair.

There was a knock at the door. Matt floated off
his bunk, which took up more than a third of the
total cabin volume. "Yes?"

"Virgins to the bridge," Button Dutton said
from the connecting tube. Matt had been warned that
there was some kind of mildly embarrassing cere-
mony in store.

He opened the door, a square of epoxy seven
decs across, drifted through into the main tube. Dutton was floating, hands folded behind his head. "All
set?"

"Yeah." He followed Dutton through the winds
of the tube, emerging on the bridge. It was a half-
sphere of glass, seats and consoles mounted every

which way. The whole crew, fourteen plus Matt, were arranged around the space.

Matt looked past them, at the flare of the Sun, reversed to black by the viewing glass. Two smaller lights hung below it. "Is that—"

"The bright one's Earth," said Eddie Yglesias, the number-one navigator and number-three cargo handler. "The dimmer one's Luna."

Matt pushed forward, to get closer to the glass. Everyone moved out of his way, without a word or a visible sign. There was a blue crescent, and a little white one, down below the black sun. He had thought —he had *known*—

He turned his back. He had been wrong. Hating the worlds, either of them, was no longer easy.

Nothing was, now.

ABOUT THE AUTHOR

JOHN M. FORD is the author of eight science fiction and fantasy novels and many pieces of short fiction, including the World Fantasy Award winner *The Dragon Waiting* and the Nebula Award finalist *Fugue State*. His stories and poetry have appeared in *Omni, Analog*, the anthology *Masterpieces of Fantasy and Wonder* and many other publications.